R
RUNS IN THE FAMILY

An absolutely gripping cozy murder mystery full of twists

JEAN G. GOODHIND

A Honey Driver Murder Mystery Book 13

Originally published as
Mord unter Brüdern

JOFFE BOOKS

Joffe Books, London
www.joffebooks.com

First English edition published in Great Britain
by Joffe Books in 2023

First German edition published by Aufbau Taschenbuch
in Germany as *Mord unter Brüdern* in 2016

Cover art by Dee Dee Book Covers

ISBN: 978-1-83526-045-6

CHAPTER ONE

SUSPICIOUS DEATH OF MAN FOUND ON RAILWAY LINE

> *The body of a man found buried in mud close to the railway line in Bradford on Avon has been identified as that of Caspar St John Gervais, owner of the La Reine Rouge Hotel in Bath . . .*

No! Surely not!

In the process of reading the news headline for the second time — Honey Driver had almost choked as she'd read it the first time — she tripped over the cat. Where the cat had come from, she didn't know, and what it was doing in the downstairs hallway of her private residence, she hadn't a clue. However, a stray cat having wandered in was too trivial to distract her from the newspaper article. Caspar was dead? How? Why?

Numb with shock, Honey dropped her hands, the paper crumpling in the middle. If a photographer had been there, he would immediately have snapped her face, the round eyes, the perfect 'o' of her mouth. It was a scary picture, reminiscent of *The Scream* but without the artistic merit.

Tearing the front page away from the rest of the paper, Honey, owner of the Green River Hotel and Crime Liaison Officer for Bath Hotels Association, headed to where she'd flung her trainers on her return from a one-mile run that should have been two miles. The run had been halved by virtue of a sudden urge for a chocolate digestive. Being fit and being famished fought for a nanosecond before the chocolate digestive won the day. . .

For some daft reason the cat appeared to have adopted the idea that the trainers were its personal territory and in need of being defended against all comers. Snarling and spitting, it sat between them and Honey.

If she hadn't been so upset, she might have given the cat a piece of her mind — plus the toe of a trainer up its backside — but she had received a terrible shock. Caspar St John Gervais, Chairman of Bath Hotels Association, was the man who had handed her the job of Crime Liaison Officer on behalf of the Association. She had reluctantly accepted the poisoned chalice — nobody else wanted the job — because Caspar had promised to keep her letting rooms full during the winter. She'd been going through a sticky patch at the time so the extra business and the revenue it would bring was not to be sniffed at.

It hadn't been something she'd wanted to do. However, the position of Crime Liaison Officer had proved interesting on a number of counts: firstly, getting involved in crime got her out of the hotel and into the world. Secondly, without it she would never have met Steve Doherty, her police liaison contact.

It hadn't been all wine and roses, however. When serious crime occurred, Caspar was on her back until it was solved.

'We must not allow crime to destroy this fair city and its unique heritage,' he had said to her.

He hadn't added that crime could also have an adverse effect on hotel takings, but she knew it was true.

Now he was dead.

OK, death comes to everyone, but Caspar wasn't the sort you found dead next to a railway line. He was the kind of man who made a grand entrance, so it stood to reason he would be inclined to make a grand exit. She couldn't imagine him dead, and the newspaper article didn't specify how he'd died. Suicide? An accident? Murder? Buried in mud. Had he slipped? It all seemed very vague.

With the cat having adopted the trainers as its day bed, Honey pulled a pair of two-tone brown ankle boots from the wardrobe. Hair awry and face devoid of make-up, she slammed the door behind her and skidded across the flagstones to the back door of the hotel.

Smudger Smith, her head chef, was in the kitchen, his face pink with effort and the heat of the flat-top range. The smell of fried bacon made her stomach rumble, and normally she would have indulged in a couple of crisply fried slices served with eggs and toast. But Caspar's death had ruined her appetite.

'Boss,' Smudger exclaimed, one hand raised in a kind of salute. Judging by his action it seemed he wanted a word.

She raised her hand in the universal stop signal, palm facing him. 'Not now. Leave any problems until I get back. Something very bad has come up. Very bad indeed. There's been a death. A quite shocking one.'

At the mention of death Smudger looked instantly contrite. 'Oh. I see. In that case, there are no problems. Well. Nothing I can't deal with. I just thought you looked . . .'

She sensed he was about to say she looked pretty pale, as though she'd seen a ghost, but stopped himself. People who lived in Bath were always seeing ghosts.

'I'll explain later.'

With that, she was gone.

Back in the kitchen Smudger shook his head. 'I was going to ask her if she minded my cat moving in,' he said to Lester, his commis chef. 'Looks a bit shaken up though, don't she?'

Lester was slicing a cucumber with astonishing speed and great verve — like an executioner on piece work.

'A member of the family?'

Smudger shook his head. 'Nobody I can think of. Her mother's getting on a bit but she's too busy to die.'

* * *

La Reine Rouge looked happily summery, trailing lobelia, geraniums and other colourfully dramatic plants spilling from hanging baskets set at equal distances all along its facade.

Knees weak from the bad news and the fact that she was pounding pavements wearing a pair of winter boots, Honey almost collapsed before the white oak reception counter.

Kevin, the freckle-faced receptionist, looked down at her, his nose quivering above his pale-cream cravat. His outfit owed much to that of a Georgian gentleman. His expression was one of exaggerated blandness.

Sandy-coloured brows arched halfway to his hairline. 'Is something wrong?'

Wrong? How could he sound so unconcerned at a time like this?

Mouth too dry to explain in detail, she handed him the newspaper, tapping at the self-explanatory headline.

'This!'

Kevin took the newspaper, holding it delicately with the tips of his fingers as though it were contaminated with something highly contagious, such as reality.

On reading the content, his jaw dropped and his tentative clutch tightened.

Honey took charge of the moment. 'Tell me it isn't true.'

Kevin's head jerked up so sharply it looked in danger of snapping off.

'It isn't true. I've just taken him a cup of coffee — thick and black, just as he likes it.'

Honey grabbed the paper back and, without waiting to be announced, dashed off down the stairs leading to Caspar's basement office.

Large as life — and his usual colour-co-ordinated self in a pale shade of yellow — Caspar sat behind his desk perusing his computer screen. A cool draught of air blew through a pair of newly installed French doors from a courtyard garden planted in Japanese style. Caspar's partner, Takardo, was Japanese and they had been together on and off for about five years. Caspar's passion was clocks, Takardo's was gardening.

A medley of clock chimes sounded eleven as Caspar glanced up long enough to assess her expression.

'Dear me. Your complexion is white as snow. Either you've seen a ghost or your mother has moved in with you.'

'No to the first and, thankfully, no also to the second.'

She barely suppressed a shiver as she sank into a chair. Her mother moving in would be an ordeal, though not quite as shocking as this.

She pushed the newspaper under Caspar's nose.

'According to this, you're dead!'

Caspar's demeanour was unchanged as his eyes caught the headline.

'The first paragraph,' said Honey, her finger stabbing the shocking words.

The calm expression stiffened to waxy paleness. Caspar was not a man to be easily ruffled, but his usually sanguine features creased to blustery anger.

'I want this man's phone number! I want his editor's phone number! This is all very unfortunate.' A well-manicured fingernail jabbed at the newspaper. 'Now, where is it?'

'Inside the front page?'

Caspar checked. She was right. Armed with the editor's details, he reached for his phone and put it on loudspeaker.

The usual 'dial one for this department', 'two to place a classified' and 'three for a marriage announcement' were quickly dispensed with. After being passed around the block a bit, he was at last speaking to the man at the top — the editor.

'Look, you stupid man. It's not me. I'm not dead. I'm alive. You can hear me, can't you? I'm alive!'

Caspar's wheeled desk chair flew out from behind him as he leaped to his feet and paced the thick pile carpet, phone clutched tightly in one hand, the crumpled newspaper in the other.

'Dead? I'll give him dead!'

'Perhaps it was a genuine mistake . . .'

'I call it careless. He could have rung here to make sure.'

'Yes, but if you were dead . . .'

'I AM NOT DEAD!'

His voice was louder than usual, but Caspar was not one to lose control, and his tone was cold.

'Caspar, you are so cool,' Honey whispered. 'I'd want an apology.'

Whatever it was about her comment, Caspar responded. Suddenly he was swearing, his face livid with anger, so much so that he could barely speak. He began to splutter so much, he passed the phone to Honey. 'Will you tell him?'

It was all quite surprising.

A fit of coughing followed and he pummelled his chest with his clenched fist. 'Bloody coffee gone down the wrong way . . .'

Honey told the editor what was happening, that Caspar St John Gervais was almost choking on his anger. She also confirmed that the identity they'd attached to the dead man was incorrect. Caspar St John Gervais was very much alive. 'And there couldn't possibly be two people with the same name. I mean, it's not as though the name Caspar St John Gervais is very common.'

Caspar glared at the very thought of it.

The editor was apologetic. 'Look. I'm sorry, his death — sorry — the death was reported to us by a reputable source.'

'Then your source was wrong.'

Caspar interjected, grabbing the phone back from her. 'I want that source. I want his address. Now!'

'I'm sorry, we can't give out details of our sources and staff to the public . . .'

'I'm not the public. I'm me. I have connections in high places. Titled connections. Now come along. Give me his name.'

'I would like to point out, Mr Gervais, that his name's on the article.'

Both Honey and Caspar took another look at the newspaper. There in bold print beneath the even bolder print of the headline was the name of the reporter, Geoffrey Monmouth.

Honey pointed. 'Ah yes. There it is.'

Caspar wasn't usually so unobservant, but the article had upset him. It wasn't every day you read a report of your death, with a question mark over the details.

The editor was unrepentant. 'We can't give you his address. I'm sorry.'

'Is he there? I'll come there.'

'Not here.' Honey detected panic in the editor's voice. 'He's a freelance. We only use him occasionally.'

Honey couldn't blame him for not wanting the Chairman of the Hotels Association barging into his office. When Caspar had the bit between his teeth — as he did now — he was like a bobsleigh going downhill without a brake handle.

Honey flicked the paper into readable flatness again.

Caspar took another look at the front page. 'I see from this he's written another article for you about the two-thousand-year-old body that was dug up on the Torrington estate some time ago. It's on the same page. Are you sure that body really was dead too? Not sat up in bed somewhere, is he?'

'There's no need to be facetious.' The editor's tone was sniffy.

'I could sue you for this. In fact I am going to contact my solicitor the moment I put this phone down.'

The editor's apology and vow to make amends was immediate and heartfelt. 'Look. I'll get it retracted. I'll publish an apology saying that it was all a mistake. How would that be? After all, no harm done. You're still alive.'

'I am.' Caspar's eyes narrowed maliciously as they met Honey's. 'So who was it really, this body you were told was me?'

'I don't know. I'll ask Monmouth to speak to his police contact. They might know more.'

'I'm sure they will,' said Caspar.

The call was swiftly terminated.

Honey saw the look on Caspar's face. His presence had become alarmingly overblown, as though he'd done the *Alice in Wonderland* 'eat me' thing and was about to become too big for the room.

'Until this moment I have refrained from getting involved in the sleazier side of life. It does not constitute part of my character. I have always left that to you.'

'Thanks a bundle,' murmured Honey.

Caspar did not appear to notice he'd been a tad insulting.

'I would obviously like to seek out this Monmouth character and convey my hurt feelings. I will also expect some form of redress. I will attend to sending notice of my intention to sue the newspaper to the editor.'

'It's probably a genuine mistake, though science and DNA stuff being what it is, I wonder how they got it so wrong. I wonder who it really is?'

Caspar tilted his head back, his eyes scouring the ceiling as though his decision were floating there, waiting to be plucked.

Honey felt the apprehension building in her stomach. She could guess what was coming next.

'Yes. I need clarification. I want to know who this man is. Drop everything. I want you to make in-depth enquiries.'

'I do have a hotel to run . . .'

'Never mind that. Take a break. Follow lines of enquiry. If there are problems at the Green River, I will send somebody over to help out.'

She knew from past experience that he would be true to his word. She was already getting a tad excited at the prospect of what was to come. The case might prove interesting. First, she had to find out exactly how the man had died. Why mud? Surely nobody could commit suicide in mud? She smelled the stench of foul play. Her mind was already whirring with what she should do next.

'Doherty is bound to know something about it and I'm meeting him later . . .' she started.

'No! Not later. Now. I want you to apply yourself to this matter as quickly as possible. Go to the place where this man died and get a feel for it. Make enquiries at the highest level. There's not a moment to lose. My disposition is shocked to the core. I need closure. Now. Apply yourself!'

Caspar was always brusque, but now his insistent attitude was sharp enough to slice off her head. Still, it was just his way. There was only one Caspar St John Gervais — there certainly wasn't room for two in his world.

CHAPTER TWO

Recovered somewhat from the shock of reading that Caspar was dead and then finding him very much alive, Honey marched along the pavement, through the motley crowd of shoppers, sightseers and people taking selfies beneath the floral baskets hanging from lamp-posts.

Doherty, the Police Liaison Officer who also shared her bed on occasion, wasn't answering his phone. Exasperated, she kept trying. Still no answer. She knew he was due to attend a team-building course sometime soon, but was pretty sure he hadn't yet left.

Again she tried, gritting her teeth while muttering, 'Where are you, Steve Doherty?'

'You trying to find me?'

His voice had not come from the phone. It was real. He was close by.

It was easy to miss seeing people in Bath, especially in the height of the season when it was swamped by tourists.

She stopped in her tracks, guessing correctly that if he wasn't in front of her then he had to be behind her. They collided nicely. She found herself slap bang up against his usual black T-shirt and scruffy jeans, his finger hooked into the loop of his trademark scuffed leather jacket, which hung nonchalantly over his shoulder.

They were in one of their 'cooling-off' periods, though cool was wont to turn hot quickly between them, like night follows day.

'I need you to tell me something,' she said, her voice low and husky.

He raised his eyebrows, a cheeky smile on his lips, and promise in his eyes.

'Is it a secret made for two?'

'Not at all. It's national news — in a way. It's Caspar. The *Western Daily Press* suggested that he's dead.'

The cheeky smile was close to outright laughter.

Before he could say something totally unsuitable, she added, 'They thought he was the body found buried in mud near the railway line in Bradford on Avon. Was it an accident? Suicide or murder?'

'Caspar?' He managed to chortle and look serious at one and the same time. 'Crikey. Glad I was away on a course.'

'So it's not your case. But it wasn't Caspar anyway. He's very much alive. Have you any idea about it?'

He shrugged. 'No idea. From the little I know of the case, suicide would be a big surprise. I suppose he could have slipped in the mud and got himself buried that way. Perhaps he was drunk and couldn't get out. Or somebody could have had a hand in it. Only the boys in the lab can work that one out. What do you know so far?'

'One thing only. It wasn't Caspar. He's in shock — or as near as he can be, bearing in mind how he usually is. I was shocked too. First the headline saying he was dead, then seeing him sipping coffee behind his desk.'

'Hmm.' Doherty's expression turned serious, then he shook his head. 'Nothing to do with me, I'm afraid.'

'But you can find out.'

'I could. If I wanted to.'

'I suppose it's understandable. You're too relaxed from your time off just now. How did the course go?'

He shrugged. 'So-so.'

'When are you off on the team-building programme?'

'Shortly.'

Their mutually agreed 'cooling-off' period was basically meant to see if they could live without each other for more than a few days. She'd missed him but wasn't going to say so — not unless he said so first.

'Can I come with you?'

'You're not a member of the police force.'

'That's not what I meant. Not the course. To the station. Caspar is keen on getting this sorted as quickly as possible and he'd like to know who it really was out there. I take it you're going to be briefed on the details?'

He shook his head. 'The incident occurred in Bradford on Avon. That's in Wiltshire, in case you didn't know, and outside the jurisdiction of Avon and Somerset.'

Honey slammed her palm hard against her forehead. 'Damn!' Police authorities guarded their given territory jealously.

'Can't put my big boot in there.'

Honey sucked in her breath. 'That's a shame. Caspar was pretty shocked when I took the piece round to him.'

Doherty grinned. 'I bet he was.'

'It's not funny.'

The serious expression returned but the laughter was still in his eyes.

'Of course it's not.' A smile continued to hover around his lips.

'I would fall apart if I read I was reported dead,' she said testily.

'So Caspar's ordered you to look into it — though it's odd him wanting to get involved seeing as it didn't happen in Bath.'

She nodded. 'Well, not exactly ordered . . .'

Doherty pulled a disbelieving expression. 'I suppose his view was altered a tad when he saw his name in the headlines.'

She put oodles of pleading into her tone. 'Can you help?'

He blew out a low whistle and shook his head. 'They won't like it. I would be treading on toes. It's not my territory.'

'OK,' she said, nodding her head slowly. 'I see where you're coming from. It wouldn't be professional for you to make enquiries — but surely you know somebody in Wiltshire Constabulary who might be able to help? Somebody I could talk to?'

He closed one eye, a habit when he was thinking deeply or suspecting that Honey was demanding favours he might not be able to fulfil.

'Sefton Goudge. He's the man who might be able to help you — as a favour to me. He used to be based in Bath but retired from active service to take a desk job in Wiltshire — one of the backroom boys.'

Honey beamed, kissed him and nipped her hands around his waistline.

Doherty murmured his appreciation, then added, 'I like your powers of persuasion and, with a view to experiencing a repeat performance, I will make a few preliminary enquiries.'

Honey leaned close and kissed him. 'Your help would definitely merit a repeat performance, perhaps on a more intimate level.'

Doherty smiled. 'That's exactly what I hoped to hear. In the meantime, go poke your nose in where you can.'

'I've no problem with that. It's a lovely day,' she said, looking round her at people in short-sleeved tops, some in shorts. 'I think I might take a drive and then a walk along the river.'

Doherty nodded. 'Uh-huh. In Bradford on Avon?'

'Seems like a good idea. Sorry you can't come.' She genuinely wished he could.

'Take care,' he said, taking hold of her shoulders and kissing her forehead. 'And don't get in anyone's way.'

He whistled as he stalked off, jacket still flung over his shoulder.

As for Honey, she did have a sudden urge to enjoy the sunshine. At the same time, it would be interesting to see where the body was found. There was bound to be some action still going on there. Odd about the false identity though — why Caspar? Yes, it was funny, but also intriguing.

* * *

Honey parked her bright-yellow Citroen in the car park adjacent to the river walk and convenient for the public toilets. She guessed that the body had been found some way downriver from the famous medieval bridge spanning the flowing water in the centre of the pretty town. She recalled the meadows sloping gently down from the treeline, the weavers' cottages, the narrow track climbing upwards into denser vegetation and the pedestrian access over the railway line. Scary really, having a railway line so open to public access. No safety fence. No nothing.

The parkland area where people strolled and walked their dogs petered out into rougher terrain just beyond the place where the path climbed upwards towards the railway line. That was where the blue tape fluttered, stretched across the path and preventing anyone from walking further. Following recent wet weather and the cutting back of foliage, a lot of mud had shifted.

Two uniformed constables were on duty, both arguing with a particularly irate dog walker who was expressing the sentiment that her dogs got very upset if they didn't keep to a strict routine, and they went walkies along the path crossing the railway line every single day. No matter how the policemen tried to impress on her that something very bad had taken place on the railway track, the routine habits of her dogs outweighed anything so mundane as a human death — or at least to her they did.

'There's been an incident, madam . . .'

'That was days ago. And anyway, you've just allowed a car to roll down here. What about that? It disturbs more ground than me and my dog, don't you think?'

'I'm sorry—'

'People commit suicide on railway lines all the time. It's not as though it was a murder now, was it?'

'Madam, we cannot possibly comment . . .'

Hearing their indecision, Honey's thoughts went back to the newspaper headline. Suspicious death. Why suspicious? If, as the dog-walking lady said, it was indeed a suicide, then it wasn't suspicious. The truth wouldn't be revealed until a full pathology examination had been carried out. But there was a question mark.

Honey felt an instant surge of curiosity. How things could change from one minute to the next. This was no longer just about finding out why Caspar's name had been affixed to the corpse.

While the dog lady continued to berate the police and their gross insensitivity to her and her dogs, Honey ducked underneath the tape. The shrubs thereabouts grew thickly at the side of the path all the way up the slope.

There was only one white incident van still there, its rear doors open to facilitate the used siren suits and bulging incident cases being thrown into the back. By virtue of the warm weather and the sticky suits, two people were mopping their brows and stretching their arms before climbing into the van and driving off.

One vehicle remained: a shiny black BMW with tinted windows and alloy wheels.

It crossed her mind as being quite an upmarket car for a policeman. It had to be a policeman. Nobody else would have been allowed to park adjacent to the fluttering incident tape. Not that he seemed to be in evidence at present. The scene was now bereft of people, the gleaming rails running in each direction and no sight or sound of a train.

Taking a quick look round to make sure nobody was watching, she stealthily approached the railway line. Bending down, she scrutinised the place where chalk marks and a spray can of white paint outlined where the body had been found, though by virtue of the terrain, only scrappily. Apart from the markings, all that remained were dark bits of gravel between the rails plus a few stains on the wooden sleepers.

It came as something of a surprise to see that she was not the first civilian visitor to the site. A stunning bouquet of orange, blue and purple flowers had been left at the scene. Closer examination revealed no note, no tender words hastily scribbled on a simple card that might have told her the name of either the victim or the person who had left the flowers. It was touching and showed someone cared.

She leaned closer, smelled the blooms but saw nothing more — except a card tucked down the back of the flowers. At first she thought it was a playing card, but then saw it was a tarot card — the Hanged Man, one foot tied to a tree.

'Can I help you?'

She swiftly tucked the card into her bra. A shadow fell over her. The new arrival's footsteps had been so soft she hadn't heard a thing.

She spun round, expecting to see some overbearing police officer wearing an officious expression and about to tell her to sod off.

He was no more than a silhouette, the sun behind him forming a halo around his head. His features remained indistinct until he sidestepped onto more level ground and out of the sunlight behind him.

Honey drank in the details. He was tall and well dressed, his hair silvery blond, flat and glossy over his skull and flicking around his collar.

She was instantly reminded of a medieval knight, gleaming hair, chiselled expression, china-blue eyes. He didn't look the sort of copper who'd ever graced a police uniform and done traffic duty, though other uniforms were distinctly possible.

Smiling disarmingly, though still businesslike, she held out her hand. 'How do you do? I'm Crime Liaison Officer for Bath Hotels Association. My name's Honey Driver. I usually liaise with Detective Inspector Steve Doherty at Manvers Street in Bath on serious crime matters that might affect Bath's international tourist trade. I realise that this man died in Wiltshire, but I'm working on a case of mistaken identity. A newspaper wrongly reported the identity of the victim, in fact naming a friend of mine. He was quite upset.'

The hand that shook hers was firm. Warm. Lingering. His smile was enticing. 'Do I call you Honey?'

She smiled, smitten. 'Please do.'

'So, you're interested in this case?'

Holding his head to one side, he looked her up and down as though he could measure her height, breadth and width with nothing more than a quick glance. It crossed her mind that he might also be able to surmise the colour of her underwear. Just the thought of it made her blush.

'My name's Dominic Christiansen. Do call me Dominic. Pleased to meet you. So, your friend's name was mentioned in a newspaper article?'

His accent was cut glass, his eyes unblinking, and he oozed the confidence of a man born into money and privilege, the product of somewhere like Eton or Harrow. She noticed that he hadn't given his rank and somehow knew that he wouldn't. Something else was going on here.

Honey gathered up her own confidence. 'Yes. He was very upset. How it happened, we don't really know. Possibly just a newspaper journalist jumping the gun.'

'Possibly. Poor chap. Nobody wants to read about their own death. Almost as bad as suffering it!'

'Yes. I read it and thought it referred to my friend. The name was the same. I went round to see if it was true and there he was as large as life. It's very strange.'

'And your friend's name?'

'Caspar St John Gervais. He's Chairman of Bath Hotels Association. After reading that little snippet I shot off to check on him. He has a hotel in Bath. It was a bit of a shock to see him sitting in his office drinking coffee, I can tell you.'

It was sudden and could have been imagined, but she perceived a sudden flash in the man's eyes, as though he'd heard Caspar's name before.

'Have you met him?'

He shook his head. 'I can't say I have.'

'Well, I do hope we can clear this up.'

'So do I. I'll be handling the investigation. Here's my card. It's my mobile number. I don't give it out to just anyone, so keep it to yourself or I'll have every Tom, Dick and PC Smartass phoning me!'

He laughed at his own joke. Honey laughed too and did her best to stop visualising him in other capacities. My, but this man was gorgeous. She barely looked at the card. She had been half inclined to shove it down into her bra but had no wish to give the wrong impression. Besides, one card in there was quite enough.

Not that she wished to impress him merely because he was good-looking. Oh no, that would be far too shallow. She couldn't help weighing him up, though. Judging by his height he would stretch full length on a bed without an inch to spare!

He said nothing.

She said nothing.

They just stood there looking each other up and down, no secret to either of them what was going through their minds. This was like standing on the edge of a cliff, hypnotised by the view and wanting to jump into it. Only the vision of Doherty with his jacket thrown over his shoulder stopped her from falling off the edge. In the meantime she would make small talk, another word for getting information she might not normally be party to.

'So! Is there anything you can tell me? I mean, do you know the true identity of the dead man?'

For a moment he just looked at her with what she could only describe as a steely gaze — the sort hot-blooded heroes adopted in her mother's romantic novels. Was he going to tell her anything or not?

Suddenly he glanced over her head as though considering his options.

At last he turned back to face her. 'Very well. Seeing as your friend was wrongly identified . . . in the strictest confidence, of course.'

She nodded. 'Of course.'

His gaze held hers. 'What do you want to know?'

'Was it suicide, an accident or murder?'

'I can't tell you that just yet. He was dead. That will have to suffice for now. We're making enquiries as to his identity and assessing the details of his death. Sorry your friend got involved. I can't imagine who gave the newspaper his name.'

'He'll get over it. I'm not sure the newspaper editor will, though. Caspar doesn't easily forgive anyone who takes his name in vain — and that includes mentioning him in front-page headlines.'

'This friend of yours sounds quite a character. I'd like to meet him — just in case he might be able to shed some light on the victim.'

'Oh, I doubt there was any chance that he knew the victim,' said Honey, shaking her head.

His face clouded. 'Perhaps you're not quite as close a friend as you thought.'

'He doesn't do Devizes,' she blurted.

Christiansen frowned. 'Devizes?'

'Wiltshire police headquarters? I understand it's in Devizes.' She fixed him with a pointed gaze.

'Ah yes! Of course.' He gave an affirmative nod of his head, but she couldn't help thinking he hadn't known what she was talking about. If he was employed by Wiltshire police, he should surely know Devizes.

However, he offered her a crumb of solace. 'He wouldn't need to go to Devizes. I can come to him.'

'That's very good of you.'

'No problem at all.'

'Look. If you need to contact me . . .'

It wasn't often she gave out her business cards. Usually they remained in her desk gathering dust, or curling at the corners in her pocket or purse. Still, she carried them just in case a special occasion presented itself. Dominic Christiansen was that special occasion.

For a moment he eyed her thoughtfully and she eyed him right back. This was a dynamite moment and she couldn't easily walk away.

'Have you got time for a coffee?'

His invitation took her by surprise. 'Well . . . Yes . . .'

OK, her response was stammered, but it wasn't long coming. He'd taken her off guard. Her thoughts were reeling.

'Get in the car. The Swan looks a good place and there's room to park at the rear.'

'There are other places . . .'

'With car parks?'

'Well, some you'd have to park in a public car park or out on the road for.'

'My car is never parked in a public car park. Come on. Let me take you for a drink.'

She didn't argue.

The interior of the car smelled of expensive aftershave and warm leather. She glanced at his profile as they drove the brief journey to the Swan.

What started off as coffee turned into lunch, and a brief sojourn became two hours, during which he told her that the dead man was very likely homeless. 'Not well dressed and not in the best of health, according to the pathologist.'

It was the only time during their lunch that her thoughts flipped back to the case.

'Goodness! Why would anyone think it was Caspar? I mean, he's exactly the opposite of scruffy. Fastidious, in fact.'

'Fastidious or not,' he said, 'the man was buried in mud, so his clothes would have suffered. But we'll look into it.'

His smile was almost enough to obliterate her need to know.

Ten minutes after taking leave of him, she was still reeling. Snippets of what they'd talked about were remembered, though dominated by his presence, his good looks, his smooth hair and deep voice. He'd asked her a lot about herself, her business, her family and her reasons for accepting the job of Crime Liaison Officer. Her suspicions were roused. He had to be a spook — MI5 or 6.

They had said their goodbyes outside the Green River Hotel.

'I'll be in touch,' he'd said. She hadn't had chance to agree before he was gone.

'Who was that?'

A pair of brown eyes watched her intently. Her daughter, Lindsey, was the crutch on which she leaned. She was also abnormally observant for one so young and, if Honey cared to admit it, ran the hotel better than she did.

Honey threw her folded arms onto the reception countertop. 'He's a policeman — kind of. Wasn't he gorgeous?'

'Very fetching — from what I could see of him. Talk about an upgrade, Mum! If Steve could see you now . . .' Lindsey's words trailed away at the look on her mother's face. 'Fabulous car, too. Where did you find him?'

'Bradford on Avon.' Honey sighed. Yes, a handsome guy. Yes, a luxury car — way beyond Doherty's pay grade. *Doherty*. There he was again. Like an itch that couldn't be scratched.

'And he gave you a lift back?'

Honey threw back her head, eyes closed in rapture at the memory of his closeness, his smell and the dancing seductiveness of his eyes. 'Yes, yes, YES!'

'So where's your car?'

One short sentence and Honey's bubble was well and truly burst. She groaned.

'Damn.'

The truth was most definitely out there, as they used to say in *The X-Files*. She was here in the Green River Hotel. The car was still in Bradford on Avon.

'Honey! I haven't seen you all day, and now that I am seeing you, there's an aura about you that's turning from gold to pink and on to scarlet. Some karma, wish-list-related, got hold of you?'

It was a nonsensical question, of course. Typical of what Honey had come to expect from Mary Jane, long-term resident of the Green River Hotel and professor of the paranormal. She cut an alarming figure as she appeared in reception, wearing what seemed to be a cotton trouser suit with Hawaiian palm trees spewed all over it. She leaned on the reception desk, towering over both of them, bright-blue eyes dancing from mother to daughter.

'Not so much karma as car. Thanks to the sudden appearance of a handsome prince, Mum's left her car at Bradford on Avon.' Lindsey was grinning more widely than the Cheshire Cat.

Honey grimaced. There were times for including Mary Jane in a conversation, and there were times when it was best to walk on by. This was definitely a walk-on-by scenario.

'No problem,' Honey said brightly, keen that Mary Jane did not offer her a lift. 'I can get a bus and collect it.'

Too late!

Mary Jane was all gushing assistance. 'I can drive you to Bradford on Avon.' Her voice boomed around reception. Any lingering guest would think what a kind offer it was. Their opinion would be based on ignorance. They couldn't know about Mary Jane's driving.

'Grandmother told me to say that she and Stewart will be arriving at nine. You can get back by then,' added a smiling Lindsey, her eyes dancing with wickedness.

'In double-quick time,' stated Mary Jane.

'That's what I'm afraid of,' muttered Honey.

* * *

Dominic Christiansen congratulated himself. Honey Driver had walked straight into a trap, though she couldn't possibly know that. Neither had he at first, not until the message had come through and confirmed their worst suspicions. The Tarot Man was in the country and the intelligence services wanted him badly.

Honey Driver would never have heard of him, of course, even though her family and his had a history, a bloody, cruel history that had been passed on from father to son.

Murdering was a hobby to him, but revenge on those responsible for his father's death was an obsession.

Catching him was a big problem. But they did know who he had in his sights as regards his professional vendetta. The opportunity to come to England had arisen and he had taken it. Now they were waiting for him to strike. The man at the side of the railway line had been a dummy run, the bait in the trap. They'd been too slow catching him this time, so they had to try again.

And now that Honey had found that bouquet — with the tarot card tucked neatly inside — things were finally in motion. Under ordinary circumstances, Dominic would never have been so negligent as to leave evidence at a scene. But the Tarot Man had eluded them so many times. They were getting desperate and determined to catch him. And if that meant breaking protocol, then so be it.

CHAPTER THREE

Honey had always wanted a bright-yellow car, so when her old Citroën bit the dust, she immediately bought a new one. Yellow. Still a Citroën, but jazzier than the old model.

She loved that car. She'd love it even more once she was ensconced safely behind the steering wheel.

The journey from Bath to Bradford on Avon went by in a whirl of speed, dodgy gear changing and even dodgier braking, all accompanied by the squealing of tyres.

'Do you want me to hang around and see if it starts OK?' Mary Jane oozed sincerity. She really didn't have a clue about the effect her driving had on people.

Clinging to the body of Mary Jane's pink Cadillac coupe until her wobbly legs were under control, Honey declined the offer. 'It's a new car. It'll be fine.'

Even if the car failed to start, she would clamber onto a bus, or even walk rather than endure another ride in the Caddy. She'd learned from Mary Jane that the word Cadillac, and indeed the word Pontiac, had been the names of Indian chiefs.

'Real wild guys,' Mary Jane had told her. 'Wish I could have met them.'

But the experience of sharing a car with Mary Jane might well have turned them into nervous wrecks.

The first thing Honey did on sliding into the driver's seat was to close her eyes, take a deep breath, then reopen them. It wasn't wise to open one's eyes when Mary Jane was driving.

Once her car was safely retrieved and returned to its parking space in the multi-storey, she felt a great sense of relief, which was immediately followed by feeling duty bound to call in on Caspar and see how he was getting on now they all knew for sure that he wasn't dead.

She found him sitting behind his desk in a handsome winged armchair in a soft shade of cornflower blue.

'I've been out to Bradford on Avon and thought I would pop in to see how you were. Would you prefer me to come back later?'

He shook his head. Without waiting for an invitation, she sat down.

Taking a deep breath, he appeared to have regained his self-control, his shrewd eyes fixing her so intently, she felt in the grip of a pair of steel pincers.

'What did you find out?'

She instantly gathered her thoughts.

'I went out to where the man was found. It's that stretch of railway line that runs almost parallel to the river where there's no fencing and no gated crossing. Everyone just kind of pops over. Except the man who was found dead didn't get the chance to pop over. He was buried there. I don't know when he was laid in the ground, but we've had a lot of rain recently, plus the foliage had been cut back so there was a mudslide. He came with the mudslide from what I can gather.'

'I'm pleased to hear your boyfriend was so helpful.'

Honey felt her face go red. She wasn't about to declare that it wasn't Doherty's old friend who had filled her in on the matter.

'Although it's terribly selfish of me to say so, Honey, it's such a relief to know it's not me lying dead. I phoned a few friends to assure them that the news of my death was greatly exaggerated. All of them reacted in varying degrees of astonishment.

'There were a few I couldn't get hold of: Simon, an old flame with connections in Fleet Street is off on assignment in Berlin. He did finally get in touch and asked if there was anything he could do — like advise me as to my rights of libel. He also said that it happened all the time and not to worry. But then he would. He wasn't the one reported dead.'

'Quite.'

'Though I am over it now. One has to get on with one's life, doesn't one?'

Honey agreed that one did. She attempted to get her thoughts in order. There was a mystery here and both she and Caspar were involved. A man was dead, but it wasn't him that kept popping into her mind. That particular space was dominated by Dominic Christiansen. He wasn't just good-looking, he was intriguing.

Caspar dragged her back to reality.

'How successful have you been, my dear girl? Is there any description of this man?'

Honey shook her head. 'It's been suggested he was a homeless person.'

Caspar's eyebrows rose. 'Homeless?' He looked appalled at the prospect of having been identified as an itinerant down-and-out.

'The man I spoke to did say that, and I questioned how such a mistake could have been made . . . Anyway, enquiries are continuing. It won't be long. Have the police put in an appearance?'

He nodded. 'I had a phone call from someone suggesting I might be interviewed at some point. That was all.'

Honey chewed over the facts, which was much easier to do once she'd placed Dominic Christiansen on the back burner.

'Someone left flowers. There was a card with them, but unsigned.'

Something flickered in Caspar's eyes. 'How very touching.'

'Yes, and a funny thing — it was a tarot card. You know, one of those fortune-telling cards. The Hanged Man.'

'I know what a tarot card is, thank you!' His snappiness was out of character and very sudden.

Although Caspar sounded indignant, Honey also perceived a nervous flicker. Never in all the years of their acquaintance had she seen Caspar display any sign of nervousness.

'The policeman who phoned. Did he give you a name?' Honey asked.

Caspar's long fingers stroked his forehead as he thought about it.

She gave him a prompt. 'Was it a man named Dominic Christiansen?'

'I think it was.'

Honey frowned. 'I'm going to ask Doherty if he's ever heard of him. He knows quite a few people in the Wiltshire Constabulary. I mean, he did give me his card . . . Though it's odd it doesn't give his rank. Did he happen to mention it to you?'

Caspar shook his head and looked away, as though the man's rank — or lack of it — didn't count for anything. Yet she perceived sudden alarm in his eyes.

Honey pushed her hair back behind one ear. Getting hold of Doherty was top priority before he left for the Brecon Beacons and his team-building exercise.

'I think I have to run this past Steve again.'

Caspar paused and frowned. 'Yes,' he said thoughtfully. 'I think that would be a very good idea.'

* * *

A woman of her word, Honey arrived back at the hotel just before nine — in time to welcome her mother and Stewart. Now she had just one thing left on her mind . . .

Doherty had not yet left for his ten days away in the misty dampness of central Wales.

She opened the door of the coach house she shared with her daughter to find him filling the gap in the doorway between the hall and the living room, an elbow resting on one side of the door surround. His look was nonchalant, a half-smile on his face.

'Are you ready for me?'

She cocked her head to one side, matching his sauciness with a large dose of her own.

'That depends on your demands.'

'I come bearing gifts — well, one gift anyway. Wiltshire is being a bit difficult over releasing details of the man out at Bradford on Avon. I had to go above their heads. We should have the details in the morning.'

She didn't know why she shivered, but she couldn't help thinking of that old saying about somebody walking over her grave. But it isn't my grave, she told herself. It's not me that's dead. The need to reassure herself that she was still alive had something to do with her suggesting to Doherty that he stay awhile. Despite the fact that they'd both agreed to take a break from their relationship, she could already feel her resolve beginning to crumble. She had supper on the go and enough to share.

'Plus a decent bottle of New Zealand white wine.'

'Sounds good.' Steve asked her if there was anything for dessert.

'We could liaise,' she said seductively.

As usual, Detective Inspector Steve Doherty was on form. He wasn't exactly a sexual athlete, but he certainly knew which buttons to press.

'Steve,' she moaned, as he snuggled into her back, his lips nuzzling her neck, his voice loaded with suggestions of what they might do next. 'Do you know an officer in the Wiltshire police named Dominic Christiansen?' She thought she already knew the answer.

His body jiggled as he laughed. 'Dominic what?' He sounded disbelieving.

She lifted her head and turned to look at him. 'Why do you laugh?'

'No self-respecting policeman would carry that moniker. It's too public schoolboy. Where did you hear that name?'

She managed to control her blush. 'Out at Bradford on Avon. He claimed to be on duty there, plus two uniforms.'

There was no real need to mention the uniforms, but she felt she had to, just in case Doherty put two and two together and came up with the correct answer.

'What can you tell me about him?'

'He had a very smart car. A black BMW. And you are right. He was terribly public schoolboy. Very upper crust.'

Doherty stopped caressing her body. His expression turned grim. 'I don't think you should get involved.'

'I didn't say I was getting involved.'

'You're lying. I know you too well. You're curious and once you get the bit between your teeth, there's no stopping you.'

Honey sucked in her bottom lip. She wasn't in the habit of lying to him. They'd always been upfront and personal — very personal — with each other.

'Honey, are you listening?'

'Steve, you must understand. I was so shocked when I read about that man and thought it was Caspar. Caspar was pretty upset too.'

Steve gripped her shoulders. The look in his eyes was sharp enough to cut liver.

'It's over, Honey. It wasn't Caspar and there's no reason for you to investigate.'

'But Caspar insisted. He's so keen to find out—'

'Honey. Didn't you hear what I'm saying? Caspar has no real reason to continue with this. I don't understand where he's coming from. It's cleared up now. Do you get me?'

Honey had to concede that he was right. There was no need for Caspar to maintain his interest in the dead man. Unless there was something Caspar wasn't telling her, though she couldn't think what that might be.

'Will you promise to drop this?'

She promised him that she would let it go, but that night she dreamed of Dominic Christiansen. Something about him was egging her on.

CHAPTER FOUR

Dominic Christiansen regarded the body lying on the mortuary slab as though he were seeing the man for the first time. At first glance one would think that the true cause of death was still visible in respect of a vivid line around his neck. But the rope was for display purposes only, to coincide with one of the cards in the tarot deck, Orlov's calling card.

The man had been buried alive after first being rendered immobile by the prick of a needle. He would have known everything that was happening to him, just like the girls back in Russia and elsewhere that Orlov had killed as a hobby. Killing old adversaries of his father was a different matter and part of his professional make-up, however. And they believed he had more planned.

He looked at the body. They should have been able to save this man but had lost him.

'Satisfied?'

He nodded and said that he was.

A plain-clothes police officer was waiting out in the foyer to ask questions. He'd get answers, of course, though nothing that would lead to any verdict — in other words, inconclusive. That was the order they were required to follow.

He responded to all their questions and couldn't help smiling at the deference in their faces in response to his dominating presence and the sound of his voice. It was a voice straight out of a public school that had educated quite a few British prime ministers, the sons of titled lords, military men, and many of the shakers and movers in the banking industry.

'Something funny, Mr Christiansen?' It was the police officer that had followed him out.

Dominic shook his head, causing his silky hair to fall forward and caress his face. He pushed it back, a little more affectedly than he would normally do, and carried on his way.

He wondered if the dead man would have found this whole charade amusing. From what he knew of him, he most certainly would. But the deed was done. His death would be recorded as inconclusive and nobody would be any the wiser.

Between leaving the double doors of the morgue and gaining his car, he received a message from Devizes police headquarters via a relay point in Cheltenham. A detective from Bath had been asking if they had a police officer named Dominic Christiansen working there. It was the Cheltenham operative's job to say that indeed they did, and would he like Mr Christiansen to call him back . . . ?

Detective Inspector Steve Doherty had left his number. Dominic called it but didn't give the policeman a chance to say anything.

'Christiansen here. I believe you were trying to get in touch with me regarding a death that occurred outside your jurisdiction.'

There was a pause before Detective Inspector Doherty answered. The thoughtful type, Dominic surmised. Watch out. A man who thinks can be dangerous.

'Sorry to intrude, sir, I have a vested interest. An old friend asked for more details. Somebody thought it was my friend on the railway line. I would be interested to know more details.'

'People have accidents all the time. The pressures of modern living and all that. I understand the vibration from a passing train was responsible for the mudslide, plus the errant weather of course.'

Again that thoughtful pause. When Doherty spoke again, Dominic heard a trace of humour.

'Nothing's run on that line for a few days. There was a signal failure.'

'You must be mistaken.'

'No. I don't think so. I think you're spinning a tale. So, what's the score? What really happened? Who was that man and how come he was wrongly identified?'

Now it was Dominic's turn to pause. There was no way he could tell the truth, so he'd have to pull rank.

'This matter is out of your league. Just let events take their natural course and everything will turn out well in the end.'

'You sound as though you have great faith — or more information than the rest of us.'

'That may be. Leave it to us, old boy. We do know what we're doing. You will leave the matter alone if you know what's best for you.'

He cut the connection.

* * *

Feet resting on his desk, a cup of coffee untouched, Doherty attempted to call the number that had just rung him. An angry burring sounded. Not a message saying this number was engaged or unavailable. His stomach churned at the possibilities. It was exactly as he'd anticipated. The number was barred.

He scratched his chin and frowned at his phone. If somebody didn't want you to see their number, it usually came up as unknown. This one had not done that. It was hidden behind a tight barrier. Only computer criminals and spooks did that, the latter well-educated individuals who worked for faceless government departments with frightening agendas.

Doherty decided to check his facts and phoned Devizes. Goudge picked up his phone on the first ring.

After exchanging preliminary courtesies, Doherty asked him a few questions. He was not surprised by the answers but wished they could have been different.

He repeated himself. 'Are you sure about this Christiansen bloke? Are you sure you've never heard of him?'

Goudge was adamant, not that Doherty really needed confirmation. He'd spoken to the bloke via a department in Cheltenham. He could guess who Christiansen worked for, but still found it unbelievable. 'What's more, there's precious little information about the case coming in here. Somebody is holding onto the forensic report for grim death. OK, he could very likely have had an accident, perhaps even a heart attack, slipped and got buried in the mud. But I don't think so. I think there's more here than meets the eye.'

Doherty told him of his experience. 'That's not all, my friend. I tried phoning Christiansen via a department in Cheltenham. He phoned me back but when I tried to return his call I found the number was barred.'

The silence between them was that of old friends, their thoughts hurtling along the same wavelength.

'Well, as I see it,' began Goudge, 'somebody doesn't want to talk to you. Could be one of the cloak-and-dagger brigade, and you're best giving that lot a wide berth. Mix with them at your peril.'

Doherty didn't confirm his thoughts on the matter one way or another. He did explain about the mistaken identity of the body, which resulted in a stony silence on the other end of the phone.

For a moment he thought the line had gone dead. 'Are you still there?'

Goudge sighed. 'Yes. I'm still here. That name. St John Gervais. It's the same as the family who own Torrington Towers. Lord Torrington, in fact. That's the dead man's name. Tarquin St John Gervais.'

'Is that so?'

Doherty's mind was made up.

'You could well be right about the spooks being involved. I fancy rattling their cage a bit. Do you want to jeopardise your pension and join me?'

Goudge chuckled. 'Don't mind if I do. Wouldn't hurt to have a little adventure to look back on when I'm nursing a beer in my rocking chair.'

'Right. As I see it, we need to pull in a favour from a friendly pathologist. Do you know one?'

'I do.'

'Right. This is the plan . . .'

* * *

Honey was just evicting the cat from her coach house when her phone rang. It was Smudger's night off and, although he'd asked to have a word with her, so far they hadn't caught up. She presumed it was him, then changed her mind and guessed it was Steve Doherty.

She leaped on it immediately and, certain it would be Doherty, she spoke first.

'Hi, handsome. Care for a late-night drink with a sexy broad?' She knew she was pushing the boundaries but couldn't seem to help herself. Old habits . . .

'What? Honey! It's Xavier! Night receptionist at La Reine Rouge. Something terrible has happened.'

Xavier was one of several receptionists at La Reine Rouge Hotel. His high-pitched voice sounded as though somebody had their hands tight around his throat.

'Mrs Driver. I'm so sorry to disturb you at this hour, but it's Caspar! The old darling's been taken into the police station for questioning regarding that body found in Bradford on Avon.'

Regardless of the confusion regarding identity, Honey wondered how he could possibly be implicated.

'Leave it to me, Xavier. I'll go there right away and see what's going on. Have you contacted Caspar's lawyer?'

'I don't have an evening phone number for Mr Featherlight, only his office number.'

'OK. Caspar might already have phoned him. If not, I'll get in touch myself. Don't worry.'

Xavier sounded as though he were about to break out in a very bad case of hysterics. Honey asked if there was someone there he could share his fears with. Xavier replied that there was.

'I've got Gulliver. He sleeps on his cushion under the desk.'

She didn't wait to ask if it was a cat or a dog. She tried phoning Doherty but there was no response. Was he on duty or had he left for his long-standing trip to the Brecon Beacons? Whatever the reason, she couldn't hang around.

* * *

The desk sergeant at Manvers Street looked up and smiled when he saw Honey enter.

'Hello there, Mrs Driver. I thought you might be along.'

'Sergeant Clark. How are you?'

'Fine to middling. Fine to middling.'

It was all he ever said when asked how he was. Honey had no idea whether he had a family or not, because his responses never went further than 'fine to middling'.

'What can I do for you?'

'I hear the Chairman of Bath Hotels Association has been brought in for questioning regarding the body found at Bradford on Avon. Is there any reason for that?'

Sergeant Clark leaned forward and whispered so nobody else could hear.

'It's all about identification. I don't know where the order came from, but I had a phone call saying they want a sample of Mr St John Gervais's DNA.'

Honey drew back, as much to avoid the desk sergeant's bad breath as in surprise.

'What for?'

The desk sergeant scratched his head. 'Apparently the wheel was set in motion by some pathologist in Devizes.'

Honey tried to think why that would be. She couldn't even begin to guess.

'Has he agreed to give a sample?'

Actually, Caspar wouldn't have much choice, but she knew how stubborn he could be. It wasn't inconceivable that he would put up a fight. Regardless, the police would be insistent. They would only have asked him for DNA if they suspected some connection. If that was so, then this case was no longer a suicide. DNA was required when a crime had been committed. It had to be murder.

'He's very subdued,' murmured the sergeant, still trying to avoid being overheard. 'However, he was persuaded. The guv'nor's asked for a quick turnaround on the results.'

Honey frowned. 'But I thought everything to do with this was going through Devizes?'

The sergeant tapped the side of his nose and winked. 'Devizes did want him taken there, but the guv'nor persuaded them that it would be quicker for us to do it.'

Honey had to agree that it made sense. She also guessed the word 'guv'nor' alluded to Steve Doherty.

'There seems to be a bit of rivalry going on here — I mean between Wiltshire police and Bath.'

The sergeant nodded. 'Seems that way, though we all know old Caspar. He's done a lot for this city and it owes him. Why put him through unnecessary hassle?'

Honey's fingers tapped a rhythm on the counter as she thought it through. It came to her that Doherty was doing Caspar a favour and playing for time. She nodded her thanks to the desk sergeant.

'Do you want to wait for the guv'nor?' he asked her, a slightly mischievous look in his eyes.

Honey smiled and shook her head. The whole station knew the history between her and Doherty. At least she knew he was still somewhere in the city.

When Caspar emerged after giving a sample of his DNA, his face was paler than the collar of the white shirt that peeped above his navy-blue blazer. He looked like the commodore of a yacht club.

'Are they letting you go?' Honey whispered.

Caspar nodded, his eyes downcast and his jaw moving as though he were grinding his teeth.

'At least they know you're not the dead man.'

She said it cheerfully, in the hope of raising his spirits.

Caspar's face remained deadpan, in fact severely concerned.

The fresh evening air outside hit them with a fine shower of drizzle. Just for once Caspar didn't have his umbrella.

They walked away from the police station, Caspar lacking his usual composure. Honey sensed there was more he wanted to say.

'What is it, Caspar? Why did they want a sample of your DNA?'

'In order to identify the man who was murdered. If it matches, then I also have to make a formal identification.'

So it was murder!

Sprinkles of rain showered from Honey's hair when she shook her head, puzzled by all this.

'DNA and a formal identification? Why?'

Caspar stopped in his tracks and took a deep breath, a strange, foreign look in his eyes.

'Because they think it was Tarquin who was murdered. They think it was my brother. One way or another, my DNA will prove that.'

CHAPTER FIVE

She tried a few times to phone Caspar after that, but on each occasion one of his bevy of receptionists told her he was busy. She told herself that he needed a few days to get over the shock.

The next time she saw him, he was sipping cocktails in Raphael's, the smart restaurant opposite the old mineral hospital, and he seemed incredibly calm.

'I understand your policeman lover is off shortly to the wilds of mid-Wales. Will you have the opportunity for some time together before he leaves?'

Up until now Caspar had never referred to her and Doherty in the same breath, or asked such a personal question. It was unlike him.

'Well, we were considering a weekend away . . .' she faltered, realising how it must sound to Caspar's ears. 'I mean, we've had a break from each other. Not necessarily permanent, just a bit of time for both of us to think where we're going. What with the wedding not happening . . .'

The planned wedding had been interrupted by a murder in the village church where they'd chosen to get married, which had contributed to putting them off the idea.

Caspar generously offered the use of a cottage he owned down near a place called Wyvern Wendell. Honey expressed her gratitude.

'It's the least I can do,' Caspar responded. 'It's on the Torrington Towers estate. A lovely little place. I'm sure you'll like it. Here's the key.'

Seeing as they'd only just discussed his cottage, it seemed odd that he had the key on his person.

'I'd very much like you to be there.'

Suspicious at his motives, Honey eyed him warily. What else was this about?

'Next weekend, if you don't mind. I'll be there too of course.'

'What's happening?'

Eyelids as smooth and big as dessertspoons hid his expression.

'It's my brother's funeral. I would like you to come. Not to keep me company, but to observe, to ask questions and so on.'

Honey found herself agreeing. After all, it made sense for her to make enquiries.

Now she just needed to convince Doherty . . .

* * *

Doherty seemed taken aback at the idea, and looked in two minds until she mentioned that she'd been invited to the funeral in a private capacity. 'Though we could linger a little longer. We're due a bit of quality time . . .'

He went on to say he had a few things to tidy up before they left. 'Mine has to be a mixture of work and pleasure. I'll probably be a bit late getting away but it might be useful — in more ways than one,' he added with a grin. 'So we're on, if you don't mind us driving down separately.'

She didn't mind at all.

The plan was that she would drive to the cottage at Wyvern Wendell on the Torrington estate and Doherty would follow on behind. On arrival, a little wearied by travelling, they would eat in.

The weather was seasonal, the Indian summer they'd been enjoying having headed south, leaving the trees heavy with colour and a refreshing nip in the air, ideal weather for an autumn weekend.

She wouldn't admit it to Doherty, but she felt good about arriving before him. She'd have time to prepare the evening's meal, chill the wine and await his arrival. Everything would go swimmingly. At least that's what she thought, until she glanced in her rear-view mirror.

The car was sleek, black and had tinted windows. Four times she looked in her mirror, each time growing more suspicious and a little scared.

It looked very much like Dominic Christiansen's BMW. But that couldn't be right. Could it?

So, she said to herself, swallowing her fear, you're being followed. Either that or you're paranoid.

She didn't think she was being paranoid. A fifth and a sixth glance and it was still there.

She found herself feeling slightly sick. Why would anyone want to follow her?

Miles more motoring and he was still there. She'd left the motorway some way back. The traffic on the main road was less than on the motorway, and lessened again once she left the main road and turned onto a minor road.

The hedges were higher, and in places it was single file with just a few passing places.

The effect was claustrophobic and definitely scary. It was the stuff of crime and thriller novels created by vivid imaginations and, although she tried to persuade herself otherwise, she knew, she just knew.

The driver's identity was cloaked in the dim interior behind the darkened glass of the windscreen. No passengers, or at least none that she could see.

Was she being paranoid? A little test would prove it one way or the other. She stabbed at the brake and saw the reflection of her brake light glowing red on the shiny chrome of the car behind. There was a screeching of locked wheels as the driver fought to maintain control and avoid kissing the Citroen's rear.

'You're driving too bloody close,' Honey shouted.

She made a rude gesture into the rear-view mirror, pushed the accelerator to the floor and shot off. Though she'd expected some kind of response — even a sounding of a horn — she received none.

The narrow road ahead needed close attention if she was to outrun the man — and outrun him she damn well would. His engine was bigger than the Citroen's, but the little car was extremely manoeuvrable on country lanes.

Determinedly, she wove along the narrow road, which became no more than a lane before she shot out across a T-junction and onto a wider road.

The sign opposite her said, *Wyvern Wendell, 3 miles.*

Without halting at the white line, she took a swift right and put her foot down, driving like a demented spider weaving a web. When she next looked in the mirror, the shiny black BMW had been replaced by a police car.

'Thank *God*!'

Honey had never been happier to see a set of flashing blue lights. The car she was sure had been following her had disappeared.

She breathed a sigh of relief and, not wishing to upset the men in blue, pulled over dutifully. Checking again for the other car, she wound down the window.

She tossed her head so that her hair splayed out like a living halo. Now that the threat of the other car was gone, the prospect of getting a speeding ticket loomed large in her mind. It was something she could well do without.

Two uniformed police officers exited the car. One of them approached her, his walk slow and purposeful, as though he were John Wayne and had just dismounted from his horse.

'Constable — I'm so relieved you're here!'

'Are you really, miss? You were travelling at over sixty miles per hour in a thirty-mile limit. Going somewhere in a hurry, are we?'

The sarcasm was feral.

'Yes. As I was just about to explain, I was being followed — no, *tailgated* — by a reckless driver in a huge black car. It was almost like he was trying to run me off the road . . .'

The policeman looked tellingly at the empty road.

'If he was, he must be the invisible man.'

'Look. I'm meeting my boyfriend. He's a policeman.'

He didn't look as though he believed her. 'That's what they all say, miss. Everyone wants to be a policeman.'

'It's true!' she exclaimed with feeling. 'His name's Detective Inspector Steve Doherty. He's stationed at Manvers Street in Bath and—'

'Can I see your driving licence, miss?'

Heaving a huge sigh, Honey dragged her shoulder bag off the front passenger seat. The bag was made of brown suede, very square with a rawhide fringe all around. Very hippy-looking, though in actuality very expensive and bought in a shop specialising in the retro look.

'Here you are, Constable.' She gave him the licence, which he scrutinised as though searching for some hidden meaning in the basic details of name, age and contact address.

His disdainful manner continued.

The writing was on the wall. There was no way he was going to let her get away with this but she was determined to give it another go.

'Look,' the words came tumbling out, 'I really did think I was being stalked by a man in a black car. Really, I did. And the way he was driving put the fear of God into me.'

He held onto the licence as he gave it back and, for a brief moment, his fingertips touched hers. His look was direct.

'I'll let you off this time. Next time I won't.'

After snatching the licence back, Honey made a big fuss about putting everything back in the bag. The tremor in her hand as she fumbled with her licence was real.

'What about the man following me? Will you keep a lookout for him?'

'He isn't following you now, is he?'

'He wouldn't be,' Honey returned hotly. 'You pulled me over because you said I was speeding. You'd be speeding too if somebody was following you.'

He screwed up his face until it looked like a withered balloon.

'Well, you're not being followed now, miss, so I suggest you carry on.'

'Perhaps not. But if I see the car again, I'll be sure to report it to someone who'll listen. In the meantime, you've seen my licence. Good day to you.'

Clenching her jaw, she slid the gearstick into first, foot to the floor, and roared off, the car's deceptively small engine pushing to thirty miles per hour in no time at all.

Taking one last glance in the rear-view mirror, she detected the policeman was standing at the side of his vehicle, speaking into his radio.

CHAPTER SIX

The sun came out from behind a cloud just after six, and although it was too late to hit an unseasonal high, it was good enough for a weekend away from it all. She found herself wondering about the use of dark glass in cars. Wasn't it illegal?

The satnav took her along the main road running through Wyvern Wendell, the nearest market town to the Torrington Towers estate.

The syrupy-voiced satnav woman instructed her to turn at the signpost at a place called Hangman's Corner. At the base of the sign was an old milestone saying ninety miles to London. She guessed that, as its name implied, there was once a gibbet at Hangman's Corner.

She avoided looking up just in case her imagination played tricks and she espied a skeleton encased in an iron cage, its flesh torn apart by crows and magpies.

'*Continue for three miles . . .*'

She wasn't entirely trusting of satnavs, having seen some unfortunate tourists end up in the middle of a Bath city thoroughfare facing the wrong way. She wanted to be sure of where she was going so had taken the precaution of bringing a map with her. At present it lay on the passenger seat, open at the right page in case she needed to do a quick referral.

Although the trees on either side were shedding their leaves, enough were left to keep the road in perpetual shade. The fact that the branches met overhead only added to the encircling gloom. It was like driving through a tunnel.

On the way to the estate where the cottage was situated she passed a few hamlets and the odd dwelling. It struck her that these outlying places seemed devoid of people, almost as though their only purpose was to pretty up the landscape.

The river dissected town and village, the road dropping from a great height into the valley. The only noticeable change was some bald patches on the highest slopes where the Forestry Commission had harvested a series of tall conifers.

A single road ran through the village of Wyvern Wendell, a place mentioned in the Doomsday Book as having a tithe barn, a church, twenty sheep, forty pigs and a 'goodly duck pond and diverse roach and perch'.

She saw a few sheep and pigs in the surrounding fields, confirming that in a thousand years things hadn't changed much. How the ducks, roach and perch were nowadays she didn't have a clue.

The buildings varied in age, those dating from medieval times of half-timbered construction, twisted and bent and leaning against the later structures for support. Colours varied from white to cream, pink and mustard. Some were thatched. Some had slate or tiled roofs.

At the end of the street was the church, hiding behind a thick hedge of yew. The village store housed the post office and overlooked the duck pond, and the ducks still wandered the village green.

The garage boasted two antiquated petrol pumps in front of a greasy garage workshop. The sign said, *Fred Cromer, Motor Engineer.* There was a man out front presently engaged in filling up a car. Probably Fred Cromer. Because the garage had only a small forecourt, the car being filled was parked halfway into the road.

Honey did a second take. The car was black with dark windows and shiny chrome wheels.

The stalker! It had to be Dominic Christiansen, but why had he followed her?

Honey slowed the car. Somehow the black car had overtaken her, but how was that possible? When stopped by the police she'd presumed her stalker had shot off onto a side road.

She craned her neck, looking for the driver. She couldn't see anyone, just the lone figure filling up the car.

It was quite impossible to see him. Whoever he was, he'd gone into the garage.

In an effort to calm her nerves, she turned up the volume on the radio. Bob Dylan was singing 'Blowin' in the Wind'. Normally she would have sung along to the old-time classic, but on this occasion she gave it a miss. She motored on, her throat dry and a feeling of apprehension chilling her blood.

* * *

Dominic Christiansen stayed in the shadows until he was sure she'd driven past.

The garage owner, Fred Cromer, had been brewing a cup of tea when he'd arrived at the garage, his glasses misted by the steam rising from the kettle.

'D'you fancy a cuppa?' Fred asked now.

Dominic shook his head. He'd seen the mugs, thickly coated with tannin.

'Then I'll leave it to stand for a bit,' said Fred. 'I don't like none of that fortnight tea — "too week",' he said, laughing at his own joke. 'Cash or credit card?'

Dominic handed him a credit card chosen from a selection nestled in his leather wallet. A present from a past girlfriend and purchased in Harrods.

Cromer curled his bottom lip before rummaging for the mobile payment terminal. Dominic didn't need to be told that Cromer preferred cash.

Dominic slid into the driver's seat. He never tired of appreciating the comfort of the soft leather upholstery. The contours of the seat moulded to his back.

He gave the garage owner a quick wave before making off down the high street. A glance in his rear-view mirror confirmed that Fred had foregone the tea he'd just made and was watering his plant pots. Red and white geraniums made a splash of colour, still flowering despite the advent of mid-autumn, positioned as they were between the two old-fashioned fuel pumps, one for petrol and one for diesel. The flowers prettied things up but did nothing to veil the stink of old oil and grease.

Once out of the village, he pushed a button on the dashboard and made a call. It was answered quickly.

'Has she arrived safely?'

'Yes. I followed her until the police stopped her. She and the copper are staying at a cottage. She's gone to it the long way round. I've noted there's a shorter route. It leads to a heavily wooded copse. I can keep an eye on them from there.'

He heard a heavy sigh on the other end of the phone. 'The sooner this is over the better. It shouldn't be any great shakes for you, Dominic, old son. She's just a bloody amateur and won't have a clue as to what's going on. Do we know where the Tarot Man is?'

'Not sure. The tail lost him. I'm guessing he might be interested in her. I don't think she knows anything about him though.'

'I must say her boyfriend's been something of a surprise. He's forced us to show our hand. It would have been better if the dead man had never been identified. The Tarot Man would have known. The girls he's killed don't matter. But he wanted confirmation that he'd killed the man he wanted to kill. Tarquin was his victim. We've given him that confirmation — in a roundabout way.'

'Exactly as planned. As for Mrs Honey Driver, I think it's a little too early for the Tarot Man to show his hand, but we live in hope.'

'We do indeed. Full marks for your finding out about this weekend retreat, Christiansen.'

'I was lucky.'

The man on the other end of the phone had a dry, humourless laugh.

'You're manipulative, Christiansen, not lucky.'

It had proved too easy to ask questions at the police station, and even easier at the Green River Hotel — until the woman's daughter had intervened.

'She's already left for a weekend away.'

'Can you tell me where?'

'You're the man she met out at Bradford on Avon.'

He'd winced under the directness of her gaze but pulled himself together quickly.

'I wanted to see her again.'

Her voice had softened a little, but she still hadn't been forthcoming. 'I think that's her business, unless she wanted to tell you herself.'

He'd decided to back off.

Straight after that, he'd bumped into Honey Driver's mother, who was leaving the hotel at the same time as he was. He heard the daughter behind reception calling her 'Gran', in response to which the older woman's expression turned thunderous.

'Lindsey. You know how I feel about you calling me that.'

'OK. Gloria. Gloria, my grandmother.'

There was a hint of contempt in the granddaughter's voice that made him smile.

Dominic had taken full advantage of the situation, opening the hotel door for the older woman, playing the charm card for all he was worth.

'Perhaps I could buy you coffee?'

It had worked swimmingly, and over two frothy cappuccinos she had made it obvious that she did not approve of the copper with whom her daughter was having a relationship.

'Neither do I approve of unmarried people going away for the weekend. And not even a hotel! A cottage in the middle of nowhere. Now, who in their right mind wants to be that isolated? Of course there is the funeral . . .'

The funeral. Ah, of course.

He had the sort of mind that was used to dealing with more than one problem at a time, so was ready to explain his findings.

'Honey Driver is no fool. Very observant. She saw me, or rather she gave every sign that she knew somebody was following her.'

'Did she now!' The man on the other end of the phone sounded displeased. 'It's not like you to be so careless.'

'I try not to be.'

'This is what I want from you.'

Dominic found himself almost yawning at the sound of the voice. Basically, he found it boring and, in order to bear it better, he took a card from his pocket — a tarot card.

The voice droned on. 'I would have halved your load and put a separate tail on the Tarot Man, but I don't have the manpower. This weekend at least you'll have to keep an eye on them both.'

Once the connection was severed, Dominic sighed. A rough weekend was in store. He'd found an old tin shed in which to hide the car while he prowled outside, keeping an eye on the cottage from the copse surrounding it.

Within the tin shed he stripped off his smart casual clothes and donned field fatigues, took out his binoculars and long-range sound-recording equipment that James Bond would have been proud to make use of, and settled down.

He'd thought his days of roughing it in combat gear were over.

'Getting too old for this,' he muttered to himself.

He took one last item from a box hidden beneath the floor in the boot of the car. A small firearm. The pair about to move into the cottage were innocent of what they'd stumbled into. At some point he might have to enlighten them, but for now it made sense to be prepared.

CHAPTER SEVEN

The cottage was surrounded by trees and approached along a single-track road. The sign had been half hidden by overhanging foliage, but with the aid of 'Ada', as she'd nicknamed the satnav, she arrived at her destination.

She found herself in a clearing, the cottage — suitably measuring up to the description of 'chocolate box' — was right ahead. There was an old Mini Clubman parked outside. It looked in decent condition. A woman appeared in the cottage door. This, Honey knew, was the woman who looked after the cottage. The old car obviously belonged to her.

'Here you are, me dear,' said the cheery-faced woman. 'My name's Mrs Cromer. I look after this place for the owner. I think everything will be to your satisfaction. There's two steaks cut thick as your finger in the fridge, plus milk and basics. If there's anything else you need, give me a call. I've left my number,' she added with a smile. 'I'm off now, on account that Mr Cromer will be wanting his dinner.'

'Can I ask you something before you go?'

Mrs Cromer looked only slightly perturbed at being delayed.

'As long as it's short and sweet, dear.'

'Did you know Lord Torrington?'

'Everybody did.'

'Did you like him?'

'Oh yes. A gentleman, but a bit of a lad — even at his age.' She chuckled. 'The stories I could tell . . .'

'Do you think . . . ?'

Mrs Cromer waved her hand dismissively. 'Oh, you don't want any second-hand tales from me. I take it you're attending the funeral?'

'Yes, I am.'

'Then you'll no doubt get some first-hand information there.' Her voice dropped and her eyes widened as she imparted a little local knowledge.

'They used to call him the Thoroughbred Stud!'

She laughed at that, waved her hand again and was gone.

A cool breeze rustled the trees as Honey stood watching Mrs Cromer drive away. Once the car had disappeared, the sun hid behind a cloud. The trees rustled more ominously and she shivered.

Glancing at her watch, she saw it would be at least another hour before Doherty arrived. Time enough to get her single piece of luggage out of the boot, plus the ready-made meals she'd bought at Marks and Spencer. Dine in for two, complete with a bottle of wine. Who needed anything else? She reminded herself that Mrs Cromer had mentioned buying in two steaks. If they were locally raised they were bound to be good.

The cottage had flagstone floors and an Aga cooker, and the living room had antique chairs with shiny wooden frames and velvet upholstery. Most of it looked comfortable.

The bedroom, approached via a spiral staircase, was pretty. A rug with motifs of pink roses and green leaves covered the centre of the bedroom floor. The walls were scattered with smaller versions of the flowers on the rug. The bed was of white-painted cast iron, quite decorative and about five feet wide. Plenty of space for two.

Dear Mrs Cromer had placed a bottle of white wine in the fridge. Honey helped herself to a glass while she waited for Doherty.

The sound of a car and headlights flashing into the descending darkness heralded his arrival. He was late.

Honey opened the front door, pleased that the table was laid and they could eat once he'd brought in his things.

'I've got something to tell you.' He entered the cottage without passing comment on how cosy it was and that something smelled good.

'What is it?'

Doherty frowned and for a moment looked at her as though having second thoughts about telling her anything.

'Well, you already know that the deceased was Caspar's brother.'

'And?'

Doherty flung off his jacket and stood in front of her, hands in pockets.

'Lord Torrington. The family name is St John Gervais. He was actually Caspar's half-brother. There's no mistake.'

Honey rolled her eyes. 'That's right, Steve. The man we're here to bury. The question is, why on earth it's been so impossible to ID him. And why they ever thought he was a vagrant?'

'He'd been in the ground for about a month, so his clothes were pretty muddied, but they were pretty grim too. Then we checked the National DNA database.' He frowned thoughtfully. 'It took longer than usual. Somebody seemed to be holding things back, but with a bit of persistence we got a result . . . Forensics came back to us with the name Crustwell.'

'Crustwell?'

Honey couldn't believe that Caspar could possibly have a brother named Tarquin Crustwell because that might mean that his own name was Crustwell. But it wasn't. It was St John Gervais. Or was it? Names were easily altered by deed poll.

'You're right,' said Doherty before she could ask the question. 'Our friend Caspar used to be called Bernard Crustwell but changed his name by deed poll. Tarquin was the legitimate heir to Torrington Towers. Caspar was his half-brother, his mother being the housekeeper. Caspar confessed.' He grinned. 'Fancy old Caspar's real name being Bernard Crustwell. It's certainly made the investigation interesting, that's for sure. And completely threw us off the scent. Who knew a man named *Crustwell* would have aristocratic heritage . . .'

Doherty went on. 'Anyway, Tarquin was ten years younger than Caspar and they hadn't seen each other for years.'

Honey tilted her head to one side and eyed Doherty quizzically.

'I thought this was a Devizes case. How come you suddenly know all this?'

Doherty sat down, his expression thoughtful, his hands clasped in front of him.

'I couldn't break through. I couldn't get any details about this case until, with the help of my old friend Goudge in Devizes, we threw a few spanners into the works. Once that happened we couldn't be ignored and Caspar was dragged in to give a DNA sample. Otherwise it might never have happened.'

'And then the family secrets came out?'

Doherty nodded. 'Yes, but only once Caspar was involved.' His frown persisted. 'I still don't think we're getting everything, but it's a start.'

Honey frowned. 'Are you saying he was murdered?'

Doherty's eyes met hers.

'He was buried alive.'

Honey shivered. 'What a dreadful way to die.'

Doherty stood up.

'I take it we have wine?'

Honey willingly took the half-empty bottle of white from the fridge and placed two glasses on the table. Doherty eyed it suspiciously.

'What happened to the first half of this?'

'Don't worry, there's another one in the fridge. A lovely bottle of Chardonnay, chilled to just the right temperature. I chose it with you in mind.' She was not going to admit it came as part of a deal along with the professionally prepared food.

'And something smells delicious.'

'Courgettes stuffed with prawns and chicken marinated in red wine with prosciutto lardons and garnished with miniature tomatoes, onions, garlic and mushrooms. Summer pudding to follow.'

He positively beamed. 'Brilliant.'

'I'm glad you think so. I've been slaving over the cooker ever since I arrived.'

He looked at his watch and frowned. 'At high speed I should think. Is that the truth?'

Honey grinned. 'No. I popped into Marks and Spencer. They were doing their dinner-for-two deal including wine. Who needs to spend time on cooking when we can spend it on each other? Though Mrs Cromer, the lady who looks after this place, brought steaks. We'll have to have them for breakfast or tomorrow night.'

'I thought we might go to the pub tomorrow night.'

'OK. We can take them home with us after the funeral.'

The food was good and they discussed further what they expected regarding Caspar's brother, though without it putting a damper on the evening.

Honey was feeling mellow and replete. 'There will be people there who might know something.'

Doherty lowered his eyes and fingered his glass.

'I have to repeat this here and now. I think it best you back off. I've got a bad feeling about this.'

Honey leaned forward, her hand on his knee, her face upturned to his.

'I know where you're coming from, Steve, but you have to understand how obliged I am to Caspar. He's been good to me, filling my rooms and all that. Even though he can be overbearing, sniffy and downright selfish.'

Doherty agreed, though listlessly. She presumed he was feeling tired.

She drained her glass and threw him a suggestive look.

'Ready for bed?'

They both regarded the dishes as they might be a killjoy about to burst their bubble.

'The dishes can wait until the morning,' said Honey. 'There's something I have to tell you. I was followed here. I'm sure of it.'

Steve said nothing but maintained a less than surprised look. Finally he yawned pointedly. 'It was a long drive.'

While he visited the bathroom, she opened the bedroom window and sniffed the evening air.

The smell of the last summer flowering of old-fashioned roses was tinged with the scent of cow dung. Luckily it wasn't too overpowering.

The trees fringing the grounds were black against an indigo sky and their shadows moved with the breeze. The sky was full of stars. Apart from that, the darkness was total, black shadows falling across the lane.

She was about to turn away when something caught her eye. Something moved.

She leaned further out of the window.

'Something interesting out there?'

Doherty had returned.

'I thought I saw something or someone move among the trees.'

She felt the heat of his naked arm and torso as he squeezed into the small gap beside her and the window frame and looked out. His eyes narrowed.

'Mammal or man?'

She shook her head. 'I'm not sure. Probably nothing. A deer? A stray cow?'

'But you reckon you were followed.'

'Aha.'

Doherty reached for the window latch. 'Everything's locked and bolted downstairs. Let's close this.'

Honey stepped back. It wasn't a chilly night, but all the same she couldn't help rubbing her arms.

'You need warming up,' he said, at the same time wrapping his arms around her. 'That was a lovely supper. I need to express my gratitude.'

The chill nervousness left her body. She smiled and did the same to him. There was comfort in clinging to each other, them against the world beyond the window. They still clung together when they were lying in bed.

Eventually Doherty left her arms, turned onto his side and began to snore.

Half dozing, Honey lay there on her back looking up at patches of light on the ceiling. Was she falling asleep or were the patterns changing?

It's just your imagination, she told herself. She rolled over onto her side and, tugging the bedclothes over her head, blotted out the ceiling.

CHAPTER EIGHT

The Tarot Man imagined her undressing. Closing his eyes, he took deep breaths, smiling at the visions he could see in his mind. He could smell the subtle sweat of her body, breathing it in until he could almost taste her essence, the scents and the feel of her that made her who she was.

Cloaked by darkness, he reached out a hand, his fingers folding gently inwards as though tracing the shape of a bra cup.

He opened his eyes. The light in the bedroom was still on. Just one more item of underwear and she would be naked. The man nicknamed the Tarot Man sniffed the air. His concentration was total as he breathed in the more distinct aroma of lace-edged panties — expensive items bought in upmarket places in upmarket cities.

She was blonde, she was beautiful, and yet . . . and yet . . . she was ugly because her soul was ugly, because the wealth, the power and the prestige of her class made her that way. And it was all down to her father, one of those who had fought the undercover war, the one where enemies were just as likely to be friends and vice versa.

Women like her were the epitome of all that was ugly about the Western world, the democracies that trumpeted their fairness but were not fair. Hence the reason for his hobby, this presentation of the fact that no matter how rich, how fair, how gifted, these girls and women were no different from anyone else. Fashioned from clay and to clay they would return. This was his homage to what he believed in.

A sound disturbed his revelry. He became aware of another presence, perhaps one of the rangers who worked for the estate on which the cottage was situated. Like a shadow, he melted into the undergrowth.

* * *

Dominic Christiansen was aware of somebody close by. Keeping low and treading stealthily, he crept through the undergrowth. Hearing a rustling of foliage, his hand leaped to the bulge beneath his armpit. He would only use it if he had to.

He came to the spot where he thought he'd seen movement. There was no one there — but someone had been. The smell of a smoked Russian cigarette lingered, but his prey was gone.

'Damn.' He swore under his breath.

He went back to the ruined stump of the ancient elm tree, its interior rotted away and big enough to get inside. From there he had a good view of the cottage. Honey Driver would be safe until morning.

CHAPTER NINE

'Hey, babe. You didn't ask if I'd brought a black tie.'

Doherty's lips brushed her shoulder.

Cursing her lack of resolve, Honey turned to face him. The very sight of Doherty sent shivers down her spine. His hair was tousled and he was wearing a seductive grin — nothing else. Resistance was futile.

'I take it you have.'

'And you?'

'Black trousers. Black cowl-neck top.'

'How about afterwards? Do you fancy a country walk?'

'That depends.'

'Questions, questions, questions.'

'There's a chance we might learn something.'

'From grieving relatives? Perhaps.'

Over an hour later, Honey was frying bacon while Doherty prepared scrambled eggs. Fresh coffee was brewing and the kitchen window was open to the freshness of the morning. The funeral service was at eleven in the village church, the cremation in private grounds owned by the family.

Honey voiced her thoughts. 'In the grounds. Not at the crematorium. Odd, don't you think? How do I look?'

He finished fixing his tie and grinned. 'Sexy without being disrespectful.'

'I look good in black.'

Doherty took on a pondering expression. 'I wonder if there's any significance in that. I mean, why outdoors and why so swiftly? I've never known a body be released this quickly before, especially without having found the culprit. It all seems a little rushed to me.'

'I'm glad for Caspar's sake that everything's being finalised. I must say I'm looking forward to it. Torrington Towers. It sounds quite grand. I didn't realise Caspar came from such a well-heeled family.'

'I didn't even know he had a brother,' Doherty added. 'Or a pile in the country complete with a zoo. What an expense that must be!'

'A safari park. Not a zoo.' Honey had to agree about the running costs, though pointed out that it was open to the public.

'That should help pay to feed the lions.'

Doherty shrugged his shoulders into the sleeves of his black leather jacket. His shirt was white, his trousers were black, and so was his tie — the latter the only gesture to this being something of a formal occasion. At other times Steve Doherty never wore a tie.

* * *

The church was full and not the place one could go asking questions about a man's lifestyle. That would have to wait until they were at the wake, which was being held at the same time as the cremation at Torrington Towers itself.

A lion roared some distance off in the park as the cars of mourners jostled for space around the front of the house, overspill from the private car park at the rear.

'Quite a pad,' murmured Honey.

'So why was Caspar's brother living like a tramp?'

'Perhaps he wasn't. Being eccentric, perhaps he was getting a taste for the life of a down-and-out.'

Doherty looked at her sceptically. 'You don't really believe that?'

Honey pulled a face as she thought about it. 'No. Not really.'

Doherty made no response but frowned and looked straight ahead.

'Hello. What's this?'

Several security men were stopping cars before checking them into a parking place.

'My word. Are they worried somebody's going to steal the casket?'

Doherty pulled rank and waved his police ID. The security guard looked unimpressed.

'I'm sorry. You have to have an official invitation to this funeral.'

Now it was Doherty who was unimpressed. 'You're joking!'

The security guard's face was impassive and there was a hard look in his eyes.

'Will these do?'

Honey flashed the invitations Caspar had given her.

The guard winced and, although he waved them through, she got the distinct impression he would have preferred to refuse them entry.

'He didn't want to let you in,' she said to Doherty.

Doherty shook his head while gripping the steering wheel as though it were the guard's neck.

'Since when do you need an invitation to a funeral?'

Honey had to admit the same thought had occurred to her.

'There was something decidedly shady about Caspar's brother, this whole thing hinting that he was a vagrant when he obviously was not. He'd have had to be the direct opposite of his brother to be like that and I don't believe he could be. All siblings have some likeness to each other, however small.'

They were locking the car door when a familiar voice called to them.

Caspar looked dapper and almost otherworldly, head to toe the epitome of the lord of the manor.

After the initial greetings, Caspar held onto Honey's hands. 'I am so glad you could come, my dear. Your attendance is much appreciated. Yours too, Doherty. I see you're wearing a tie.'

'Hired just for the occasion,' returned Doherty. 'I didn't even know you had a brother.'

Caspar pointedly declined to answer. 'There's champagne and canapés in the drawing room. Do help yourselves,' he said, his expression as grey as November.

He wandered off. Honey was tempted to go after him, but Doherty stopped her, his hand landing on her arm.

'This is weird.'

'"Curiouser and curiouser," said Alice.'

'You're not Alice and this is not a dream!'

'They've got lions here. Did you know that? Once the cremation's done and dusted I'm going to look for them.'

Doherty eyed her suspiciously. 'You're going to wander around this place looking for lions?'

She looked up at him with innocent eyes. 'Isn't that what I just said? Anyway, I like lions.'

They were directed to where the event was to take place. Caspar's brother was being cremated in a walled garden, a place of peaty ground, long grass and late-season vegetables. The rain was holding off. White clouds suffused with hidden sunlight slid like sailing ships across a sea of sky.

Caspar had set himself up at the arched entrance to the walled garden, accepting condolences and sympathy with a wry expression.

Honey did the same as everyone else, although she'd already expressed her condolences back in Bath.

Doherty dawdled behind, seemingly uninterested, but in truth observing everything that was going on.

A man passed her by and Honey felt a strange ticklish sensation, like feathers floating inside her. Straightaway she knew it was him, Dominic Christiansen. He was wearing a navy-blue suit, white shirt and black tie.

For a moment their eyes met. Before she had chance to speak to him, other people had crowded through the archway, blocking her view.

But she knew it was him. She looked for Doherty. He saw her serious expression and asked what the problem was.

'He's here. Dominic Christiansen.' She pointed to where she'd seen him. 'Oh. He's gone.'

Things were crowded in the walled garden. The earth had been left fallow and was soft with rotting vegetation. Great for vegetables. Hell for high heels. The female guests were sticking to the narrow gravel paths that ran in a loosely oblong arrangement around where carrots and potatoes were usually planted. Honey was no exception.

Doherty held her elbow as she picked her way through the mud.

'Trousers are practical. High heels are not,' Doherty rebuked, glancing down at Honey's attire.

The funeral pyre had been erected in the central square area. The guests milled around it, slowly inching along like a column of black crows. The pyre was a neat construction of interlocked logs.

Doherty leaned close and whispered in her ear. 'The gardener told me the logs were mainly pine, though a few from a recently felled apple tree have been included.'

'Is there some significance to that?'

'Of course there is. Apple logs give a nice perfume to the wood smoke.'

'Oh. They could kill two birds with one stone and cook a few jacket potatoes in the embers. Should prove quite delicious.'

'That wouldn't be respectful.'

Honey reminded herself that this was the funeral of Caspar's brother and conceded he had a point.

'I think it's time we split up.'

Doherty's eyebrows arched in feigned surprise. 'I've done something to offend you?'

'Stop playing the fool. We're supposed to be giving each other space, remember? And besides, we can cover more ground if we circulate separately. You ask your questions and I'll ask mine.'

Doherty grumbled something that sounded like agreement, then added, 'I thought we were on a weekend away.'

'Oh, come on. Don't be such an old grouch. We are away. The cottage is lovely, isn't it?'

'I am not being a grouch,' he said sulkily.

She threw him a disapproving look to which he responded.

'Honey, my idea of a weekend break is walking in the countryside and perhaps — no, most definitely — ending up eating and drinking at a lovely little wayside inn. Funerals do not come high on my list of things to do on a weekend away.'

'There'll be food and drink after the fire's lit.'

Doherty shook his head. 'Sometimes I don't quite know what planet you're on.'

'Shoo,' she said, waving him off to mingle, meet and ask questions of the mourners.

As she watched him go it came to her that he was less than willing to get involved in this case and she couldn't work out why.

Suddenly she spotted Dominic Christiansen again, standing head and shoulders above everyone else, his eyes scrutinising the gathering with deadly accuracy.

Before she had chance to filter through the crowd to speak to him, a soft hand touched her arm.

'He lived as he wished and died doing what he loved.'

The speaker was a fine-looking woman with white hair and high cheekbones. She wore sadness in her eyes and affection on her lips. Honey couldn't think why she'd picked her to speak to but sensed it might be something of a bonus.

'I'm sorry. I don't think we've been introduced,' said Honey.

'Clara Witchell. I do believe I was his first.' She didn't offer to shake hands.

First of what, wondered Honey? One possibility loomed higher than any other. Thinking it rude to presume, at the same time as introducing herself, she asked what first Clara Witchell might possibly be referring to.

'His lover. Women were very fond of Tarquin. And he was fond of them. Not that he maintained any long-term associations. He couldn't, seeing as he disappeared for months, even years, at a time. An odd fellow. Odd life.'

Honey recalled the nickname Mrs Cromer had imparted. The Thoroughbred Stud.

'So he travelled a lot?'

The woman nodded. 'A very great deal. He was clever with languages, you know. Quite debonair too, a true jet-setter. You know, yachts, nightclubs, pretty girls . . . but he always came back here. A bit like James Bond. He loved this house.'

Honey eyed the formidable-looking turrets of Torrington Towers, the family's stately home.

Clara Witchell had a very direct look. 'Am I right in thinking you're a friend of his brother?'

Her question took Honey off guard. She didn't know anyone here except Caspar, so hadn't expected anyone to know her.

'That's right.'

Clara shook her head. 'Following his half-brother's demise he'll take over the title. Two entirely different sorts. Both debonair in their own way, but Tarquin was fun. *Casino Royale* as opposed to *Priscilla, Queen of the Desert*.'

It seemed an odd comparison to make, but Honey let it pass until she rethought the *Casino Royale* aspect.

'Did Tarquin play cards?'

Clara laughed a deep, throaty laugh. 'You mean did he gamble? Oh yes. He gambled all right.' Her eyes sparkled.

Honey wondered at the kind of man who made a woman's eyes sparkle even after he was dead.

'Ordinary playing cards?'

'What other sort are there?'

Honey recalled the card found on the dead man's body. 'Tarot cards?'

Clara shook her head. 'Oh no. Tarquin was a very realistic though sensory man, the sort who makes the future rather than foretelling it.'

The two women regarded the pile of wood.

'They'll be lighting it soon,' Honey said to her.

'Very theatrical,' Clara said softly. 'He'd have liked that.'

An old gentleman of military bearing held what looked like a flamethrower. He reminded Honey of the Statue of Liberty as he waited for the word to touch flame to timber.

'That's Uncle Theobald,' Clara informed her. 'He's a general and a bit deaf.'

'I didn't know there were any living relatives,' said Honey.

'Oh, there are. Though some of them only get wheeled out for christenings, weddings and funerals. They're the last of the old generation and for the rest of the time they're best left locked away!'

Although the comment was just a little cruel, Honey couldn't help smiling. No wonder Caspar was the way he was.

'It's what he would have liked,' Clara went on. 'The alternative was a plot of earth marked by half a ton of carved stone cross.'

Honey concurred. 'At least this way he's going out in a blaze of glory, so to speak. Well, certainly a blaze.'

Clara agreed.

Honey deduced they were now on familiar terms so threw in a question.

'Who do you think killed him?'

Clara sighed. 'Well, knowing the man he was . . .'

'Which you certainly seem to do,' Honey said, by way of encouragement. Flattery always helped loosen tongues, and suggesting Clara knew the deceased better than anyone seemed a clever idea.

'An angry husband, boyfriend or father. Or it could have been something to do with his work.'

Honey frowned. 'I thought he'd inherited a fortune and didn't need to work.'

'Everyone needs to work, my dear, and darling Tarquin was not the sort to vegetate, burying himself in the country behind these splendid walls and dealing with the tenant farmers and villagers.'

'Was the safari park his idea?'

'His father's. The only way the family could hold onto the place.'

Honey gazed around beyond the garden wall where the turrets of Torrington Towers pierced the treeline.

'I would have stayed here. It's lovely.'

'Then you haven't got the same itchy feet that he had. He was an adventurer through and through. Not that he talked much about his adventures — not in any great detail.'

'Do you know who he worked for?'

Clara eyed her curiously. 'Well, don't you know, my dear?'

Honey blinked. 'No. Whatever made you think that?'

Clara's grey eyes deepened to velvet. Her look was cool and calculating. 'Simply because you ask so many questions.'

'Call me an interested party.' Honey couldn't help the guilty blush that stained her cheeks.

The clock in the tower above the stable yard struck noon, the allotted time for the fire to start.

An aged woman pushed herself into sight between Honey and the fire. She had orange hair and the figure of a rubber banana.

'I am Great Aunt Maude,' she intoned in a high squeaky voice. 'You may kiss me.'

'I don't think—' Honey protested. It was no good. There was no escaping the long arms that clasped her to a bony bosom. Great Aunt Maude's cheek was as soft as a peach and she smelled of cologne. What with the orange hair, the long arms and the hairy face, Honey was reminded of an orangutan. Only the over-applied cologne helped dispel the image.

Caspar stood straight and silent surrounded by relatives. Judging by the look on his face, he wished they would vanish.

However, it was impossible for him to escape. The words of condolence kept coming.

'At last,' Honey murmured under her breath as the pyre was finally lit. The flames were hot and high.

Once the logs were crackling, Caspar sauntered over with a glass of champagne in his hand with which he had toasted his brother's personal barbecue.

'Thank God that's all over,' he muttered. 'Now. Have you found out anything?'

Honey frowned. His tone was very abrupt and slightly disrespectful given their present circumstances.

Caspar read her expression.

'Don't look at me like that. My brother and I never got on. In fact I would go so far as to say we didn't like each other very much.'

'But you still want to find out who killed him even though you didn't like him?'

Caspar looked oddly taken aback. 'Um. Yes.' His fluster was uncharacteristic. He was usually so forthright and always chose the right words.

He immediately seemed to collect himself.

'Of course I do. Blood is thicker than water. However, my brother was insufferable. Totally selfish and an out-and-out philanderer. I felt like killing him myself on many an occasion.'

Honey raised her eyebrows. 'The Thoroughbred Stud?'

Caspar raised his eyes in surprise. 'Who called him that?'

'Everyone. I understand he didn't spend much time here, that he was away a lot with the work he did.'

'Yes.'

'What did he do?'

'He was a diplomat. Something to do with the Foreign Office. He was always away at some embassy or another.'

Ah, thought Honey, remembering Clara's cryptic comment about *Casino Royale*. This was where Doherty's suspicions were heading.

'Why didn't you tell me before?'

'I didn't think it was necessary. Anyway, you might not have wanted to get involved. In my estimation only somebody on the outside is likely to find out what really happened. Government departments are famous for policing themselves and covering up anything that reflects badly on them.'

What he was saying made perfect sense and explained why Doherty had had trouble getting anyone at Devizes to tell him anything. No wonder he'd warned her against getting involved. This type of thing was way out of their league.

One of the park wardens, the man who looked after the lions, came across to ask Caspar about the situation regarding the employees.

'I know it's not really the right time, but if you don't mind . . .' he mumbled while shuffling his feet.

Caspar sighed impatiently. 'Get to the point.'

'The thing is, do you think you're likely to change things here? Do you think jobs might go?'

'Perhaps now is not the time. The one thing I am sure of is that the paperwork will be tremendous.'

Turning his back on the park ranger, he headed for the arched gate, a gaggle of mourners following him.

Doherty reappeared. 'I don't know about you, but all I've found out is that Caspar has a lot of dotty relatives. When can we go?'

She glared accusingly up at him. 'You knew, didn't you?'

His eyes turned darkly intense, as though he had something to say and was just waiting for the right time to say it. Just as suddenly they became guarded.

'My suggestion is that we head for the local pub for lunch and compare notes.'

'Never mind the pub! I know when you're hedging, Steve Doherty.'

It wasn't like her to lose her temper, but she was certainly losing it now.

'No wonder you didn't want to come here. You knew Tarquin was something at the Foreign Office and you were warned off investigating. Isn't that the truth?'

Doherty shrugged his shoulders and took a deep breath. 'Confession time. Yes, I became aware that something was off kilter when Devizes gave me the runaround, and also when the smooth-talking friend turned up at the scene of the murder.'

Honey paused for breath and to consider how swiftly Dominic Christiansen had charmed her with his looks and glossy accoutrements — a cool, black BMW with shiny wheels, his come-to-bed eyes and a muscular form beneath an Italian suit.

'Are we into something *very* dangerous?'

Doherty rubbed thoughtfully at his chin, which today was clean shaven, with no sign of his usual stubble.

'What you're asking is whether it's too late to pull out.'

'Am I?'

She hadn't really thought she was asking that, but on reflection it seemed backing out was a sensible option if personal danger was likely to be involved. Government departments were either ruthless or careless when it came to matters of national security. Either one could get you killed.

CHAPTER TEN

It was a week or so later when Honey called in on Caspar at La Reine Rouge, just to see how he was in the aftermath of his half-brother's send-off.

The duty receptionist rolled his eyes when she asked after Caspar's well-being.

'His temper could be better,' he confided, with a pat of his bright-yellow hair. 'You'd think he'd be cock-a-hoop inheriting a title and a fortune.'

'Do I need to call him your lordship?'

'Not if you want a dark scowl and cussing under his breath.'

Honey made her way down to Caspar's office, quietly rapping on the door and waiting for his permission to enter before opening it.

'Just an old friend to see you,' she said, poking her head around the door.

It wasn't like Caspar to be turned towards the window, his back to his desk, although the courtyard garden beyond was lovely.

He looked pale and there were dark rings beneath his eyes.

'You look terrible. Have I come at an inconvenient time?'

'Yes. Not that it's likely to go away if you go away. The bad time is here to stay. Thanks to the dutiful dictates of my brother!'

Honey took a guess at what his brother might have done to annoy him so. Not leaving him anything? So who got the stately pile?

'Is this something to do with your brother's will?'

'He's left me Torrington Towers.'

'Well, that was nice of him. I understand he was your half-brother, wasn't he? He didn't have to leave you anything, did he?'

Caspar's scowl deepened. 'He's left me the responsibility — subject to a proviso.'

Rising from his chair, he loomed over Honey like a praying mantis, his eyes like dull-grey marbles.

Honey felt something — her courage possibly — shrinking inside.

'My dearly departed brother put a clause in the will that requires me to run the place for five years.'

'Oh!' Honey held her breath for a moment. Caspar was his own man. He didn't like being organised by anyone, so being told he had to live in the ancestral home and run a safari park and other entertainments open to the public was not to his liking.

'Five years?'

That doleful nodding again. 'Absolutely.'

'OK,' said Honey, not quite over the initial shock. 'Plan B. How about getting rid of the animals, closing the safari park and taking it back to being a private house.'

Even before she looked up at him, she knew she was going to see that doleful head-shaking yet again.

'Keeping and continuing to run the safari park is also a prerequisite of me inheriting Torrington Towers.'

'You're joking?'

The head-shaking ended abruptly. 'I never joke.'

No, thought Honey. You rarely laugh either. Carefully, she thought through her next question before pitching it.

'And if you don't move into the house?'

'The whole lot goes to the National Trust.'

It was a tricky thing to say, but Honey just had to do it.

'Who needs a big, old house anyway? It's not your life. This is your life.' She spoke breezily and waved her hands around to signify that the building they were in was his life, not the house he'd known when he was growing up.

Caspar was unmoved. 'That's not the point. Granted, fairgrounds and wild animals are not my thing, but it's a matter of honour that I inherit.' A glimmer of sadness flashed in his eyes and his Adam's apple moved as though he were swallowing something that tasted bitter. 'I also owe it to my mother, God rest her soul.'

'Oh!' Honey was again speechless. Caspar was being emotional about another human being — his mother. He hadn't spoken of the circumstances surrounding his relationship to Tarquin and she hadn't pried. It was now all coming out.

'Did Tarquin's mother die at a young age?'

Caspar looked startled. 'Young age? The old cow lived till she was eighty.'

'So your father divorced Tarquin's mother . . .'

'No!' Caspar's jaw tightened as he grasped for the courage to tell the truth. 'He and my mother never married. We lived in a cottage in the village. My father had visiting rights — to my mother as well as me. He hated Esme, his wife, but loved my mother.' Suddenly he fixed her with an intense look. 'You will never disclose this to anyone! Never!'

Honey gulped. 'I wouldn't dare.'

'Even Doherty.'

'I won't say a word.' She took a deep breath, ready to make amends. 'So it's a matter of pride, you getting the stately home.'

'Most emphatically. It is said by those who have plenty that money doesn't make one happy, but it certainly helps. Not that I am ever likely to warm to the idea of running the place. Oh, how mortifying.'

Honey made as if to catch him as he slumped back into his chair, both hands covering his face.

'Five years of smelly animals and smelly visitors asking stupid questions about the house and family. Children wanting pony rides and permission to touch the giraffe.'

'Perhaps he had good reason for leaving it to you. Perhaps he felt guilty about your mother and all . . .'

He did not respond, his face hidden and his head in his hands.

'Don't take this the wrong way, Caspar, but . . . doesn't all this make you the prime suspect for Tarquin's murder?'

'I've no idea.'

In her opinion the police had every right to suspect him. He'd inherited a huge stately home on his half-brother's death. People would kill for that.

She paused before leaving as a more mundane thought occurred to her.

'Seeing as the situation currently seems set in stone, do you think you could see your way to giving me some free tickets? I could do with a day out.'

'Get out!'

CHAPTER ELEVEN

In the deep, dark depths beneath the rolling grassland of the Torrington estate, Dominic Christiansen tagged through the steel door that protected the entrance to the facility, went to the communications room and made his report.

The man sitting across from him had dark, arched eyebrows over wide-set eyes. Beneath that, his face seemed to contract inwards, ending in a sharply pointed chin. He perused the report thoughtfully.

'So the Tarot Man is still around. You know he's as nutty as a fruit cake, don't you?'

It wasn't often the man known as GR to his subordinates — GR standing for Grave Robber on account of his skull-like features — cracked a joke. He wasn't the joking kind.

Dominic was careful not to smile too widely.

'I do.' He wanted to add that perhaps they should inform the woman that her life was in danger, but the creaking gears of government intelligence regarded such disclosure as tantamount to treason. Nobody must know anything, and nobody in this case meant any ordinary member of the public.

'Does anyone suspect who you work for?'

'They're both suspicious — to a certain extent.'

'Understandable that he has contacts. I trust you made it clear that it was not a police matter.'

'I did, and he understood the warning. I think he's done all in his power to persuade Mrs Driver not to pursue it — but of course we want her to.'

The man nodded and said nothing. Like Dominic, he was a man of few words. However, he was a man used to interrogation, to sensing a thought beneath a tone of voice.

'I sense you have reservations.'

'She's headstrong and very curious, the sort who, if given interesting information, can't help poking her nose in. I saw her talking to the Witchell woman, an old friend of Tarquin. I caught a little of what she told her.'

'And?'

'She was talking about who Tarquin was, his travels, etc.'

The man with the cold eyes folded his bony fingers beneath his chin.

'Hmm. Well, if it helps to keep her poking her nose in . . .' He threw the report onto the desk in front of him.

'She's no fool, but I don't think she's got a clue about her father's past and how he fits into all this.'

'Good. It's best she doesn't know that he too was a "diplomat", though only in the widest sense of the word. The Cold War made many into secret agents.'

'Even though she may be targeted by Tarot Man?'

The man across from him pursed his lips. 'That's the way this department operates and that's the way it should stay. We did what we thought was right, even down to the funeral request.' A broad smile brightened his face. 'And we did it before the pathologist could delve too deeply. To the Tarot Man his death was something of a ritual. A modern equivalent of hanged, drawn and quartered, except in this case the ingestion of mud was the equivalent of being drawn. His signature.'

The man's deadpan expression returned and his chill eyes went back to the report. 'He's here to take his revenge on those who killed him. The hotel woman's father is dead, but she is alive. He wants revenge on relatives of those he feels are guilty. Excellent work, Christiansen. We couldn't have hoped for better bait to set the trap.'

CHAPTER TWELVE

The Cats' Liberation Society was holding a meeting in the small conference room at the end of the first-floor landing. It was being chaired by Honey's mother, Gloria.

It was a mystery to Honey as to why her mother had joined such an organisation seeing as she didn't own a cat.

'I was a cat in a former life. Luckily for me I lived in the lap of luxury, but there are so many cats leading such miserable lives, I felt I had to step in and do what I could.'

Honey didn't bother to ask how she knew she'd been a cat in a former life, though she had to admit there was something of the feline about her. Mary Jane, their resident professor of the paranormal, had a lot to answer for.

Before her mother marched off to take charge of the meeting, Honey caught her halfway up the main staircase.

'Mother, are you responsible for the cat that seems to have moved in with me?'

Her mother blinked. 'What cat, Hannah?'

Honey ignored the use of her given name.

'The one I keep finding in the coach house.'

Her mother shook her impeccably coiffed head of beige-blonde hair. 'I don't know anything about a cat. I told you, my interest in the society is purely because I'm a kindred spirit to felines everywhere.'

The sound of sneezing came from behind the reception desk.

'There,' said Honey. 'Lindsey's always been allergic to cats. We've got to stop it coming in. If I catch it again I'll take it to the stray dogs and cats home.'

'I haven't been allergic to cats for years, Mother. I've got a cold.'

'Sorry, dear.'

Honey gave up. There were too many other things to occupy her this morning. Smudger had asked to have a word and she'd promised to speak to him as soon as possible.

Despite having attended a funeral, she felt refreshed. It hadn't all been dark and dire. She and Doherty had had some time to themselves.

'Oh, I almost forgot. A man left this,' said Lindsey. She passed her mother a brown manila envelope. 'He said he'd promised he would send it to you.'

'Did he leave a name?'

'No. He said you would know who it's from. Dishy, though.' Lindsey smiled. 'Not a rival for your affections, is he?'

Honey gave her a blank look. 'I wouldn't think so.'

Not unless it's Dominic Christiansen, she thought to herself, and only just managed to stop blushing profusely.

Aloud, she said, 'Not the guy who drove me home that time? The gorgeous kind-of policeman?'

'No,' Lindsey shook her head. 'Definitely not that guy.'

'So, what did he look like? This latest mystery man?'

'Tall, large frame, short hair, chiselled features, nice suit.' Lindsey nodded and repeated the bit about the suit. 'It was the most notable thing about him.'

'Not very helpful. It's not ringing any bells so far . . . Let me know if he drops in again, won't you? If anyone wants me I'll be over in the coach house.'

The coach house sitting room was cool, the chair comfortable. Honey gave the envelope the once-over before opening it. There was nothing in it except for a tarot card, this one of a goddess dressed in blue. Her thoughts went back to the tarot card she'd found at the murder scene. She'd forgotten she had it. Now she had two. There were two people who could enlighten her about its meaning. One was her daughter, Lindsey, who could trawl the internet and find out. The more immediate option was Mary Jane. Anything to do with the occult — including tarot — was right up her street, and on balance she knew more than any internet source.

CHAPTER THIRTEEN

Caspar arrived mid-afternoon to ask whether there was any progress with the investigation. Honey suggested they convene in her office so they could talk in private.

'Have you decided what to do about your inheritance?' she asked him.

Caspar cleared his throat before answering.

'What am I to do?' He rolled his head as he said it as though his brain were trying to escape.

Now it was Honey who cleared her throat, unsure what to say next.

'The funeral went well — don't you think?'

'I go to too many of them nowadays. Never did like them. Always preferred dinner parties. So did Tarquin, though in his case the wilder the better!'

Honey refrained from raising a surprised eyebrow.

'Still, if it was what he wanted . . . The old man with the flamethrower . . .'

Caspar pursed his lips and threw her a disapproving look.

'I don't know that it was what he wanted, though all that melodrama would have been right up his street.'

Honey frowned. 'He didn't ask for it?'

'Well, if he did, he didn't put it in writing.'

'And you didn't arrange it?'

He shook his head and shivered. 'Definitely not. Special permission was gained for the burning in private grounds, his ashes scattered in the pond where sea lions swim for goodness' sake! To my mind it was in appallingly bad taste.'

'The family must have misunderstood his wishes.'

'What family? I was his closest relative and our decrepit aunts and uncles assure me it was nothing to do with them, even the old uncle who lit the fire.'

Honey looked at him, puzzled.

'So if the family didn't arrange it then who did?'

'I don't know.' As he shook his head a look of pure confusion crossed his face.

Caspar's declaration scared her. This case was proving the most complicated she'd ever been involved in.

There were the issues regarding the police investigation for a start, along with Doherty's reluctance to get involved. The mystery surrounding the funeral arrangements was even more curious. What was the point? Unless there was something more incriminating about the body than met the eye of your average pathologist.

'Who would have wanted to kill him and why? An old flame? An old flame's husband?'

'I cannot enlighten you. Tarquin was admired by both men and women. A man's man. A woman's man.'

She thought about mentioning the tarot card she had received but decided not to.

When Lindsey had handed her the envelope, Honey had been almost certain she knew the identity of the sender. Mysterious, flirtatious Dominic Christiansen, purely because she couldn't think it could be anyone else. And he'd been there, hadn't he? The day she'd found the first card . . .

But Lindsey was pretty adamant it wasn't him.

If not Dominic Christiansen, then who . . . ?

Honey felt a strange sensation prickle across her skin as she let the thought take shape. She'd read the cards as a kind of harmless flirtation. But what if she was dealing with something altogether more sinister?

She decided it was about time she mentioned it to Steve. Goodness knows what he would make of it.

* * *

The meeting of the cat ladies finished at around four thirty, once they'd consumed pots of tea, cups of coffee and a delicious array of cream cakes, cucumber sandwiches and salmon mayonnaise vol au vents.

'I've decided it would better suit my understanding of both myself and the world of cats if I purchased a cat,' her mother declared.

Honey eyed her mother's matching outfit of turquoise cashmere trimmed in a contrasting sable.

'What sort of cat?'

Her mother closed one eye and regarded her with what could only be described as disdain.

'I wasn't being sarcastic,' Honey added quickly. 'I was just wondering whether you knew that kittens scratch wood and upholstery and pull threads in woollen suits.'

'I still think I would like one. Not a long-haired cat. I understand that involves a lot of brushing and talcum-powdering.' She shook her head decisively. 'I don't think I could do that.'

'And nothing too expensive. What about Stewart? Will he mind a cat around the place?'

'If it pleases me then he's pleased!'

Her tone was resolute. Honey wasn't so sure her mother's new husband would be so keen.

'As long as he's not allergic or anything.'

'I just want a pet.'

Honey thought of the stray that kept appearing in the coach house.

'Tabbies are nice. Or tortoiseshells! Yes. Tortoiseshells are quite rare.'

'Are they?' Her mother's eyes were round with delight. If there was one thing she liked it was to be one up on everyone else, and what better way than to own a cat of rare colouring. 'Where can I get one?'

Honey put her arm around her mother and placed a kiss on her cheek.

'Leave it with me. I think I know where I can find one.'

* * *

Back in the coach house she looked for the cat. 'Here kitty, kitty!'

There was no sign of it.

'Well, isn't that just typical. When you don't want it it's there, and when you do want it it's nowhere to be seen.'

Lindsey came in, humming to herself prior to showering and going out on a date with a lecturer in historical forensics who'd been quite a regular boyfriend of late.

'Have you seen the cat?'

'What cat?'

'The one I was telling you about that I've found in here a few times.'

Lindsey shook her head. 'I've already told you, Mother. I haven't seen a cat in here.'

'Not in the last few days?'

'No.'

'Not ever?'

'Absolutely not. Must dash. Shower and change then Frederick's Bar at eight.'

Slumped on the sofa, Honey listened to the sound of running water from the bathroom. Her mother didn't have to give the stray a home of course, but it would have been nice.

Thoughts about the cat melted into thoughts of Dominic Christiansen. Despite the card, and seeing him at the funeral, there'd been no contact between them.

Lindsey didn't take long getting ready.

'You look good enough to eat,' Honey said to her as mother and daughter exchanged kisses.

Lindsey grinned mischievously. 'I'm hoping Sean thinks so.'

She winked and made a clicking sound before exiting. Honey sat there thinking about her next move when it struck her how chirpy her daughter had seemed. No other boyfriend had made her behave like that before. She wondered if Sean was the one, then dismissed the thought. Her daughter was happy with the way things were.

Her thoughts went back to Dominic Christiansen. She reached for the business card he'd given her and dialled the listed number.

There was the usual ringing tone then a click before the ringing continued. It did seem odd, but there were so many private companies running what used to be public service utilities nowadays. They all had their own little foibles.

'Hello. Is that Dominic Christiansen?'

'Honey. I wondered when you would ring. How can I help you?'

Honey fingered the card. 'I picked up a card at the murder scene. It was with the flowers some kind soul had put there.'

'A card?'

'A tarot card.'

'Ah.' It was a comment that meant everything and said nothing.

'You know something about it?'

'I'm not into fortune telling, but I know someone who is.'

'So do I.'

She'd asked Mary Jane, who'd gone into a long history of tarot cards and how they'd had an unfair press, how they weren't a portent of doom but a pack of markers reaching into the future.

It had been far from what she'd wanted to hear.

She'd also got round to telling Doherty about the one left with the flowers. He'd declared that it was some kind of prank. She'd retorted that he wasn't taking her find seriously. 'Tarots have a kind of magical significance.'

He'd laughed and said that she sounded like Mary Jane. Was she going nuts herself?

She'd slammed the phone down.

It seemed Dominic was listening to her, however.

'I just wondered at its significance. There is some kind of significance attached to it, isn't there?'

'You didn't tell me that you'd picked up a card at the murder scene.'

'I didn't think it was important. It was left with a bunch of flowers. People do that a lot nowadays, leave bunches of flowers at scenes of great tragedy.'

'That is true.'

She'd met with no disbelief or comment about her being nuts. He was listening. In one way it flattered her. In another it made her feel even more curious about who he was and what he'd been doing at the crime scene.

Impatient to find out more, she deftly quipped, 'How about dinner?'

'I . . .' The question seemed to catch him off guard.

'I promise I won't sweet-talk you into going to bed with me. Strictly business. How about it?'

Doherty's reaction to the tarot card had annoyed her. If he wasn't careful, this temporary break in their relationship might well become permanent.

She felt pleased with herself. What a feather in her cap it would be if she solved this case despite Doherty's warnings not to get involved. Dining with the mysterious Dominic Christiansen was bound to yield results. Wasn't it a wise move to ask him questions over dinner?

'OK, Mrs Driver. I'll check my schedule and be back in touch with a time that works.'

It wasn't until the call disconnected that she realised he hadn't given her a say in the matter. She concluded he was a man used to giving orders and not asking favours. She also wondered what she was letting herself in for.

She might have pondered more if she hadn't seen the cat lying across the stairs, lazily cleaning first one fat paw then another.

'Stay right where you are,' she said softly as she got to her feet. 'Let me just make sure the door is shut . . .'

After shutting the door, she turned round, ready to pounce and claim the tortoiseshell cat for her mother. Instead, she stood empty-handed. The cat was gone.

CHAPTER FOURTEEN

'So, what do we really know about Tarquin St John Gervais?'

Doherty and Honey were sitting knee to knee on a couple of high stools at the bar in the Zodiac Club. It was Saturday night and heaving.

She scanned his face over the rim of her glass containing vodka, tonic, ice and a slice.

'We know that he's dead,' Doherty said.

The answer was compact and his expression bland.

'Caspar said he was a diplomat. But that can mean so many things.' Pausing, she leaned closer. 'Perhaps he was a James Bond type — licensed to kill.'

'But got himself killed? Couldn't have been much of a spy. Certainly not up to 007 standards.'

Honey narrowed her eyes. 'You're being facetious.'

Doherty looked deeply into her eyes. 'Honey. Leave it alone. It isn't a police matter.'

'But you wish it was, don't you? And don't deny it. I can see it in your face. You want to be involved but you've been warned off.'

Doherty shook his head and looked away. 'That's the way it is. We've all got our job to do and we don't go treading on departmental toes.'

'He was Caspar's brother.'

'Half-brother.'

'That doesn't make him a bad person.'

'Leave it.'

'I'm having a day out at Torrington Towers. I asked Caspar for tickets and he gave me some kind of pass that will take me all over the house and the safari park. Do you fancy coming?'

He shot her a warning look. 'You're not to go poking your nose in.'

She threw up her hands and gave an innocent look. 'I won't if you're with me, but if you can't come I can take my mother. She's into cats at the moment, the ones that curl up on the hearth rug and catch birds in the garden. I thought the lions would be fun.'

'Lions are never fun. They eat you.'

* * *

Wearing sensible shoes and taking raincoats with them, Honey and her mother duly arrived at Torrington Towers.

They were early so joined the queue of cars at the gate.

'Just a few minutes,' said Honey, glancing at her watch.

Her mother was not amused. 'I thought we had a special pass. To my mind, if we have a special pass they should let us straight through without having to queue with the public.'

'I'm not sure of the procedure,' ventured Honey, turning over the pass with one hand while the other remained on the steering wheel of the car.

By the time she'd scanned the card to see if anything was mentioned about the queuing arrangements for those with a free pass, the passenger door was left swinging in the breeze.

'Mother!'

Although of only average height and slim build, her mother cut a determined figure in red (including her wellington boots), charging towards the gate where a uniformed man was eyeing his watch, waiting for that moment when he had to spring into action and open the gates.

She closed her eyes and moaned. 'Oh no! Mother, why couldn't you be just a little patient?'

Patience was not one of her mother's virtues. Discerning the catwalk trend for the year ahead was more up her street, despite being well into her seventies.

She came back beaming.

'He says that seeing as we are friends of the owner, we are to go round to the side entrance. There's a small car park there close to the big cat houses.'

Once the gates were open her mother lost no time in giving Honey instructions to jump the queue and head to the right.

Angry looks and the odd car horn came their way as they swept forward and to the right.

Directed by first one security guard, then another, they came to a small car park where Land Rovers used to traverse the safari park were parked cheek by jowl with staff cars.

Honey found a gap and parked up.

'Phew,' said her mother, fanning her face as she stood next to the car. 'That's a pretty strong smell.'

'Big cats. Wouldn't you like to see the house first, Mother? It's probably full of sweet-scented flower arrangements.'

Her mother decided in a trice that she would prefer that.

'Then after that we can get in our car and drive through the safari park. The lions and tigers roam free here. They're not kept in cages.'

'Just the sick ones,' somebody said, 'and the old ones who can't be bothered to go out.'

The speaker was an elderly man pushing a wheelbarrow full of manure, the waste product of the big cats if the smell was anything to go by.

'Are the cat houses worth looking at?' Honey asked him.

'Not really. Nero's at home and so is Octavia — separately, of course. Can't put them in together or they'll kill each other.'

Honey asked her mother if she'd like to see the old lions. Her response took Honey by surprise.

'I think I should. Seeing as we're esteemed guests with a free pass from the owner, who just happens to be a personal friend of ours, I think a private viewing would be very much appreciated.'

The statement was for the benefit of the old man who worked there.

Honey cringed. When it came to putting on airs and graces, her mother was miles ahead of anyone else.

The cat houses were stout, long and purpose-built. The lions were housed in big cages with strong bars, a thick bedding of sweet-smelling straw, water on tap and half a sheep on demand.

The old man told them his name was Crompton.

'I used to be a ranger here, but only help part-time nowadays. Me knees 'ave gone,' he said nonchalantly. He pointed at a black-maned lion snoring its head off in among a thick bed of straw.

'That's Nero.'

After a few tottery steps he pointed at another cage where a lioness was sitting on her haunches, peering at them through half-closed eyes.

'She's a bit short-sighted,' Crompton explained. 'All the same, it's not wise to get near her, not unless she knows you.'

'I'm thinking of getting a cat,' said Honey's mother. 'That's why I'm here.'

Crompton eyed her speculatively.

'Well, bully for you, though I must warn you that owning a big cat isn't for the faint-hearted. What sort of cat are you thinking of?'

'A tortoiseshell,' Honey interjected. 'My mother is keen to acquire a tortoiseshell cat, the sort that can cuddle up to her on the sofa and lap milk from a saucer. A pet cat.'

Crompton looked amused, his bushy eyebrows flapping up and down. 'Don't fancy a bobcat or a cheetah then?'

Gloria held onto her superior veneer. 'I live in a flat with no outside space.'

Honey couldn't resist adding, 'Think of the litter tray.'

He grunted. 'That's a shame.'

The lioness opened her jaws in an almighty yawn. Even at this distance Honey could smell the carnivorous breath.

'Have they ever eaten anyone?'

Crompton jerked his head at the pair of old lions. 'No record that they have, but I know different!' He tapped the side of his nose. His eyes were unblinking. 'They told me so,' he said, his voice barely above a whisper.

'Who told you so?'

'The lions. They talk to me. They've always talked to me. We talk to one another.'

Honey exchanged a slightly worried look with her mother. Gloria was frowning deeply, wondering if she'd heard right.

'That's nice,' said Honey. At the same time she was thinking: Right! Here I am talking to a man who thinks he's the Torrington Towers version of Doctor Dolittle.

'They don't talk to many people,' he said, his voice a drawn-out drawl, 'but they do to me. And I talk right back, don't I, Octavia?'

The lioness stretched her neck at the sound, her head turning in the direction of the voice.

'I see.'

Out-of-the-ordinary events had been happening lately, and things weren't getting any better. If she was confused before, she was more confused now.

Still, the old chap had made the effort to give them a guided tour and she appreciated that, although she was swiftly concluding that she'd entered a lunatic asylum.

'How close were you to Mr Tarquin?' she asked him.

'As close as anyone. A born gentleman, he was.'

'I believe he worked for the government in foreign embassies and such like. Did he ever speak of his job with them?'

Crompton made a strong sucking sound and shook his head.

'Oh no! Well, he wouldn't, would he? He'd signed the Official Secrets Act. He couldn't say anything, could he?'

'No,' said Honey, inclined to agree with him, 'of course not.'

'Your father knew Tarquin,' her mother said as they made their way to the main house to peruse its history. 'A young whippersnapper, he said, who fancied himself as an international agent.'

'Father knew him?'

Honey was doubly surprised. Number one, her mother rarely spoke of her father, and number two, it came as something of a surprise to hear her father had known the deceased.

'I know Dad worked for the government, but you never said which department or anything.'

'Overseas trade,' returned her mother. 'That's why he was away a lot, negotiating trade deals and such like. It wasn't good for our marriage being apart so much. Me left alone with you, and him jet-setting from Timbuktu to goodness knows where.'

Honey knew they'd divorced and that her father had died some time shortly after that.

'I didn't want to know about his job and he wasn't inclined to talk about it. Said it was just boring stuff about contracts and treaties referring to the supply of things made in England that people wanted.'

'What kind of things?'

Her mother shrugged. 'I've just told you, we never discussed it.'

'Are you sure he wasn't a spy?'

Her mother looked at her as though she'd lost her mind.

'Don't be ridiculous!'

'Why is it ridiculous?'

'Your father wore pinstriped suits, a bowler hat and carried a rolled-up newspaper!'

'Even when he was abroad?'

'Well, I suppose so! I wasn't with him.'

Her mother frowned and fell silent. Honey knew she was rattled, and she herself was amazed that her mother had never questioned his job and his travels.

Because Honey had lost him when she was only a child, her father had remained a distant figure. She recalled seeing him on occasion, up until the day they told her he was gone for ever . . . Honey had been just ten years old.

Racing thoughts occupied her mind more so than the house they were visiting, which proved a disappointment. The oriental rugs and carpets were a little threadbare, the furniture in need of some tender loving care, and the tour guide a bit listless.

'The vases at the end of the mantelpiece are Wedgwood. The ones on either side of the clock are Ming dynasty . . .'

The disinterested voice droned on and on.

Honey made a conscious effort to fall back from the tour group they were attached to.

'I can't stand her voice any longer,' she muttered to her mother. 'Let's explore on our own.'

The tour guide was as disinterested in the group she was leading as she seemed to be in the house. Honey and her mother fell away unnoticed to go wandering from one room to another.

After a fair amount of walking, her mother sat down on the soft cushions of a window seat, took off her shoe and rubbed at her toes.

'It's not that interesting a house. The National Trust own all the good ones.' She sniffed. 'This place smells musty. It could do with a good spring clean and redecorating.'

Honey had to agree with her. 'Caspar doesn't want to live here.'

'I don't blame him. I wouldn't live here either.'

'He said it goes to the National Trust if he doesn't.'

'So what are you hoping to find out?'

'What makes you think I'm here to find something out?' Honey asked, her face a picture of innocence. 'We came here for a day out. Mother and daughter.'

Gloria narrowed her eyes. 'I know you. What's afoot?'

'His lordship was Caspar's brother. He was killed recently. I came here to the funeral. It was a decidedly odd affair. They cremated him in the walled garden.'

'In the walled garden? That's outrageous!' Gloria looked seriously dismayed. 'You can't just set light to somebody like that, as if it were November the fifth and you were burning Guy Fawkes. Not the real one, of course — just an effigy dressed in old clothes with a turnip for a head.'

'This was a very well-organised affair. Totally above board — well, as far as I can tell. And the whole thing must have worked out a damn sight cheaper than what funeral directors charge. Yet it was still quite dramatic.'

Honey's mother looked at her in horror. 'Promise me here and now that you will never, and I repeat never, consider disposing of my remains in that manner. I want a church. I want flowers. I want to be sent off with the singing of hymns and the sound of an organ.'

'Whatever you want, you only have to ask.'

'An oak coffin with brass handles. And remember to invite your Uncle Percy.'

Honey frowned. 'Who's Uncle Percy?'

'He's not strictly your uncle. He's your father's cousin. They were very close.'

Honey leaned back against the window. This was the first she'd ever heard of her father's cousin.

A faraway look came to her mother's eyes. Sighing, she recounted an old memory about the phone in the house where Honey grew up, which had been out of order for some time.

'Your father and I were separated at that point, of course, and he got very angry about it — I think it bothered him, you see, having no way of checking in with us at all. He was constantly on at me to get it rectified. He came over one day to visit and it was finally fixed. He phoned Percy to tell him about it. I didn't hear the gist of their conversation but they did arrange to meet in order to get it sorted out permanently.' Her mother sighed. 'If he hadn't gone to meet Percy, he might still be alive.'

Honey knew her father's car had hit a tree. His head had hit the windscreen. She had known nothing about the meeting with Percy. She hadn't even known Percy existed.

'So have you learned anything about this case?' her mother asked her.

'Only that I have an Uncle Percy — strictly a second cousin.'

'I mean about the case.'

'Caspar's brother was here the day before he died. Nobody saw him leave. Not that the police have been asking too many questions. Caspar thought if I stayed here I could ask questions at my leisure.'

'That seems a good idea. What does your policeman boyfriend think?'

Honey thought about lying.

'Your silence speaks volumes. He doesn't like the idea. I call it kind of selfish myself. You haven't been seeing so much of each other lately.'

Honey grunted. 'I don't want to go into it.'

'Is it a permanent arrangement? Have you finished the relationship? I'll be over the moon if you have.'

'It's not necessarily a permanent thing!'

'No need to shout. Now come on, let's take a good look round. I told Stewart to expect me when he sees me. He won't mind if it's late when I get home.'

Stewart wouldn't dare, thought Honey. Her mother, although only recently married, was of independent mind — and means, come to that — a factor resulting from having had four husbands.

'Anything else while you're here?' her mother added.

'I wouldn't mind visiting the walled garden on our way back to the car.'

'Then let's get going.'

Because they'd peeled off from the official guided tour, they found themselves outside and passing a row of cottages they hadn't seen on the way in.

'Very pretty,' remarked Gloria.

Honey had to concede that she was right. They were like something out of 'Hansel and Gretel': honeycomb-coloured, with small square windows, one either side of a plain green door. Leafy green foliage curled up around the door, swamping the stonework all the way up to the eaves. They bore a similarity to the one she'd stayed in with Doherty, though much closer to the house.

It occurred to Honey that these simple dwellings had been loved and lived in over the centuries. People had planted roses round the door, and the flowers in the garden were mature and old-fashioned.

The heavy heads of cabbage roses long past their best hung over the narrow path, their scent still pungent despite the dying season.

One of the windows was open and music was coming out.

'I'll just take a peek,' whispered her mother.

Before Honey could stop her she was tiptoeing up the garden path to the open window.

'I don't need your help,' Honey hissed. The bull in the china shop aptly described her mother — and her propensity to put her foot in it. 'Mother!'

Gloria ignored her.

Honey rolled her eyes and muttered an expletive. This was a police case. Murder had been committed, but her mother had the bit between her teeth and was off.

Honey prepared to run, or at least make an excuse as to why her mother was being so nosy. If anyone asked she might tell them that her mother was on a day out from a nursing home specialising in dementia. It seemed the most fitting excuse, though her mother would be furious. Perhaps it might be better to run.

Honey didn't breathe easy or discard her excuses until her mother was picking her way back along the garden path.

'It's a very pretty sitting room. If anyone had been at home I might have asked them for a guided tour.'

Honey uplifted her eyes to heaven and thanked God that nobody had been there.

'Strange though,' her mother said as they resumed their walk to where they'd left the car. 'One does not leave a window open and music blaring when one is not at home.'

'One does not,' Honey agreed.

'I think he was at home,' said Gloria once they were in the car and halfway back to the main gate.

'Why do you think that?'

'There was a wallet on the table and a pack of cards spread out face down. I think somebody was playing solitaire.'

'Playing cards?'

'What other sort is there?'

'Never mind.' Honey was not convinced. 'I'd like to meet Uncle Percy some time. Is he still alive?'

'Of course he is, dear.'

'You have an address?'

'I can get it. Now, about this cat you told me about. I've made enquiries. Tortoiseshell cats are very rare, males rarer than females. Do you happen to know if this cat is male or female?'

* * *

The Tarot Man slid silently from behind the open door. Peering from the upstairs window, he'd seen them walking past, the old lady stopping and having the temerity to walk up the path and peer in the window. He didn't expect her to make anything of the items he'd left on the coffee table. He had had the use of the cottage for some time and he was here for a purpose. He'd had it on good authority that Honey Driver would shortly also be staying on this same estate.

CHAPTER FIFTEEN

Following their excursion to Torrington Towers, Honey's mother accepted the offer of a cup of tea and followed her daughter into the coach house.

Honey did a quick look around the place, opening her bedroom door, the bathroom, even the odd kitchen cupboard. There was no sign of the cat, and Honey's first priority was to kick off her shoes and put the kettle on. The sighting of the cat, let alone the sexing of it, could wait.

'That cat gets in here from somewhere. It has to be a stray.'

'Poor thing. Here, kitty, kitty.' Her mother made tweeting sounds.

Honey set down the tea tray and left her mother to select sugar, milk or lemon. She opted for sugar and lemon.

'Do you have a phone number for Percy?' Honey blurted suddenly, knowing that if she didn't ask now she might never work up the nerve.

Gloria eyed her over the rim of her teacup. 'Why this obsession?'

'I want to know more about my father's death. I want to know the *exact* details.'

For a moment their eyes locked. That in itself seemed to unsettle her mother.

'Why resurrect the past?'

Honey frowned. Why indeed. Her father only came to mind in the middle of the night when she wondered how things might have been if he'd lived. She remembered so little about him.

Her mother sighed. 'You're thinking that there's more to your father's death than meets the eye.'

Honey nodded. 'Yes.'

She could almost hear her mother's internal anguish, but now she'd started, she couldn't let it go.

'I can't help thinking that there's a history to all this.'

The whole truth and nothing but the truth would bring the colour back to her face.

'I'm not that stupid,' Gloria muttered. 'I always thought there was something but put it down to affairs with other women. That's why I divorced him. Uncle Percy knew more of what was going on. He was covering for him. I'm sure of that now. Shady character at the best of times.'

'Uncle Percy knew?'

'More than he let on. He was a born liar, was Percy.'

Her mother sipped thoughtfully at her tea. 'Anyway, I was lonely, him being away all the time.'

Honey would have commented but the phone interrupted.

It was Caspar. 'I've made all the necessary arrangements. You're booked in at Torrington Towers to investigate further.'

'Right! Are you coming with me?'

She sensed it would be a negative.

'No. I don't want to go near the place.' Another pause. 'You're not going to let me down, are you?'

Honey sighed. Awkward cuss that he was, she was quite fond of Caspar, and the swiftness with which he'd made the arrangements amazed her.

'I could do with a few days away.' She bit her lip. Doherty would disapprove, so Doherty mustn't know.

Caspar expressed his gratitude and went back to whatever he was doing.

Her mother peered at her, face alive with interest.

'You're going to stay there for a few days? How about I come with you?'

CHAPTER SIXTEEN

Before setting off for her stay at Torrington Towers, Honey tracked down Uncle Percy. After he'd expressed his surprise and asked her how her mother was doing, he finally asked the reason for her call and suggested then and there that she wanted to talk about her father.

'Am I right?'

She told him he was.

'Was he a spy?'

She perceived a jerky sound to his voice before Percy laughed. 'You've been watching too many of those 007 films, my girl.'

He sounded condescending. It was only what she'd expected.

'Do you know a man named Lord Torrington? The family name is St John Gervais.'

A pregnant pause. His hesitation was enough to answer her question.

'I'm not sure . . .'

'I went to his funeral the other day. It was a very odd occasion, a funeral pyre in an orchard at a stately home. His death was suspicious. The police are very hands-off and I've been asked to investigate by a close relative of the victim. In doing so I've uncovered a link between him and my own father.'

'Have you indeed?'

She couldn't help thinking that he sounded displeased. Nevertheless, she soldiered on.

'Do you happen to know anything about tarot cards?'

Total silence until, 'Where are you, my dear?'

'Bath. I run the Green River Hotel.' She gave him the address.

'Is your mother with you?'

'My mother is never far from me.'

'Good.'

He didn't sound as though it were good but went on, 'I would love to meet up with you. We have so many things to discuss.'

'Yes. That would be nice.'

Once they'd said their goodbyes the phone line went dead.

Honey harboured an uncomfortable feeling. Although he'd suggested meeting up with her, she'd sensed hesitancy, which made her suspicious.

Her father had spent a lot of time away from home and travelling the world — goodness knows where. She really should have pressed for more details on the phone. Questions came to her mind one after the other. She wanted to know more — right now! When she redialled, the number was engaged so she left a voice message.

* * *

At the other end of the phone Uncle Percy, a big man with white hair and a tight chest, was trying to get his breath. His lungs were shot — too many rich cigars and French brandy. Hearing the bad news about Tarquin's murder hadn't helped. Somehow the Tarot Man had been resurrected. Whoever it was had to be a relative of the original, the one who'd reached his zenith of operation in the midst of the Cold War. A few enquiries and he knew for sure. The Tarot Man had taken on his father's mantle and was out for revenge. All Percy could do was call in a few favours and hope he was wrong — that his cousin's daughter, Hannah Driver, wasn't one of those in the firing line.

* * *

Honey's room at Torrington Towers had a high ceiling from which clusters of plaster hung down from an intricately patterned background. The clusters were intertwined leaves and brambles ending in a Tudor rose. Dark oak panels adorned the walls, and the carpet beneath her feet was thick enough to drown in. A four-poster bed of splendid proportion dominated the room and a lead-paned oriole window afforded a breathtaking view of the grounds.

Her mother had the room next door. It had similar proportions and both had bathrooms.

'Thank goodness,' stated her mother. 'I wasn't looking forward to trotting down a draughty corridor in the middle of the night.'

Honey wasn't entirely sure what her mother's role would be during the investigation, but was glad of the company. Doherty would have been a hell of a lot more useful, but as he didn't approve of her getting involved, she hadn't told him. Anyway, he was going on a course that coincided with her stay at the stately home.

Honey decided also not to tell her mother that she'd spoken to Uncle Percy. It would do no good to dredge up old memories her mother was loath to revisit.

A Mrs Crompton made sure they had everything they needed and told them when dinner would be served. She was very chatty and told them as much as she could about the old place and when Mr Tarquin — his lordship — had last been seen there.

'He wasn't here that much. Always gallivanting. That's what I told the police. The last time I saw him I made him breakfast, but he didn't seem that hungry.'

‘Did he have much to say?’

Mrs Crompton shook her head vehemently, which sent her double chins quivering.

‘No. But then he never did. Mr Tarquin enjoyed his food. You could say he concentrated on his food.’

‘But he didn’t have much to eat that morning.’

‘No. He did not.’

‘A man who eats a hearty breakfast one day then doesn’t the next has something on his mind.’

Honey knew her mother was right. All the talk of food had made her hungry. She looked at her watch. There was just enough time to wash and change before dinner.

‘I’ll meet you downstairs,’ Honey declared.

‘No. I’ll call for you.’ Gloria looked around her tellingly. ‘This old place is very grand, but the shadows get longer at twilight. I think Mary Jane would call it a house of history, where ghosts lurk in the shadows. Who knows what things have gone on here?’

She had a point, so Honey fell in with her wishes.

Her mother was disappointed to find they were to dine in the servants’ hall.

‘But I’m not dressed for the servants’ hall!’ she exclaimed, indicating the pure-silk dress she was wearing.

Honey sighed. She had emphasised that she was here on business and needed to interact with the staff, but obviously her words had fallen on deaf ears. Her mother had had visions of them staying in five-star style with knobs on!

Not all the staff were at dinner, but those that were offered what help they could, though most of it was pretty much along the lines of what Mrs Crompton had told them.

There was only one exception. Adrian Sayle was the head ranger with overall charge of the safari park and dressed the part: khaki shorts, khaki shirt with lots of pockets, and a bush hat complete with corks dancing from the brim. The clothes were very Indiana Jones, but his ruddy face and frequent swipes at his nose with the back of his hand were a world away.

'Somebody from his past. That's who I reckon it was.'

Honey pasted on an interested expression.

'Have you seen any strangers around here?'

'There are always strangers around here,' he exclaimed, a chunk of steak and kidney pie speared on his fork. 'We take bed and breakfast guests in some of the cottages out back. Not all of them, just those not occupied by members of staff.'

Honey was fascinated. Adrian Sayle had cast aspersions on person or persons unknown.

As a hotel owner, she was very aware that few people stayed in bed and breakfast accommodation for longer than one or two days. Tourists liked to see all they could as quickly as they could.

'Were there any who stayed longer than normal?'

The brusque, rough-looking man, his muscular calves bare beneath the long legs of his shorts, responded to her interest.

'Not many. The longest was some historian bloke who was doing research into the family and the ancient burial sites around here. Then there was some naturalist studying the mating habits of big cats and wanting to study those in captivity. He was here quite a while.'

'And there was the artist,' one of the zookeepers added.

'She was just a girl,' Adrian Sayle pointed out. 'A girl couldn't have killed him, not one like her anyway.'

'Was she pretty? Petite?' asked Honey's mother.

The ranger looked flustered. 'Well. Yes . . .'

'Well, that just shows what *you* know.' Gloria scoffed at the stupidity of the man. 'A pretty girl doesn't need to be strong. She could have led him anywhere — if he was that way inclined.'

'I knew there was a reason I brought you here,' Honey whispered to her mother.

Honey added things up. If his old friend Clara was telling the truth, he was certainly that way inclined. If her mother was right, the girl could have been a honey trap, and dear old Tarquin could easily have fallen into it.

‘Do you have names and addresses of those people who rented the cottages?’

Miss Vincent, the estate secretary, said that she did. Apparently she didn’t live at Torrington Towers but drove in each day from the village.

‘I only stayed here tonight because Mr Caspar said that you were a very well-respected detective and I should help you all I could. Mr Caspar always was a nice boy. So obedient compared to Tarquin, who used to get up to all manner of mischief.’

To Honey it seemed a pretty good summing up of what Caspar was like. It was easy to imagine him as a small boy looking as prim and proper as he did as an adult.

Honey made notes. It wasn’t lost on her that Miss Vincent was likely a mine of information on Caspar’s past as well as that of his lordship.

‘Did you see Mr Tarquin leave on the last morning you saw him?’

Miss Vincent shook her head, then paused and looked thoughtful. ‘I did pass a car on the road, but didn’t recognise it. I presumed it was one of the bed and breakfast people.’

‘OK.’ Honey nodded her appreciation for the list Miss Vincent handed her.

Her first act the following morning was to ring Professor Lionel Collins, the historian who had stayed at the cottage for about six weeks.

Honey explained her reason for calling.

‘I’m just checking to find out if you saw Lord Torrington leave and whether you saw him with anyone else.’

‘I’m a historian, not a private detective. I wasn’t here to spy on him.’

Honey applied her most sugary voice. ‘I notice you live in Dunster. That’s not too far. I don’t mind driving down . . .’

‘I’m sorry. That’s not possible.’

He explained that he couldn’t spare much time as he was off to give a lecture in Amsterdam the very next day. He still had much to do to prepare for it.

'Seeing as you don't live that far away, was there any particular reason you stayed for six weeks?'

His response was abrupt. He'd moved into a converted Methodist chapel in the village about a year ago that needed some building work. The builders had moved in and he'd moved out.

'I trust they did a nice job.' Actually, she'd never liked church and chapel conversions very much because they never ceased to resemble what they were. 'Look, I'm sorry to have troubled you, but the brother of the deceased has asked me to look into the death. He's quite unhappy about it. I'm sure you understand.'

'OK. Well, if you want to drive down for the briefest of chats, you'll have to do it now.'

Honey jumped at the chance. 'I'm at Torrington Towers. It won't take me long.'

She persuaded her mother to stay behind and keep an eye on things.

'Can I snoop with impunity?' her mother asked.

Honey assured her that she could.

* * *

She set out immediately after breakfast and got to Dunster at around eleven thirty.

The converted chapel had a circular window of coloured leaded glass above a pillared entrance porch.

Lionel Collins answered the door wearing the typical professor attire: corduroy trousers, denim shirt and tweed jacket with leather inserts on the elbows. A pair of wire-rimmed spectacles hung from a bootlace around his neck.

His hair was awry, a veritable lion's mane of grey receding from his forehead and hanging around his shoulders. Honey assessed him to be around fifty-five years of age, though judging by the way he moved and the directness of his manner, he pretended he was younger. About six feet two inches tall and well built, she had to concede that he must have been a handsome man when he was younger and was still worth a second look.

'Enter,' he said, extending his arm in a flamboyant flourish. 'Straight ahead.'

He directed her along a narrow passage and into a room with a vaulted ceiling.

Honey tilted her head back and eyed it with interest. She felt it was only polite to make a complimentary comment.

'Impressive.'

It was the best she could come up with. Her eyes took in everything else. Both man and house were best described as shabby chic.

Although the interior had been tastefully modernised, the arched windows were still in situ, the bottom halves letting in light to the ground floor, the arched upper halves to the upper storey. The lower halves were crowded with bookshelves stuffed with books.

At one end was the gallery where worshippers used to sit, gazing down on their pastor and the pews beneath. Dark-red oriental rugs covered oak floorboards.

Honey declined a drink but accepted the offer to sit in a cane armchair with a peacock-style backrest, the sort used in magazine shots where long-haired models with skinny legs gaze out with elfin innocence.

Professor Collins poured himself a coffee and sat down opposite her, a ready smile on his face. His eyes were intently blue.

'From what you told me on the phone, I doubt I'll be much help, but fire away.'

'Do you mind me asking what aspects of family history you were researching?'

'The family tree going way back, but particularly the family's involvement in the English Civil War.'

'Did you find out anything interesting?'

'No more or less than I expected. Like a number of other families, they were in the habit of changing sides depending on who happened to be winning.'

'I drove past Dunster Castle. Wasn't that involved in the Civil War?'

'It was indeed.'

Her attention was drawn to a glass display cabinet beneath an overhead gallery.

'Fascinating stuff,' she said on taking a peek at what was on view, mostly ancient weapons, their blades holed and rusty with age. 'Are they valuable?'

The professor invited her to step closer, then shook his head. 'Not in money. But knowledge?' He shrugged. 'They are old. Look at them and wonder how many people this blade or that blade would have killed. The one advantage old weapons have over modern weapons is that at least you looked your enemy in the eye — not like today. One ICBM and we're all blown away.'

'Bad world,' said Honey.

He looked pointedly at his watch. 'Much as I would love to spend more time with you, I do have a plane to catch in the morning — and much to be done before then.'

'I do apologise, but if I could ask you one more question. I understand there was a young lady staying in one of the cottages at the same time as you. Her name was Hermione Standish. Do you recall her?' This was the information Miss Vincent had given her.

Lionel raised his eyebrows. 'Now, let me see. Yes. I believe I did see her. She spent quite a bit of time with his lordship . . .'

'Right.'

It popped into her mind that if Caspar inherited, he would acquire the title, something he had failed to mention. My word, but he was pretty insufferable at the best of times. Referring to him as 'my lord' would only make him worse.

'Did you see Mr . . . his lordship leave on the morning he was killed? It would have been more than a month ago.'

The professor shook his head. 'No. To tell you the truth I'd had a bit of a shindig at the pub in the village the night before. I went to bed late and got up late — me and a ruthless headache, that is!'

'I take it you were in good company.'

'Very jolly company.'

'Male or female?'

'Are you enquiring about anything specific?'

'No. Just anything that struck you as odd.'

He shook his head, his eyes twinkling behind the lenses of his spectacles.

On the drive back to Torrington Towers she diverted into Bath, telling herself her mother couldn't possibly get into any trouble while she was gone.

No matter that she'd been absent for less than two days, she couldn't get it out of her head that the Green River could not run at full proficiency without her.

Lindsey didn't look surprised to see her.

'We're still here. Nobody's burned the place down, none of the guests have complained about anything and the chef has not attacked any of the diners with a meat cleaver.'

Somehow disappointed by this — nothing going wrong made her feel kind of unwanted — she lay her palms face down on the reception desk.

'Have there been any bookings or is November still as barren as the Sahara Desert?'

'We've picked up a coach party for a two-day stay, plus a honeymoon couple, plus a minibus of senior citizens from Alabama. Oh, and the Walsall Psychic Society have booked a two-day conference. I think Mary Jane had something to do with that.'

Feeling unwanted, Honey finger-tapped the desk.

'How about Doherty? Has he phoned?'

Lindsey shook her head. 'No. Were you expecting him to break silence at this course he's on?'

'Of course not!'

Of course she was. OK, he was on some outward-bound camp in the middle of nowhere, living off the land and doing all that self-development stuff, but he could still have found the time to phone her.

'We're managing quite well,' Lindsey added reassuringly on noticing her mother's faraway look.

Honey sighed. 'I just thought I'd pop in, in case there was something . . .'

Something did spring into her head. Caspar. She dialled his mobile number.

'Honey! You're back.'

'Am I speaking to Lord Torrington?'

There was silence. Eventually Caspar gathered himself.

'I didn't want to advertise the fact, dear girl. You know how people are. People put two and two together and make a hundred and forty-four. And before you ask me, I did not kill Tarquin for the title. I did not because I never wanted it!'

'Do you still wish me to pursue this investigation?'

'Absolutely! You must. You simply must. He was my brother. I want to bring the person responsible to account.'

CHAPTER SEVENTEEN

Miss Vincent, his late lordship's secretary, was amazingly efficient.

Honey asked her how well she knew Caspar and whether there had ever been animosity between him and Tarquin.

She shook her head. 'Definitely not.'

'It's been suggested that his lordship—'

'Mr Tarquin,' Miss Vincent corrected. 'He didn't like being titled. He preferred to be ordinary.'

'But he wasn't ordinary,' Honey pointed out.

Miss Vincent shrugged. 'It was how he wanted things.'

'What about the professor? Did you have much to do with him while he was here?'

'He was friendly enough, and I was always courteous. He was a guest, after all.'

'He tells me he was looking into the family history.'

Miss Vincent frowned. 'Yes.' Her frown deepened. 'He spent a lot of time in the library. He said he had full permission from Mr Tarquin.'

'Did he?'

'I'm not sure. Mr Tarquin never mentioned it and the professor just breezed in and out each morning as though he had every right to be there.'

At around 2 p.m., Honey informed her mother that she was going to the village for a pub lunch.

'Just for a change.'

Her mother didn't wait to be invited. 'Good idea.'

The smell of steak and kidney pudding and the sound of piped music wafted around the bar of the White Hart pub.

The smell was appetising and Honey ordered a bar meal. Her mother desisted.

'I have a figure to take care of. Now, do you want to know what I found out?'

They settled themselves in a window seat and sipped their drinks. Her mother leaned closer and lowered her voice.

'Mrs Cromer who does the cleaning reckons that Mr Tarquin was afraid of something or somebody. He'd gone off his food, you see.'

'Mrs Crompton did mention that.'

'Oh, really? She's not so forthcoming as Mrs Cromer.'

Honey's phone rang. The number surprised her. Doherty had slipped a phone onto a no-phone course. From what she had gathered, all technical gadgets were out of bounds. They were in the wilds of Wales — the Brecon Beacons — and supposed to rely on natural skills and team-building efforts.

'Where are you?' he asked.

'I'm having lunch with my mother.'

She did not add that she was staying at Torrington Towers investigating a case he'd expressly told her to stay clear of.

'I thought you weren't supposed to contact anyone when you're on this course.'

'I was bored. Somebody else managed to smuggle in a tablet and a Wi-Fi connection. My mind was going stale. I turned to a bit of research to relieve the boredom.'

'So, what kind of research have you been up to?'

'That funeral we went to. It wasn't legal.'

Honey had to concede that she'd never been to one like it before and had wondered at the time. But the aristocracy could move mountains if they wanted to.

'So what did you find out?'

'I found out that it's illegal to cremate a body on private land and can only be done in extenuating circumstances by special licence. Unless a special licence is issued cremation has to be carried out at designated establishments, i.e. crematoria provided by the local authority.'

'So who gave permission for it to be done the way it was? And why?'

'No idea but I'm working on it.'

He paused.

'Have you seen anything of Christiansen?'

'No. He's keeping a low profile. But then, why would he continue to tail me — apart from the fact that I'm terribly attractive and he can't possibly resist!'

She waited for him to laugh. He didn't.

'Promise me you won't stray far from home. OK?'

Great. He still thought she was in Bath. 'OK!'

'Right. Gotta go.'

'Bye.'

A creepy-crawly sensation spread from her spine and all over her back. Doherty had warned her not to leave Bath and here she was at Torrington Towers.

She became aware that her mother was peering at her, waiting to be told the details of the conversation.

'Something about the funeral?'

Honey nodded. 'It was all very odd.'

Her mother pulled her chin in, eyes popping. 'You bet your life it was! That's how you get rid of rubbish, not bodies. Right. All this sleuthing has given me an appetite. I think I'll have a chargrilled steak.'

Clearly, her mother had forgotten all about her figure. But Honey had no complaints. The meal was good, main course only, no dessert. The waiter came to collect the plates just after Honey's mother had headed for the bathroom. The dirty plates were replaced with the bill presented in a neat little cover.

'My treat, I think,' Honey murmured and opened the cover. The bill was inside. So was a tarot card. Seven of Swords.

The colour drained from Honey's face. Once recovered, she called for the waiter.

She held up the card so he was in no doubt as to what she was referring to.

'Where did this come from?'

'The gentleman over there asked me to give it to you.'

Honey looked to where he was pointing. A solitary wine glass stood on an empty table.

'Can you describe him?'

The waiter adjusted his spectacles. 'Well, my glasses were a bit steamed up, so I can't be accurate . . .'

'Be as accurate as you can be.'

'Tall. Blondish-white hair. A long face . . .'

'Did he pay by credit card? Do you have a name?'

The waiter, looking nervous at being asked so many questions, shook his head. 'He paid cash.'

Honey reached for a paper napkin then sprang to her feet. 'I'll just see if he's left me anything else.' She swooped on the glass, holding it carefully between two fingers with the napkin.

'Madam, that glass belongs to the White Hart!'

She passed him a two-pound coin. 'There you are. That should cover it.'

She was outside by the time her mother came to find her, her footsteps crisply tapping the flagstone path.

'Hannah, I thought you were waiting for me inside.' Her indignation faded once she saw Honey's perplexed expression.

'What is it? What's happened?'

Honey showed her the tarot card. 'It was with the bill. Somebody asked the waiter to put it there.'

'Did he say who it was?'

Honey shook her head. 'No. He described him as being tall with blondish-white hair and a long face. Have you seen anyone looking like that?' Honey, of course, had her own ideas.

'No. And you don't know who he is?'

'No. I do not.'

She made a decision about the glass she'd taken from the table.

'Mother, can you be very discreet?'

Her mother looked mortified. 'Of course I can.'

Honey wasn't so sure, but time was of the essence and she wanted the fingerprints on the glass analysed.

She explained her plan to her mother. 'Take it to the police station in Bath. Seeing as Steve Doherty is away, you'll be redirected to one of his officers. Tell them that I'm being stalked and ask if the fingerprints on the glass can be analysed. Don't smudge them!' She carefully rewrapped the glass in the paper napkin. 'Be as quick as you can. Take my car. I'll stay here and hold the fort. I want to ask a few more questions. I don't like being sent things I can't understand.'

'You mean the card?'

'I do indeed. It's some kind of message and it's a pound to a penny that it's linked to the first and second cards I found and the murder. Unfortunately, I haven't a clue what it means, except that someone is playing games.'

* * *

She was still here. He'd watched the old lady drive off. He knew what they were up to. Clever of her to notice the wine glass he'd left behind. Not that she would find anything out from that. Yes, his fingerprints were on there, but they would only lead to a dead end.

Bitterness left over from the death of his father back in the Cold War had imbued in him a cold thirst for vengeance, and Honey Driver was his target. The tarot cards were about fate — the hand he dealt to each of his victims. They were never going to escape what was coming to them.

As for the blonde girls . . . His mother had been blonde and of the West. She'd left him behind with the father he'd worshipped back in the Soviet Union. She'd left him and she was no good — that's what his father had told him.

* * *

Caspar phoned that evening to ask if there was any progress.

Honey mentioned the information passed on from Mrs Cromer, that her employer had been off his food and seemed to have something on his mind.

'She is only a cleaning lady so I don't know how reliable—'

'Caspar, you can be such a snob at times. I know from past experience that if you want to know anything about anything or anyone, ask the cleaning lady. I frequently take tea of a morning with my cleaning lady, Mrs Roper. She keeps me informed of everything that's going on in my establishment. She's better informed than I am!'

She told him about the incident in the pub.

'I don't really understand what this tarot business is all about,' he said. 'Have you asked your friend Mary Jane?'

'She's been visiting friends in the Cotswolds — not that I think she'll be able to throw any light on the subject.'

'What you mean is, she'll immediately begin doing a reading,' Caspar responded somewhat acidly.

'Possibly.'

Dinner was at seven and tonight she'd been asked out by Professor Lionel Collins. He'd called her up quite suddenly, in the hope that she'd be free.

'I would suggest the Maple Tree,' he told her over the phone. 'I'll meet you there.'

Despite the fact that she'd eaten a big meal at lunch time, dining in more salubrious surroundings appealed to her, and seeing as she was here by herself, her mother having gone back to Bath, why not take advantage of the opportunity?

As she donned her favourite little black dress, she asked herself whether dining out should be part of her investigation. What would Doherty do? She came to the conclusion he would go out and enjoy the meal.

Seeing as her mother had taken her car, she flipped and flopped between borrowing a pool car from the estate and driving there under her own steam or calling for a taxi. On seeing Adrian Sayle checking his team down in reception, she took the third option and asked him to drive her.

'If you don't mind, that is. I don't want to keep you from your evening meal but my mother's gone off in my car.'

It wouldn't have been unreasonable for him to say that he was not employed as a bloody chauffeur, but he said that, yes, he would drive her.

'I ate a big lunch. I can wait outside until you're ready to come back,' he said, beaming at her.

'Do you know where it is?' she asked him as she slid into the front passenger seat of his car.

'Yes.'

Leaving the reassuring lights of the house behind, they journeyed down the drive, the gravel crunching beneath the wheels, the trees on either side waving like widow's weeds in the chill wind. The narrow road wound through dark fields, the far trees like black paper cut-outs pasted against the darkening sky.

Neither of them spoke, which Honey found quite strange. She couldn't help but get the impression that he wasn't speaking because there was something he didn't want to tell her. He'd been friendly enough back in the house, but now he was quite taciturn.

The urge to ask him outright was overpowering, but somehow she reined herself in, counselling that whatever it was he'd tell her in his own good time. She wouldn't push it.

However, her patience was soon worn down. Silence could be a bit of a bore. Even trivial conversation helps make a long journey short. Not that it was far to the village and the Maple Tree. One of them was going to have to break this silence, and Honey decided it might as well be her.

'Did you think the funeral a little odd, Mr Sayle?'

'Those were his wishes.'

He sounded pretty cool, certainly unflustered.

'Did it surprise you?'

'It was different. But up to him.'

'It's been suggested that something was worrying him. Do you know what it was?'

'No. Something was on his mind, though.'

‘Would it surprise you to know that I think I’m being followed?’

He glanced at her. ‘Now why would that be?’

‘I don’t know. I think I need a bodyguard.’

‘That’s it. You’re the body. I’m the guard.’

She heard the edge of amusement in his voice and smiled.

‘I’m dining with Professor Collins tonight. Was he very friendly with Mr Tarquin?’

‘I wouldn’t know about that. My job is with the animals.’

‘Of course.’

There was no point asking whether he knew Caspar. He was too young to have been at Torrington Towers when Caspar was growing up. Still, at least his manner had improved. He was talking to her.

‘Is there anything else you’d like to tell me about the family?’

She noticed his hands tightening on the steering wheel.

‘I don’t think it’s my place. And p’raps it’s not yours to ask. You’re not police, are you?’

‘I’m Crime Liaison Officer for Bath Hotels Association. I’m acting on Mr Caspar’s behalf. He wants to know who killed his brother and why.’

‘I can’t help you there.’

Three gables pointed skywards above the shop-style frontage of the Maple Tree. A brass bistro rail ran the length of the window, the mesh curtain hanging from it resembling fishing net — fashionable and very popular at the moment. The heads of diners bobbed through the clear glass above the rail. There were lots of them. It looked as though the place was pretty popular.

‘You don’t need to collect me,’ she said. ‘I can get a taxi back.’

‘Have it your way. If you get stuck, give me a call.’

She dashed to the entrance, already fashionably late — well, ten minutes anyway.

She smiled to herself as she entered the restaurant and saw Lionel Collins rising like a gentleman from his table.

* * *

Dominic Christiansen laid his head back and closed his eyes, pleased that he was here. There had been no sign from the car in front that he'd been spotted. Now he would wait for her to emerge. She would be safe enough inside. Once she was outside he would not let her out of his sight.

CHAPTER EIGHTEEN

The Maple Tree had linen tablecloths and the waiters and waitresses glided between tables, their service seeming effortless.

The professor's eyes met hers. His smile was lascivious and it was obvious he'd been drinking.

'I didn't think you'd come,' he said, filling her wine glass before sending for a second bottle.

Honey's radar was on full alert. The professor was way ahead of her with the wine.

'When do you go to Amsterdam?'

'Tomorrow morning. I really shouldn't be here . . . But I can't get you out of my head, Honey Driver. I've been looking forward to this all day,' he whispered, closing on her across the table. 'Now let me see. You're a hotelier who dabbles in crime. Is that right?'

'Yes.'

'And you're single?'

'I'm a widow.'

'Ah! Now, that's a novelty nowadays. Most women of your age are divorced. Do you have children?'

'A daughter.'

'And a lover?'

This was too much. 'Look, Professor, I'm not here to discuss my family or my relationships. I came here on behalf of a friend to investigate the death of his brother.'

'Half-brother,' he said brusquely. On seeing Honey's expression he made an effort to smooth over his snapped response.

'Have you had many lovers in your life, Mrs Driver?'

'That is none of your business!'

She fancied his smile cut like a butter knife into the heart of most women. But she wasn't most women and his comments, accompanied as they were by too much drink, annoyed her.

'Of course it isn't,' he said to her. 'I do apologise. Please. Study the menu. I will purchase anything you like.'

She had to admit the menu was worth looking at. She was about to voice her preferences when Professor Collins took charge.

'Let's not waste time. I'll order for both of us.'

His choice turned out well, especially the plum and marzipan dessert.

Their conversation was like a fencing match. No matter what Honey asked him, he seemed to dance away from actually answering.

Probing him about his stay at Torrington Towers proved to be a complete waste of time. He couldn't remember his way home let alone staying in a cottage a few weeks before.

She noticed he kept patting his hair above his sweating brow, as though afraid it might have come adrift.

At the end of the meal he rested his elbow on the table, supporting his chin as he smiled at her.

'You know there's always a price to pay for a good meal, don't you.'

She knew exactly what he meant.

'If you're hitting on me, Professor, go take a hike!'

Declining coffee, she headed for the door. The fresh air was welcoming after the interior of the Maple Tree. Outside,

Adrian Sayle was waiting for her, even though she'd declined his offer.

'Thank you. I didn't expect you to be here.'

'Taxis are as scarce as hen's teeth around here. I thought I'd wait.'

The evening had not been as fruitful as she'd hoped and she still wanted a few questions answered, but only when the professor was sober and not trying to hit on her.

The next day she tried phoning him to ask if perhaps they could go for a coffee somewhere and start again. As the phone rang, her mind began to wander, straying to the end of the night before . . . She'd seethed all the way back to Torrington Towers. The road had been almost as dark as on the way to the Maple Tree. She only recalled one set of car headlights, and they were behind her. Only now did she wonder who they might have belonged to.

There was no answer from the professor's number, which didn't come as any great surprise. Already halfway to Amsterdam, no doubt.

Her mother called. 'Hannah. There's been a bit of a problem.'

Honey groaned. It wasn't often her mother sounded contrite, but she did now. Her mother had taken the wine glass for fingerprint analysis to the police in Bath. One of Doherty's subordinates would have helped her with the details. It should have been straightforward. However, this was her mother. And her mother was not a creature of straightforward habits.

'You haven't smashed it, have you,' Honey said slowly, dreading what was likely to come next.

'No. I did not. I was very careful. They've done the finger test and there was a set of fingerprints on there.'

'Great!' Honey punched the air. 'Who's the culprit?'

At first there was silence. Then a tiny voice.

'Me.'

Honey's jaw dropped. 'You? How did your fingerprints get on the glass?'

'I was being careful. I had the paper napkin you gave me and carried it carefully. Unfortunately I called in at my friend Megan's on the way home and put it down on the table. She picked it up, so of course I had to wipe her fingerprints off.'

'Don't go on! I can guess the rest. You polished off her fingerprints and plastered on your own.'

'Um. Yes.'

This was bad news indeed. She'd been so looking forward to finding out the identity of the man who had inserted a tarot card into the bill folder at the pub.

Honey made a conscious decision and sighed.

'Mother, I need to stay here.'

'That's fine. I won't be coming back down. Megan has had a fall and needs somebody to take her to the hospital for X-rays and other things.' She paused. 'You don't mind if I don't come back, do you?'

'No. I don't.'

'Are you sure?'

'I'm sure.'

However, she did need a car. 'I'll come home on the train or somebody can come and pick me up.'

'Leave it with me. I'll make sure you're picked up.'

The lack of fingerprints, and thus a suspect, and nothing wound up neatly and tied with a big red ribbon was a huge disappointment.

Dinner was spent with the staff. Honey roast gammon, followed by toffee apple crumble.

Now and again she caught one or two of the staff eyeing her suspiciously. She wasn't sure about Adrian. Though he did draw her aside afterwards and give her his phone number.

'If you hear anything that worries you in the middle of the night, give me a ring.'

She promised she would, though she couldn't quite believe his concern was purely with regard to her safety.

Later that night she bumped into him at the top of the stairs and nearly jumped out of her skin.

'Sorry. Did I startle you?'

'No,' she lied. 'Not at all.'

'Your mother's not back yet. Does that mean you're staying here longer or going home?'

'I thought I might cadge a pool car,' she said to him. 'Only until somebody comes down from Bath to pick me up.'

The truth was, she couldn't see that as an option. Somebody would have to drive her car and somebody else would have to follow them in order to give them a ride back home.

'I can arrange that for you. And if you get stuck I can give you a lift. As long as I'm not working, that is.'

She thanked him. 'A pool car would be ideal. There's something I have to do tomorrow.'

'I'll make sure there's one waiting for you.'

In the morning, choosing to leave by the main entrance, she shot off down the drive but got no further than the main gate. To her amazement a familiar face leaned into the driver's side window and asked her where she was going.

Dominic Christiansen!

Initially, she was tempted to tell him to mind his own business. On second thoughts it could prove quite interesting to see his reaction when faced with the truth.

'I'm going to see Professor Lionel Collins,' she said to him. 'In case he's home from Amsterdam by now. Want to come?'

She was taken aback at the speed with which he got into the car. Should she be scared? You bet she was!

'Why are you following me?'

'I'm not. I'm here to tell you to go home. You're safer there.'

Honey frowned. 'That's ridiculous.'

'Protecting yourself is ridiculous? I don't think so.'

'Isn't it time you told me what this is all about?' She was so angry she couldn't stop herself yelling at him.

'It's purely on a need-to-know basis.'

Look at him, she thought to herself. So smoothly dressed. So beautifully groomed and smelling so nice . . .

She reined in her automatic responses. Damn those hormones. At her age they should have gone walkabout by now!

'Are you kidnapping me?'

'I can't be. You're driving.'

His voice was calm and precise, his manner unflustered.

'What was the purpose of Tarquin's funeral — his lordship, as I should rightly call him?'

'I suppose I can disclose that. It was a ruse, a theatrical stunt to advertise the fact that he was indeed dead and of no danger to anyone. Which he is not. And was not.'

'You talk in riddles.'

'Sometimes I have to.'

There was a degree of sobriety in his voice that Honey had not heard before.

'You followed us when we stayed in the cottage.'

'I happened to be attending the same funeral as you.'

On a straight stretch of road she noticed his eyes sliding to the rear-view mirror, then the wing mirror, then back again.

'Are we being followed now?' she asked him.

She sensed an initial reluctance to respond and guessed he was making up his mind about what to say.

'Could be.'

She thought of a number of reasons why someone might be following them. Number one was her driving — she cringed at the thought of her most recent brush with the traffic police.

She checked her speed and found she was doing less than fifty. My word. This would never do. She stepped on the gas. They would never get to Dunster at this rate.

Dominic made no comment about the increase in speed. His behaviour was unchanged. Despite his sleek appearance, he had nerves of steel and possibly the strength of a sumo wrestler, though certainly not the figure. Not at all.

She parked in a visitor's space in the heart of Dunster village. The professor's house had little parking and it wasn't far to walk.

Knocking on the door brought no response, yet his car — a blue Ford Focus — was parked outside.

'He's been away — on a lecture tour,' Honey said, as though that explained everything.

'What is he to you?'

The question surprised her — just as Dominic's sudden reappearance had surprised her.

'Nothing. He rented a cottage on the estate while researching the family background.'

'And this is his house?'

There was something about Dominic's tone as he eyed the converted chapel that made her nervous, as though he knew something that she didn't.

'Yes. I visited here and asked him some questions.'

Dominic glanced over his shoulder. The village centre was not unduly crowded. A few visitors wandering from coffee shop to gift shop and along to the road that led up to the castle.

'I'll be questioning you later,' she said to him in a forthright manner. She was still convinced that he was the man stalking her. 'I want some explanations.'

'Are you sure he was going away?'

'Yes. On a lecture tour.'

'To where?'

She shrugged. She had thought Amsterdam was the only destination, though she couldn't be sure.

'Amsterdam. I think. But I was under the impression he'd be home by now.'

'Indeed,' he said, edging down the side of the building.

She watched him closely, the way he was moving along the side of the house, clambering up onto the window ledge and peering through the window.

She sensed his sudden disquiet. 'Is something wrong?'

'Get back in the car.'

'I beg your pardon?'

'Get back in the car.'

His voice was firm and his phone was clamped to his ear.

She didn't wait to be told a third time. She went back to the car, but she didn't get in. Instead she watched until Dominic had finished his call and joined her.

'Is he dead?'

It was a guess, but a pretty good one even before he answered. He pushed her into the passenger seat and took the wheel himself.

'Very.'

'How about calling the police?'

'The professor will be taken care of.'

Honey narrowed her eyes. 'What is it with you? One minute you're tailing me, then you disappear, then you reappear. And why now? Who do you work for?'

He kept his eyes on the road, a stalwart expression on his face.

'I'll tell you when I can.'

'What does that mean?'

'It means when I have permission to tell you.'

'Spook! You're a spook!'

He didn't answer.

CHAPTER NINETEEN

'You've got a nerve,' Honey shouted as Dominic got out of the pool car at a car park behind the White Hart pub. He headed for the familiar black BMW.

He stopped, looked back at her and shook his head.

'I'll explain later.'

He'd already told her not to disclose anything until he said so.

The moment he was out of sight she got back into the pool car and phoned Doherty. The line switched to voicemail.

Damn. He was still on the course and enjoying getting lost in the Brecon Beacons.

Back at Torrington Towers, Honey discovered there was a lovely view from the conservatory, a place of cool fountains and rich foliage. The Green River Hotel boasted a conservatory but it was a garden shed compared to the one here.

A member of staff brought her coffee. It smelled good and was very hot, just as she liked it. She felt incredibly saintly avoiding the sugar.

Out of all the cases she'd been involved in since becoming Crime Liaison Officer, this was the most complex. There was Tarquin, Caspar's brother who turned out to be his half-brother, supposedly buried alive in a mudslide, and now

Professor Collins had been found dead. Why would anyone want to kill him?

The biggest enigma of all was Dominic Christiansen. He'd popped up at the murder scene at Bradford on Avon, tailed her for no apparent reason and had now popped up again. Where had he been in the meantime?

She would have gone on pondering but was interrupted by the same member of staff who had brought her coffee rushing in as though she might have served cyanide by mistake.

'I'm sorry to bother you, Mrs Driver, but there's been a bit of a fracas down at the front gate. A woman who says she's come to drive you around while you're here.'

The jury was out on the issue of feminine instinct, but in Honey's view it was definitely working. She knew, she just KNEW the identity of the driver.

She covered her eyes with one hand and groaned.

'She says her name is—'

Honey cut the woman short. 'I know who it is.'

Mary Jane came bouncing in wearing purple harem pants, a Rolling Stones T-shirt in dark green with gold lettering, and a silk turban with long gold tassels. She looked like everyone's idea of a fairground fortune teller. In a way she was, though La Jolla, California was her patch and by profession she was a professor of the paranormal.

'Honey! Darling!'

After throwing a gold-and-pink carpet bag to the floor, Honey was enveloped in the longest and thinnest of arms. Mary Jane was over six feet tall and had the figure of a broomstick. It was possible she might also have considered riding one at times.

'Mary Jane. So nice to see you,' said Honey once she'd unwound herself from the clinch. 'Would you like coffee?'

'Green tea if you have it,' Mary Jane said.

The woman who'd brought the coffee nodded amiably and said she thought they had some.

'So where's my car? And where's my mother?'

'Your mother's got a cat. Stewart bought it for her. She's keeping it in the spare room.'

Honey hid her disappointment that her mother had not adopted the stray that kept wandering into the coach house. Never mind.

'And my car?'

Mary Jane sucked in her bottom lip. 'It's been clamped. But Lindsey is dealing with it.'

'Clamped?' Honey felt sick. This shouldn't be happening.

Mary Jane shrugged. 'I guess you left it in the wrong place.'

'It should have been in the usual place. I have a season ticket.'

'It was clamped in Brock Street.'

'Why was it in Brock Street? You've got to be an alien from Mars to leave it there! Everyone who parks there gets clamped.'

'I'm not an alien,' Mary Jane said quietly, 'and I got clamped.'

This came as no surprise, but Mary Jane was Mary Jane and Honey was Honey and knew beyond doubt where her car was supposed to be.

'My mother!'

Mary Jane's green tea arrived. One sip and she was asking whether Honey had found anything out and generally admiring their surroundings.

'This is a grand place. I can feel the vibes of history,' said Mary Jane, closing her eyes and breathing in the atmosphere along with the steam from the tea.

Honey outlined what she could, omitting only the information that had come via Doherty.

Mary Jane latched onto the details about the tarot cards. Honey didn't know what it was, but there was something in the look she gave that was downright unnerving.

'Tarot never used to have any meaning at all. They were just playing cards. It's just those who practise the occult who gave them meaning.'

'And the ones I received? What do they mean?'

Mary Jane shook her head, pursed her purple lips and tutted.

'Have you got something to add to that?' Honey asked, unnerved by the audible disapproval that sounded vaguely like machine-gun bullets.

She nodded. 'You've had a warning.'

A statement like that was enough to make any girl's heart turn cold. Honey's certainly did.

'What do you mean?'

'Caspar was reported dead.'

'So what?'

'Have you considered why that article appeared?'

'It was a mistake,' said Honey.

'Or was it placed there for the purpose of unnerving Caspar? That's one possibility. Or did it appear so that you would get involved?'

Honey spread her hands. 'For what reason?'

Mary Jane stroked her chin, tugging at a few sprouting grey hairs.

'It's almost as though somebody is playing a game. Getting Caspar wound up and then getting you wound up. Maybe it's to do with something that happened in the past, or something that hasn't happened yet.'

Honey didn't like what she was saying. 'Mary Jane, you've spooked me. Satisfied?'

Mary Jane cleared her throat and what Honey called her mystical look appeared in her eyes.

'In order to help matters, I had a little séance before I left. Just a few close friends, including your mother.'

Honey sighed. She'd never joined one of Mary Jane's séances, but her mother was a frequent attendee.

Honey resigned herself to hearing that some eighteenth-century ancestor had come through and decided to haunt the Green River Hotel, perhaps ousting the one they already had.

'And?'

'Your father came through. He said you were in danger and everyone had to look out for you.'

This was the second time her father had been linked to the present investigation and Honey was unnerved.

'Did he really?' She tried to sound offhand. Dealing with the realities of this case was complicated enough without warnings and help from the other side.

'I promised your father I would look after you. I aim to do that.'

The offer was warming and unexpected.

'OK.'

And Mary Jane was true to her word, though in Honey's opinion she took things a bit too far. Everywhere she went, Mary Jane was at her side. Honey stopped abruptly at the bedroom door and turned to face her. 'There's no need to follow me around indoors. I think I'm safe enough in my bedroom.'

'I'm here if you need me.'

'I don't,' Honey replied tersely, and slammed the door behind her.

Later, she found Miss Vincent in her office, slogging through a mountain of paperwork.

'Anything interesting?' she asked.

Miss Vincent sighed. 'Not unless you count the solicitor, bank manager, accountant and HMRC as interesting. Which I do not! Even death isn't enough to divide the tax man from his dues,' she added gruffly.

'What with all this extra paperwork you've got at present, I do hate to have to ask you for anything, but would it be possible for you to let me have a list of past employees — casuals and such like. I know the estate employs a lot during the summer months. Could you oblige?'

Miss Vincent eyed her suspiciously and for a moment Honey thought she'd have no chance.

'It's confidential.'

'It's very important.'

'I will have to get permission from the trustees.'

'But I have Caspar's permission and he's the heir.'

Miss Vincent eyed her disapprovingly. 'It isn't all settled yet. The lawyers have the last say.'

She was right, of course. Caspar had to agree to the terms of the will in order to inherit the house, the property and a hundred acres of safari park. Who wouldn't agree?

Honey eyed the piles of paperwork spread over the huge desk in front of Miss Vincent's diminutive figure. It looked a mess. Finding something must be like one of those games where a card or a dice is hidden beneath one of three cups. The trick was to guess which cup either card or dice was under. Miss Vincent was using piles of paper and she wasn't winning.

Too impatient to wait for the trustees' permission, the only way Honey was going to snoop through the paperwork was to wait until Miss Vincent was out of the room. And only one thing tempted Miss Vincent away from her work: food.

Yesterday lunchtime she'd exited the study to indulge her taste buds in steak and kidney pudding. Today it was liver and onions. All Honey had to do was wait until the drool dripped from her chin and she left to consume yet another homely lunch.

Like an honest-to-goodness intruder — or rather, dishonest intruder, seeing as intruders are by definition unlikely to be honest — Honey sneaked — even snaked — through the house. The oak staircase was carved from Jacobean oak, almost black, the banister smoothed by centuries of sweaty palms. The stair carpet was threadbare in places and on the first landing a huge stained-glass window threw a rainbow of colour, somehow making it seem plush again. Apart from the carpet, which years ago must have cost a fortune, Torrington Towers was in pretty good shape.

Miss Vincent had mentioned something about a new carpet being on order and due to be laid in the next two weeks. Honey had commented that it must be costing a fortune. She'd smiled and said that his lordship had insisted.

'No expense spared,' she'd said resolutely, through misted eyes. 'His lordship liked everything to be top notch.' She'd smiled in a secretive way as she said it, as though the same saying applied also to his sex life — a fact Honey did not doubt.

Honey had retorted that she hoped the estate's income covered the outgoings. Miss Vincent had merely laughed and said that of course it did, as though anything else would be quite absurd.

There was something about Miss Vincent that was both efficient and formidable. Honey decided it had a lot to do with the fact that she'd been here longer than any other member of staff. And she had a touch of the Wallis Simpson about her. Like Simpson, who'd married a king and inspired him to abdicate for love of her, Honey also felt that Miss Vincent had an agenda, though didn't have a clue what it might be. Now she was working for the estate as she had for his lordship, but at one time she had been much more than that. Loyalty shone from her face and there was affection in her voice.

So here Honey was, sneaking along the landing, intent on going through the heaps of filing without Miss Vincent around.

Torrington Towers, with its wide landings, was ideal for moving around unseen. Oak coffers and court cupboards vied for space with chiffoniers and gargantuan settees with gilded frames and cabriole legs. And there were shadows. Old houses were designed to keep out the cold, not let in the light. Hence lots of shadows.

Honey lingered, hovering behind a court cupboard until the smell of liver and onions spirited Miss Vincent away to the cafeteria, where no doubt the main course would be followed by prunes and custard. Miss Vincent was a great one for traditional British dishes. Lord knows how she kept so thin. If her secret could be bottled and sold, Honey would certainly be buying.

The moment she'd locked the door and disappeared, Honey was there with the key she'd purloined from the housekeeper's cupboard. Being a super-efficient employee, Miss Vincent always locked the door.

Honey's footfall was soft on the pure-wool carpet, which was the colour of milk chocolate, very new and deep enough to drown in.

The piled-up folders were still where Miss Vincent had left them, and two more piles had been added.

Honey quickly found the latest list of employees. Ever efficient, Miss Vincent had made one original copy of the list plus two extras.

Taking a deep breath, Honey glanced over her shoulder. For a moment she had the feeling of being watched. But there was nobody there — well, nobody drawing breath. One set of eyes glared at her from a Victorian portrait. The woman wore a black poke bonnet and her icy stare was enough to turn a saint to stone. The other glassy-eyed gaze was from the head of a stuffed antelope.

They were both scary in their own way and the sooner she got the job done and was out of there the better. Discretion being far and away the better part of valour, she took a copy based on the logic that it would not be so missed as an original.

Clasping the list against her bosom, she scarpered to the gallery, a wide affair running the full length of the house, windows on one side and doors on the other. This was the place where in times past ladies in farthingales had taken exercise when the weather outside was less than amenable.

Once she was safely hidden, she scrutinised what she had taken. The list was disappointing. She scanned the piece of paper again and again just in case there was something she was missing. Mrs Cromer was there. Meercroft the butler was there, and so was the ranger, Adrian Sayle, along with other people still in service whose names she recognised.

There were three names listed as having terminated their employment. A Miss Isobel White, though a 'c' beside her name listed her as casual. Honey guessed she worked summers at Torrington Towers but was laid off at the end of the season. Another name was Patricia Garner. She too was listed as casual only.

The only other was that of Keith McCall. A note said, 'Left without giving notice.' It also said that he was chief ranger. Adrian Sayle was now chief ranger. Had he been promoted or was he a new replacement? Miss Vincent would know.

Not wishing to be caught, Honey hid herself in a window seat halfway along the landing. The window overlooked the rear of the house. From there she had a good view of the paved courtyard, the neat terraces leading down to a crisp, green lawn.

The courtyard was bounded on three sides. Below her she could see the door leading into the kitchen. Directly opposite was a row of colour-coded bins ranged along one wall. Along the other were stone structures with sloping lids. They looked like some kind of storage units, perhaps for coal.

A continuation of the front driveway ran between the lower terrace and the grassy lawn. This was, of course, the tradesmen's entrance, the vehicular access for the butcher, the baker and whoever else happened to be delivering or here on maintenance business.

Thinking she heard the sound of Miss Vincent coughing into her handkerchief as she pitter-pattered in her low heels along the landing, Honey hid herself behind the thick tapestry curtain and didn't emerge until the sound of a door being slammed reverberated along the landing.

A sudden light-headedness made her realise she'd been holding her breath.

'Get a grip,' she muttered to herself.

Her body responded and accordingly she felt her whole self relax. Before leaving her hiding place, she took one more look out of the window to the courtyard below.

Adrian Sayle was down there. He was not alone. The man he was talking to was instantly familiar. It was Dominic Christiansen.

Had Adrian Sayle caught him nosing around? Or were they already acquainted? The warning she'd received nagged at her mind. Be careful. Trust no one.

First things first. Ask Miss Vincent for clarification.

She found her sitting behind the desk patting the little bowl of a tummy where liver now swam around with prunes and custard. She was frowning at the paperwork stalagmites in a very disapproving — no, a distrusting manner. It occurred to Honey that she might have X-ray vision and could actually tell that something had been disturbed.

In the meantime it would do to impress, so Honey adopted her most superior air, the kind his lordship's ancestors would have regarded as quite the norm for people of their status. In Honey's case she was doing it purely to boost her confidence.

'Miss Vincent, there's something I have to ask you.'

Miss Vincent tilted her pert little chin upwards. Her expression was deadpan.

'I'll help if I can, though as I've already said, we have the will and the lawyers to consider. They oversee everything we do.' Her tone was firm. The staccato of her voice reminded Honey of plucked violin strings.

'Adrian Sayle. Has he been here long?'

'About six months.'

'I take it he replaced Mr Keith McCall.'

A fleeting look crossed Miss Vincent's eyes. She would be careful answering.

'He did. Mr McCall left without giving notice. Mr Sayle replaced him.'

Honey ran her finger down the list. 'I can find no record of salary payments on this list or when he started here.'

Miss Vincent shook her head, though her bobbed hair stayed still, as though it were glued in place. 'I don't know how you got that document, but it's confidential,' she hissed. 'I know nothing about the financial arrangements between his lordship and senior members of staff.'

Honey frowned as she considered what the other woman had said.

'There were separate financial arrangements?'

'Only between Mr Sayle and the estate. Not between him and his lordship *personally*.'

Again that shaking head. Again her hair stayed in situ.

'With whom and on what basis were these payments made?'

Miss Vincent shrugged her narrow shoulders. 'I've no idea. Perhaps Mr Jerwood, the solicitor, would know? If not, you could ask his personal assistant, Miss Belvedere. I believe she was privy to the matters of the Torrington estate. Otherwise, might I suggest that you ask Adrian Sayle direct.'

Honey couldn't help getting the impression she was daring her to try it.

'Where did he work before coming here?'

'I would have to find his application to tell you that.'

'Will you do that for me?'

'Only when Mr Jerwood, the solicitor, allows it.'

CHAPTER TWENTY

Mary Jane had found the library and its amazing collection of books on the occult.

'Honey, you've got to see this stuff. I could spend all day in here.' Suddenly remembering that she'd come down to offer her constant company and instead had found the library, she looked up. 'You don't mind, do you?'

No. Of course she didn't mind.

'Read till your eyes fall out. I'm off for a walk. I need to ask Adrian Sayle some questions.'

Mary Jane's nose went back into the book she was reading.

'Funny how people seem to disappear when you're around.'

For a moment Honey held that comment. Did that include people who had died? She knew Mary Jane was joking, but in a way she did have a point. Wherever she trod a dead body appeared — his lordship, for one. And now Professor Collins.

She felt she was sinking deeper and deeper into this morass of intrigue. It wasn't like her to feel so out of kilter with a case. She found herself wishing Caspar had come down here to do his own investigations.

Never mind, she said to herself. Go for a walk. Clear your head.

The autumn sunshine was muted, smothered with the fog of humidity that would inevitably be followed by driving rain. The clouds were already frowning over the funfair and the animal pens.

Donning a waxed jacket, jeans and a pair of green Hunters, she set off along the narrow path leading towards an area of woodland. Despite being narrow, the path was straight and eventually led to a ravine that in turn led to a railway tunnel and the entrance to a series of caves.

The ravine appeared to run parallel to the old railway tunnel, which was locked and barred, the iron railings protecting roughly two-thirds of the tunnel's arched entrance.

She headed to the side, taking the uneven path through the ravine. Occasional gusts of wind brought down the last leaves of autumn. The curled fronds of dying ferns dripped water onto her head and into her face. It was quite refreshing.

The stony ground made swift progress almost impossible. It was also slippery so she was glad she'd donned her boots, which had a thick sole. Even so, she could still feel the sharper stones cutting through.

Every dozen steps or so she paused to look around and above her. Thick bushes pushed through the alternating layers of rocks and earth all the way up to the top of the ravine some twenty or thirty feet above her.

Stumbling, she reached out, her hands clawing at the stones and soggy vegetation.

There were pillars outside the cave — three of them in fact. Innocuous at first, on closer scrutiny it became obvious that these were not natural phenomena. They'd been placed there in such a way that the cave's entrance was hidden. The pillars were the ancient comparative of bi-folding doors — though of course they didn't close, they merely camouflaged.

She slid through the first two, then through the gap left by pillar number two and pillar number three and switched on her flashlight.

‘What am I doing here?’ she muttered to herself. She’d come out for a walk but also to find Adrian Sayle. She wanted to know where he’d come from, where he had worked before Torrington Towers. There was no sign of him. Well, there wouldn’t be, considering he was more likely to be with the animals, not here in a secluded and decidedly creepy cave.

Inside smelled of damp earth and there was the sound of trickling water. The cave started off large in size. She supposed it looked, from a wider vantage point, as though the entrance resembled a yawning mouth, the pillars like upward-growing canines. But it wasn’t possible to see the full perspective — the channel through the ravine prevented that.

The cave narrowed, becoming little more than a passage hewn from solid rock by centuries of water ingress. The ground beneath her feet sloped downward, so steep that it was difficult to stop herself from picking up speed and careering headlong into the darkness.

A wall of rock was picked out by the flashlight. She’d come to a dead end deep beneath the earth. She was now standing in a huge cave. Above her the vaulted ceiling rose like the nave of a cathedral.

The air was freezing and her breath turned to steam, swirling wraithlike in the light from her torch.

A pool of water had gathered at one side of the cave, stalactites hung from the ceiling, and stalagmites rose like pillars of doughnuts from the floor.

Ahead of her the flashlight picked out a stone-lined pit in the floor. She held her breath. This was not just a pit. She was looking down into a grave. It was empty. She breathed a sigh of relief.

She brushed the sweat from her forehead. All this thinking was giving her a headache — though the meagre light probably had a lot to do with it too.

She turned to leave, then paused, thinking she heard something. Not human, not animal, but mechanical. Something humming, not close but far off, perhaps in front of her, perhaps above ground.

She couldn't work it out, but couldn't stay to investigate. Caves were not her favourite place — the smell, the feeling of being enclosed in stone caused panic to set in. Suddenly she needed to get out.

Staggering now, she made her way back along the narrow passage. Was it her imagination or was that methane she could smell?

Her head was swimming. Her legs were growing weak. Everything was turning black. With a sudden surge of willpower, she forced herself to go on until there it was: a pinpoint of light.

The pinpoint grew in size, and the bigger it grew, the more strength she found to stagger towards it, until eventually she was outside and gasping for air.

A sudden movement from the mouth of the old tunnel to her right caught her attention and made her start.

Startled eyes looked at her from between the bars of the gate guarding the railway tunnel before the fox slid through and ran off into the undergrowth, a piece of meat hanging from the side of its mouth.

'Bloody fox,' she shouted, purely in relief.

* * *

Mary Jane was waiting for her when she got back, an animated expression on her face. 'Where have you been?'

'For a walk. I told you.' She instantly regretted her abruptness. 'Mary Jane, I'm sorry.'

'I only meant where did you go for a walk. Purely out of interest.'

Honey saw there was no hurt look in her eyes. Mary Jane looked excited.

'What's happened?' asked Honey as she threw off her jacket and pulled off her boots. She eyed her soggy socks where a stone or two had broken through the rubber wellingtons, then she took them off too.

'There are no bones in the garden,' exclaimed Mary Jane. 'And no history of a member of the family ever having been cremated in the garden — or anywhere outside for that matter.'

Honey sat there for a moment examining her toes while digesting the information Mary Jane was giving her. She eyed her with some surprise. 'You're a dark horse, Mary Jane. I thought you were immersed in library books.'

'It's all part of my plan,' hissed Mary Jane in conspiratorial fashion. 'I made a promise to your father to look after you and I am. But I have to be cunning. So I'm letting everyone here think that I'm only interested in books on the occult. Actually they're old hat. Outdated thinking.'

Honey expressed surprise. It had never occurred to her that anything on the occult was actually outdated. She'd thought the whole point was that it was ancient knowledge and unchanged through the centuries.

'Leaving the books aside, what is it you're saying about the cremation?'

The answer sprang to mind, but she wanted to hear it from Mary Jane — just in case she was wrong.

'I went into a trance. No spirit lingered.'

Honey frowned. She knew Mary Jane believed in an afterlife, but still . . .

'I'm not sure what you mean.'

'There was no body in that coffin. I guarantee it. No body was burned.'

Honey shook her head. 'No body? I can't believe it.'

'Believe it! Notice that nothing was done about the ashes. A grieving family would've had them scooped up and taken away. Wouldn't you think they would prefer them scattered?'

Honey shook her head. This was all so complicated. What was the point of it? The deceased had been autopsied. Caspar had identified the body. DNA had been matched.

She voiced the nagging question. 'What was the point?'

Mary Jane shrugged. 'Search me. Now, I'm thinking I might hold a séance. If the atmospherics are OK we can expect a visit from your father.'

Honey looked at her in alarm. Although he'd been long dead, she didn't particularly wish to make contact with her father. She wished him at rest.

'I'm not your girl for attending a séance,' she said uneasily. 'Why not wait until you've got my mother on hand?'

There was a sparkle in Mary Jane's eyes. 'You scared, Honey?'

'You bet I am!'

She shook her head. 'Aw, come on. You'll enjoy it.'

'No way, Mary Jane. No way!'

Honey headed for the door.

'Where are you going?'

'I'm going to visit the walled garden. I want confirmation.'

Mary Jane waved a bony hand. 'OK. Have it your way. I'll have a word with your father by myself. I'm sure he won't mind doing without a circle.'

Honey pulled on her boots but left her coat behind. She shook her head as she made her way outside. Mary Jane was only trying to be helpful, but really, contacting the other side just didn't cut it for Honey. After having Mary Jane living in her hotel for some time, rubbing shoulders with whatever spirits she reckoned lived in the old place, Honey still refused to confront what might be. It was hard enough facing this world.

There was only ash where the fire had been, most of it trampled into the earth. It certainly seemed there should have been more. Perhaps Mary Jane was right. It might not be possible to detect DNA, but she'd like to think it was possible to identify ash from someone who had once been alive from cinders of just burned wood.

Seeing as Doherty was out of bounds, she rang Cecil Street, the pathologist who'd carried out the post-mortem on Tarquin St John Gervais. He was hesitant but finally confirmed that unless subjected to a very great heat, that of a cremation furnace, there would be bones left. A funeral pyre is never as hot as a furnace.

'There are sometimes even fragments left in a cremation furnace — along with the twisted metal of false hips, false teeth and the odd watch, thanks to a sloppy funeral director. But a bonfire? Small fragments of bone could be left behind.'

'The ash seems to have been taken away for burial, and I presume what bones were left with it, though I can't think why someone would do that,' Honey stated thoughtfully.

The pathologist's response was suitably cryptic. 'Perhaps the gardener wanted to plant a few spring onions.'

CHAPTER TWENTY-ONE

Doherty had been less than enthusiastic about enrolling on the team-building course. For a start he reckoned he had bonded enough over the years with his colleagues, and secondly, he disliked camping. He had gone on camping holidays as a child. He'd hated them then and he hated them now. More so seeing as they were not camping close to some pebble beach on the Dorset coast, but in the wind- and rain-swept Brecon Beacons.

After enduring a couple of days sharing a leaky tent with his colleagues, totally isolated from civilisation, it was a welcome surprise to see a helicopter hovering over them, despite the propellers adding to the wind strength.

All of them were of the opinion that the helicopter was only flying over. The last thing they'd expected was for it to set down some way from their bedraggled tent, the blades coming slowly to a halt.

Doherty narrowed his eyes. There were two men in the helicopter, the pilot and one other. It was the other man that drew his attention.

The man's strides were long and purposeful as he alighted from the helicopter and headed Doherty's way, his tie flying over his shoulder. He was wearing a dark padded jacket over a charcoal-grey suit. And even though the wind was playing with his hair, Doherty could see it was an expensive cut. He also noticed the man's facial features: strong jaw, dark eyebrows, intelligent eyes. His instinct said the man had come for him and his instinct proved right.

'Steve Doherty?'

The voice was familiar.

'Who's asking?'

'The name's Christiansen. I think we need to have a chat. Get your stuff and come with me.'

CHAPTER TWENTY-TWO

Back at Torrington Towers, the gloom outside seemed to seep indoors, settling like a smog in the study. It didn't help that the room was furnished man-style: dark carpet, dark wood and lots of books, the dark decorations swallowing the light.

Honey switched on a desk light. Mary Jane sat across from her, yet another book open on her lap. She seemed absorbed in it, but somehow Honey knew she was not.

'You were right. About the bones, or lack thereof.'

'Uh-huh,' she said, without looking up.

'I still haven't seen Adrian Sayle. I presume he's over in the animal houses. Lions and stuff must take some looking after.'

Mary Jane looked up. 'I did it.'

'Did what?'

'Held a séance. Well, not quite a séance. More of a one-to-one. It turned out quite well. Tell me, did you know your father was a spy?'

Honey blinked. She'd totally forgotten Mary Jane's intention, though was glad the séance had occurred while she was out in the garden.

'He confirmed it, did he?'

'Yep! He was a British agent. Just like James Bond. No wonder you're such a good detective. It runs in the blood.'

Honey wasn't so sure, and the flattery unnerved her.

'I take it he also confirmed that he was friendly with his lordship.'

Mary Jane beamed from ear to ear. 'Better than that. They were pictured together. That's what he told me.'

The thought of seeing her father in his cloak-and-dagger days intrigued her. Just this once, she sorely wanted Mary Jane to be correct.

'I wonder where that picture would be?'

Mary Jane shrugged. 'They used to meet up here. Far from prying eyes. Wouldn't you have liked to be a fly on the wall?'

Mary Jane's comments clicked together in Honey's brain. Her gaze journeyed over the shelves of books. Some looked old, though the gilt still gleamed on their spines.

Inside the pages of a book . . . that would be a good place to hide a photograph, she thought to herself.

She passed slowly in front of each shelf, her fingers tracing over the spines at eye level.

This is crazy, she thought. You cannot open each and every one of these books to search for a photograph. It did occur to her that it might have been placed in a frame, but she discounted that idea immediately. If so, she would have found it by now.

And then it came to her. Photographs were records of family events, though the one she was after wasn't exactly of a conventional family. It was friends all in the same profession. But it would fit snugly into an album along with other photographs.

It was a long shot, but maybe with Mary Jane's help, she stood half a chance.

'See if you can find a photo album.'

Gilded spines shone brightest on the newest books and size mattered. Albums were usually of A4 size at least. Guessing at the size narrowed her search to one area of one shelf in particular.

'Nothing here,' said Mary Jane.

Honey's fingernails tapped on the possibles. One bulging spine shone brighter than the rest. It was also too big for the shelf it had been placed on.

Trusting her instinct, Honey dragged it out.

'Here goes.' She laid it flat on a desk topped with green leather.

Flicking through pages of smiling families, she began to feel she'd guessed wrong . . .

Then, finally, it was there in front of her eyes. A brace of young faces looking out at her from a black-and-white photograph. They looked happy and confident, in the prime of their lives.

'They've signed it,' she said, pointing to the signatures all made with the same ballpoint pen.

Honey read her father's signature, Tarquin's — which of course took up the most room. Percy Bullington — her father's cousin. The signature that most drew her attention, though, was that of Keith McCall. She recalled him as the park ranger before Adrian Sayle.

In the old photograph he was a fresh-faced young man with a shock of fair hair and intense eyes that looked at the camera as though daring it to present him as anything but handsome.

Honey frowned as a question popped into her mind.

'They weren't all spies, were they?'

Mary Jane shrugged. 'I can't tell you everything. Oh, one more thing. Your father told me to warn you to be careful. The sins of the fathers and all that . . .'

'Sins? What sins?'

Mary Jane shrugged again in her characteristic manner, bony shoulders almost touching her ears.

Honey studied the photograph again. 'Five young men but only four signatures.'

The fifth man's face was sideways on, a sweep of dark hair hiding half his features. Either he was camera-shy or he didn't want to be recognised.

She felt Mary Jane's eyes on her.

'You're thinking the same as I am, aren't you, Hon. That fifth man is doing his darndest to hide his face. I think because that young man is the key to everything.'

Honey stared at the photograph as though she could detect the scraping signature of a pencil perhaps. There was nothing.

'We need to find out his name.' She reached for her bag, got out her phone and dialled Uncle Percy.

It took a few goes but eventually he answered. His voice sounded cracked, like an old vinyl record that's been scratched to distraction over the years.

After the normal niceties were exchanged, she asked him about the photograph.

'It looks as though it were taken some time in the seventies if the bell-bottom trousers and glossy locks are anything to go by.'

She outlined who was on the photograph besides himself.

'There's just one that we can't identify. He looks as though he might be camera-shy. Luckily for him he had plenty of hair to hide behind.'

'Ah. Really. How interesting.'

His response told her nothing. There were no platitudes, just exclamations that said nothing and went nowhere.

She went on to describe the man as best she could.

'You must know him, Uncle Percy. After all, you were standing in a line together, looking chummy and having your picture taken. So who was he?'

'You shouldn't be worrying your head with all this, you know.'

Honey counted to ten. Uncle Percy had been young in a time when most women were still glued to the kitchen sink. He wouldn't know he was being condescending. Or would he?

Well, two could play at silly buggers!

'But Uncle! His hair is to die for. I'd love hair like that. Perhaps he could advise me where he got it cut and how he manages to keep it looking so glossy!'

A sharp silence ensued before he answered.

'It's not so glossy now,' he growled.

Of course not. The man must be at least seventy. He probably didn't have any hair left.

'I'd like to meet him.'

'You can't. He's dead.'

Honey wasn't so much taken aback as curious as to why her uncle was so reluctant to tell her the man's identity. She still wanted to know.

'So what was his name?'

She imagined her uncle grinding his teeth but couldn't understand his reluctance.

'Ivan. His name was Ivan.'

'And the second name?'

'Orlov. Ivan Orlov.'

'Is that a Russian name?'

'Yes. It is. We were all students together. He was the grandson of a White Russian — a dissident who came over just after the Russian Revolution.'

Her mind raced in circles once she'd disconnected the call. At first she'd considered it nonsense when it was suggested her father was a spy. Her mother's response had been pretty much the same. But now there was a photo of all those young men together with a Russian, taken when they were all at Oxford University. She'd read articles on how the Russians had recruited well-educated young men into their ranks from the privileged halls of residence. Had her father been one of them or had he acted for the West? And what about Orlov? Just because his grandfather had been a White Russian didn't mean that he was.

The only person who knew the real story was Dominic Christiansen. How could she get him to tell her the truth? Could she possibly beguile him into imparting some of what he knew?

A single word came to mind. The obvious one. Sex.

She gritted her teeth at the thought of using her femininity as a weapon. Let Christiansen believe he had her exactly where he wanted her. That she was so blinded by his charms she couldn't see what was behind it all. He'd regret the day he ever underestimated her . . . she was going to make sure of that.

Never mind Honey Driver. She would look as sexy as Honey Ryder in that scene from the first James Bond film, *Dr. No*. All she had to do was find him. At present he was nowhere in sight, though she had seen him with Adrian Sayle and she couldn't find him either.

Mary Jane came looking for her, insisting they take a look at the animal pens.

'The lions are in,' she said with great enthusiasm.

Honey was at a loose end, her thoughts making her head feel like a spinning top that wouldn't quit. She was already dressed in jeans, boots and a thick sweater, so let herself be manhandled out of the house, around the path at the back and through the gate into the animal enclosures.

At some point she wanted to find out about this ranger Keith McCall. Yet another peg in the Ouija board! One mention and Mary Jane would be attempting to make contact with him too. Not that Honey had any evidence that he was dead. It was just that his departure from his position at Torrington Towers had been sudden, and it was only a month before Adrian Sayle had stepped into his shoes.

CHAPTER TWENTY-THREE

Nobody knew that the old sausage factory contained nothing but this well-lit foyer. Behind it was an empty factory, long denuded of the stainless-steel machinery once housed therein. A tunnel connected the lower level of the factory to the abattoir, also disused. It had been a long time since the tunnel had echoed to the terrified bellowing of animals on their way to being butchered.

The car park surrounding the factory was full of cars, ostensibly those who worked at the factory. The smoke curling from the sixty-foot chimneys helped maintain the illusion that it still operated, though it hadn't done for years.

Dominic Christiansen drove slowly up to the entrance. Alex Patterson was waiting for him on the steps, his hair tousled as usual, his face pale against the black polo neck and leather jacket.

Alex waited until the car had come to a halt before descending the steps.

Dominic Christiansen wound down the window.

Alex glanced over his shoulder before leaning his arms on the car roof and talking through the gap. His expression said it all.

'He gave us the slip.'

'I heard. Where is he now?'

Alex shrugged. 'You tell me. After all, you should know the guy better than anyone, DC. You were the guy shadowing him. Don't let Lord Torrington blow his cover — remember?'

'He's a professional. Damned nuisance, though. I sometimes think it might be better if he really were dead and we didn't have to go through all this melodrama!'

'So, how's our girl?'

Dominic grimaced. 'So far she hasn't been intruding into the supposed death of Lionel Collins, but at some point she's going to question cause of death and even ask to see the body.'

'And there isn't one.'

Dominic clenched his jaw. Lord Torrington was a pain in the ass.

'And the policeman boyfriend?'

'I've had a word. Gave him the gist of things and told him to back off.'

'Was he game?'

Dominic shrugged his broad shoulders. Even covered by a cashmere suit, designer label of course, his muscularity was still obvious.

'For now he's being debriefed. He won't be allowed to go until we've finished with him. The last thing we want is him galloping into this like some gallant white knight and destroying all the work we've done, the plans we've laid.'

'The Driver woman is going to feel lonely.'

Dominic smiled. 'I think I can help there, purely for the sake of the realm, of course.'

Alex, a friend for a very long time, raised his eyebrows. 'Would that be such a chore?'

Dominic smiled. 'Not really. As long as her policeman is kept out of the picture. I don't think he'd be too pleased.'

'You sound confident of success.'

A slow smile crossed the face of the well-educated, ruggedly handsome Dominic Christiansen. He'd been working for MI5 for some time, a definite asset being that he spoke seven languages fluently. Speaking Swedish, Norwegian and Icelandic had been thanks to his Swedish father. His mother was English. He also spoke Russian, Mandarin and Portuguese.

'I aim to pull out all the stops.'

Before parting they exchanged the knowing look of professionals familiar with the cut and thrust of a world hidden from what passed as civilisation. The underworld they worked in was savage and totally without conscience, but they were brothers in arms, dwelling in the shady world of international intelligence.

Both were instinctive. Both knew that Keith McCall was dead. It was just a case of finding the body.

They were interrupted by an electronic beeping. Dominic reached for his phone. The application sparked up a single word. Intruder. The tracker device was something agents kept on them at all times. Each blinked with an individual ID. This one was blinking with Keith McCall's number. Up until now they'd presumed it had been destroyed somehow. Sometimes these gadgets reacted to dampness or were deactivated by movement. Another movement must have reactivated it.

This was nothing but a stroke of luck. All he had to do was follow its low-tone bleep.

'Gotta go.'

The car throbbed into life and roared like a lion when he slid the gearstick into first.

The pulse from the reactivated tracking device kept blinking and bleeping as he followed.

It crossed his mind that someone might have found the device and activated it in order to draw him in. Under the circumstances, he was willing to chance that. McCall knew so much.

The copse of deciduous trees hid the old railway line and the tunnel from the house. Back in the nineteenth century a Torrington ancestor had insisted on his own private branch line terminating in the cellar beneath the place where sick animals were caged. It was pointed out to him that ventilation shafts would have to be built in a line across the verdant parkland. The view would have been ruined. The old man settled for a manually operated wagon running on rails between the house and his own private station. The copse had been planted to hide the station from the house. The copse remained, but the station was boarded up — locked and barred against intruders.

He left his car in the gap between the copse and the entrance to the tunnel and drew his gun.

Dominic stood at the tunnel entrance, letting his torch skip over the rocks piled along both sides of the curving walls. The rocks gave the appearance of instability, as though the structure might collapse at any minute.

It couldn't be further from the truth. The curved stonework had withstood the test of time. The rocks had been placed there to misinform, to keep intruders out. It didn't always work.

He opened the gate, bits of rust flaking from the iron bars as he pulled it open.

He heard rustling, some movement.

'I know you're in here,' he called out.

His voice echoed and bounced back to him.

He was giving whoever it was the benefit of the doubt. All the same, he cocked his gun, just in case.

Potholers, kids smoking their first cigarette, and even couples looking for a little privacy found their way into the tunnel. And poachers.

Dominic knew more about Torrington Towers than Honey Driver would ever know, simply because she didn't have clearance. He did. And so had his lordship.

'Is that you, Fred?'

Fred Cromer, who ran the village garage, was the biggest poacher around. Green fingers he might have from watering the pots out front of his garage and cottage window ledge, but Fred also had a yearning for fresh meat and salmon acquired without cost. There were others hereabouts who dabbled in poaching, but Fred was a regular and damned good at what he did. If the garage proprietor could no longer make his living mending, selling and hiring cars, he wouldn't starve.

Dominic stopped and listened. The slow drip of water running through the fissures sounded to his right. A rotting downpipe spewed excess rainwater from the few feet of guttering to the side of the tunnel's yawning arch. The water never stopped running, hollowing out a large hole to one side, big enough to bury a man in. Or a woman.

The smell was of dusty vegetation, damp rock and rat droppings, not overpowering, but far from pleasant.

He remained motionless and waited. Nobody came out of hiding.

One more chance. 'Hey! It's not safe in there. There are mantraps.'

He wasn't kidding. The torch picked out the cruel metal teeth. *A mantrap*. Someone had set them here. Step on one, the jaws would close, ripping into a man's calf, maiming him for life.

The darkness intensified, swallowing the light thrown by the torch.

Mindful of the sound of his own footsteps, he stopped, listened and tried not to breathe too deeply. The smell of decay was stronger here. Not plants. Not fetid water. This was the smell of dead meat. Dead flesh.

Even before he came to the second mantrap, he knew what he would find.

The torch danced over a face gnawed by animals, rancid flesh hanging from cheekbones, eye sockets empty, the juicy snack of a fox, a rat, even a weasel. It was likely one of them was responsible for reactivating the device. No one else had been in here for some time. Word got round, even among poachers.

Taking care not to step into the thick soup of flesh and mud, he skirted the corpse, knelt down and shone the torch on the mangled leg.

Starting at the scuffed boots, he traced a line upwards over the leg, the ripped jeans stained with things on which he had no wish to speculate.

Nobody would have heard this man screaming for help. A vivid picture came to mind, of McCall being lured here, trapping his leg.

Even before he stepped on it, he knew he would find a gun on the ground. He also knew what he would find in the man's breast pocket: a tarot card. In the light of the torch he picked out the Seven of Swords.

This had not been an accident. This was the work of the Tarot Man, though for some reason McCall had not been buried in mud like his other victims. Perhaps he'd been disturbed before he was able to finish the job.

A rat would have gnawed off its leg to escape. A man wouldn't do that. The gun on the ground was beyond McCall's reach, as though purposely placed there, sweetening the moment for the man responsible for his death. McCall had died here. The animals had done the rest.

His family would have to be informed. It was a damned nuisance. Another murder to be explained away. In this case, due to his age, at least they could say his death was natural. A heart attack. Something like that. The autopsy report would say whatever the service wanted it to say.

Dominic turned off his flashlight and made a phone call. It wasn't his job to clean up this mess. There was an entire department to do that.

* * *

Yet again, Honey was wandering towards her favourite place on the whole estate when she espied Dominic's car sitting on the track that ran parallel to the ravine.

She slid her way across the damp grass until she was looking from the top of the ravine towards the railway tunnel. It was dark down there, but his headlights were on. She shouted down to him.

‘Mr Christiansen! I want a word with you.’

It was twilight, and all around things were getting darker.

His torch flashed in her direction. Shielding her eyes against the sudden light, she tried to focus on his face, but he had the advantage and remained in darkness.

The torch stayed trained on her face until he was there, standing before her wearing an unpleasant expression.

‘Are you following me?’ She sensed the ghost of a smile. ‘I’m flattered.’

She smiled right back. ‘Why not? You’re a handsome man, Mr Christiansen.’

‘Call me Dominic. You know you want to.’

She heard the humour in his voice, but also conceit. Dominic Christiansen thought highly of himself.

‘What are you up to, Dominic?’

‘Out for an evening stroll, just like you.’ He stifled the urge to look over his shoulder. She must not see the body. ‘How about we go to the pub? We’ve been saying we’ll get together . . . Dinner’s on me. Are we on?’

This was it. The first step to flirting with a very handsome man in order to gain information. Could she carry it off? Of course she could.

‘OK.’

‘Stay here,’ he said. ‘I’ll drive up.’

CHAPTER TWENTY-FOUR

Honey was no shrinking violet, and although she did feel just a teeny bit guilty that she was playing away — Doherty was still off on his team-building course — she forced herself to believe it was purely business. Just because he smelled good and looked good when dressed didn't mean she wanted to know what he looked like with nothing on. This was all about gaining his trust so he would open up to her.

Dominic was thinking pretty much the same thing. He smiled at her, placed a protective arm around her shoulders and pulled back a chair for her to sit on. When he asked her if she wanted a drink, his voice had that hushed quality that made her think of bed rather than a drink.

'Get a grip,' she muttered to herself when he went to the bar.

'They're coming with menus,' he said. 'Is this table OK for you?'

His eyes were the colour of a sun-kissed sea. His voice lulled her into a kind of semi-consciousness. This was not quite what she'd had in mind. Her plan had been to seduce him into spilling the beans. Instead she was putty in his hands. And what hands! Long, sensitive fingers that looked capable of bending an iron bar.

Her hormones were begging for his undivided attention. They wanted him. Telling them that this wasn't the plan and that they should go lie down and play again tomorrow was only marginally successful.

Still, the job had to be done.

Dominic was Prince Charming and showing a genuine interest in the more routine side of her life. He asked her about the Green River, who was running it while she was away, how many staff she had, if there were times she wished she had done something else . . . all the usual things she'd been asked a thousand times before. She was flattered, but also suspicious. The more time she spent with him the more her opinions were coloured by the thought that he had ulterior motives. All the same, each question was delivered in a low tenor that tickled her hormones no end.

She found herself answering as though she were doing so for the very first time. Like a virgin, she thought to herself, making her face glow like a summer sunset.

'You don't think that your friend Caspar was a bit selfish asking you to stay here?'

'Caspar? Selfish?' She almost laughed. 'Of course he is. But I know if anything went wrong at the Green River, he would make sure it was put right. My business will never go to rack and ruin while he's around.'

Her own words surprised her. She'd been appalled when she'd read the newspaper headlines indicating that Caspar was dead. But she'd also been shocked and saddened. Caspar, despite his superior and outrageously fastidious ways, was a good man. He would always do what he could. His oddness of late was purely down to the circumstances he had found himself in.

Dominic tasted the wine before allowing it to be poured.

The wine was dark and fruity. The man sitting across from her was blond-haired but just as tempting.

Now go careful, girl!

Honey rested her chin on her hand, adopted her best heart-melting look and gazed into his eyes.

'Do you ever tell the truth?'

His smile was amazing. 'Of course I do.'

Top-quality aftershave wafted across the table.

'So tell me this. Where is the body of Tarquin St John Gervais? I mean the real body.'

For a moment she thought she saw mockery in his eyes, a hint of lust perhaps that was suddenly guarded.

'Ashes to ashes.'

Honey shook her head. 'I don't think so. The fire wasn't hot enough to destroy *all* of the bones. There should have been a few left, but there were not, and it looks as though the ashes themselves were scraped away. Besides that, he should never have been cremated the way he was. It's illegal except in a place reserved for such purpose.'

His fingers had been stroking hers. Delicious and very distracting, which she surmised was his intention. He wanted to put her off guard, to make her the pliable one.

There was purpose in letting him carry on doing that. Let him think she was putty in his hands. Behind her smile her mind remained sharp.

She kept smiling at him, hoping he'd be beguiled into careless talk. Perhaps he guessed that. The caresses ceased.

'Have you heard from your boyfriend?'

'You're changing the subject. Who is it you work for, Dominic? What is the underlying story in all this?'

His eyes crinkled at the corners and for a moment it looked as though he wasn't going to reply.

'Spies and counterspies, Mrs Driver, but I thought you already knew that.'

She frowned. 'Why do you think that?' She had no intention of voicing her suspicions — because basically that was all they were, suspicions.

He looked at her appraisingly. 'You've been asking questions — the right questions.'

'Give me some answers.'

'It's irrelevant,' he said casually. 'The fact is, fate has thrown us together following terrible events. I don't think we should ignore that.'

'So how did the professor die?'

'Shot.'

'I haven't seen any report about it in the newspaper.'

She reminded herself that she needed to keep him interested if she was going to break down barriers and get him to trust her.

His eyes held hers and she was determined to brave it out and not turn away.

'This is a delicate situation. You don't have to have any part in it.'

'I suppose I don't.'

'I do find you attractive.'

She was ready for this and had an answer prepared and waiting.

'I won't deny that the feeling's mutual.'

'Lucky your policeman boyfriend isn't around. I don't like competition.'

She smiled. 'I get the feeling that you're the kind of guy who likes to come out on top.'

His grin widened. 'Right. I like to be on top.'

He was being saucy, but she wouldn't blush.

She withdrew her hand when he reached for it. 'Bullshit!'

He looked only faintly surprised.

'You've been leading me on from the start. You knew who the dead man was and you knew who I was.' She held up a warning finger and glared at him. 'I'm even beginning to suspect that Caspar had a hand in it. I wouldn't have got involved except I was persuaded into it.' Just as I was persuaded into the job of Crime Liaison Officer, she thought to herself.

They were between courses. The dishes containing Breton shrimp soup were cleared away. Pork loin in apple next.

'Was it you that passed me the tarot card when I went to lunch with my mother? Or maybe you can tell me who did. Someone left it with my bill.'

His smile stiffened.

'Excuse me. I won't be a moment.'

He left the table and headed for the toilets. Honey watched him go. She couldn't help wondering about him, though in one aspect she was convinced he really did work for the shadier side of law enforcement. He was a spook.

His profession did not unnerve her. What did unnerve her were her feelings for him. He was dangerous and, because of his profession, downright unreliable. He couldn't be anything else.

* * *

The gents' cloakroom was empty. Dominic checked the cubicles. They were empty too. He took out his phone and dialled the short code, after which he explained the situation and just how close the Tarot Man had got to her.

'I'm going to tell her the truth.'

The voice on the other end protested.

'I've made up my mind. It's only right that she should know.'

When he got back to the table, Honey noticed that something had changed in his demeanour. His jaw was set and there was a hard look in his eyes. She knew instinctively that he had something to say that could very well contravene all that had gone before.

She waited, unwilling to push him.

Clasping his hands in front of him, he leaned forward.

'Honey, I'm going to tell you the truth. You're being stalked by a man who wants to kill you.'

'That is one hell of a chat-up line!'

She sounded chirpy. Inside, a ball of icy coldness was building in her stomach.

'Who?' she asked when he didn't speak but kept looking into her face.

'We call him the Tarot Man.'

She thought of the bunch of flowers close to where the dead man had been found in Bradford on Avon. She thought of the card delivered to her in a brown envelope. Then the one in the restaurant. She shivered. This Tarot Man was coming closer.

Again he studied his hands. 'He leaves a card with his victims. There's no rhyme or reason for him doing so. It seems he just likes tarot cards.'

'So why me? Why would he want to kill me?'

CHAPTER TWENTY-FIVE

Steve Doherty floored the accelerator in the car, his jaw set like iron. That bastard Christiansen was everything he'd thought he was. A spook. A government agent.

He'd been kept in a private room in a private hotel where he'd been debriefed on the situation. Aware that he would not be allowed to leave until he fell in with their plans and became compliant, he'd reined in his anger. Bloody hell, Honey was totally unaware of all this! OK, he'd signed the Official Secrets Act and would be in deep water if he opened his mouth, but he could still protect her and, damn it, that was what he was going to do.

Dominic Christiansen's cut-glass voice rang in his ears.

'Up until now this project has been on a need-to-know basis, and you weren't in the loop. I can now tell you what it's all about.'

Doherty vented his anger on the car. His speed soared and he was in with a pretty big chance of getting pulled over by a cop.

Christiansen had sworn him to secrecy but accepted that his signing of the Official Secrets Act was the only assurance he was going to get.

The truth had shaken him.

'There was once a man named Ivan Orlov, supposedly related to a Russian dissident and a Western sympathiser. At least, that was what he appeared to be, but we had our doubts so one of our agents, your girlfriend's father, was ordered to spy on him during an assignment in Russia. This was in the deep, dark days of the Cold War. I can't give you all the details except to say that things went wrong. It turned out that Orlov was a bit of a wild card. Too free and easy with the old "licensed to kill" scenario. James Bond has got a lot to answer for. Anyway, to cut a long story short, it was decided that his services were surplus to requirements. He'd killed too many people without reason. Those that knew him said he seemed to enjoy it. Never mind killing for democracy — Orlov got a thrill from shooting or knifing the life out of a body. Edmund Driver was the man ordered to carry out the termination.'

It had seemed cut and dried to Doherty. Honey's father had been ordered to kill a fellow agent who had turned out to be a double agent.

'He didn't do it. Instead, he betrayed him to the KGB. Obviously they tried to turn him, but that was the funny thing about Orlov. He was a monster but oddly loyal to the West. He didn't tell them anything. But they did break him. They almost killed him more than once — hung him, cut him down. Cut him, sewed him up. Shot him, dug out the bullet and patched him up. Equal measures of cruelty and care. Psychological destruction. He still didn't give anything of value away, but they kept him imprisoned, eventually in a gulag in Siberia. Orlov swore revenge on Edmund Driver, and that if he was dead by the time he got out, then he'd kill his progeny. He would also kill the other colleagues who he'd studied with at Oxford, then worked with in the service. One of these men was Tarquin St John Gervais. Another was a man named Keith McCall. The other, your girlfriend's uncle, Percy Bullington, still lives. We think he is in danger, though his state of health might kill him first.

'We thought the Tarot Man, as his code name was, had died so we wouldn't need to worry about this any longer.

Unfortunately, we've found out that his son follows a similar profession to that of his father. He has also inherited his taste for killing.'

Christiansen had been blunt about what Doherty could and could not do.

'We don't want you playing her knight in shining armour and charging to the rescue. We need to capture this person. We need Honey to remain calm, as though she suspects nothing.'

Charging in was exactly what Doherty wanted to do. He wanted to hug her, wrap her in cotton wool and stick like a limpet to her side. But he had taken on Dominic's reasoning. It might pay to linger in the shadows, to watch anyone he thought was watching Honey.

* * *

Honey decided that the best way to deal with the unusual and downright scary was to keep doing normal things.

Mary Jane suggested going for a drive in the open air.

'The rain will hold off. Anyway, I've something to say to you. In private,' she added with a whisper. 'Actually, two things, though one I can say right here and now. You said you saw that fella Adrian Sayle talking to the suave guy in the black BMW.'

Honey nodded and said that she had.

'I asked Adrian Sayle about him. He was cagey at first but then said the guy was a guest, staying in one of the cottages just along from him.'

Honey raised her eyebrows in surprise. So Christiansen was that close, keeping an eye on her, according to him. Still, it wouldn't be a bad idea to snoop around his little homestead.

Taking a drive meant putting up with Mary Jane hurtling along country roads barely wide enough to take the width of her car, but this was urgent.

'Let's take a look at where Mr Christiansen is staying.'

They were on the other side of the gates and zooming down the road towards the village of Wyvern Wendell when Mary Jane told her why she wouldn't share her comments back at the house.

'It's bugged. Hidden cameras and microphones everywhere. Everything you do is being listened to and watched.'

'Even in my bed?'

'Anywhere you might be doing or saying something of interest.'

Honey thought of what she'd like to do to those who had done this. Blows from her clenched fists were only a starting point.

Her anger intensified on recalling how she'd lain naked on the floor this morning doing ab curls. It appeared her aching ribs were the least of her worries. And where was the camera? She blushed at the thought of the view it might have had.

Revenge burned like a volcano inside of her, but she reined it in, and not just because revenge was supposed to be served cold. To get to the bottom of all this, she needed to think straight.

First off, it seemed a good idea to contact the journalist who'd written the article saying that Caspar was dead. He had to have been given a tip-off and that might lead her to the man who wanted her dead. Her initial intention was to phone the man and ask him, but she would not do that if what Mary Jane had said was true. She did not want to be overheard.

The cottages appeared like chunks of gingerbread from a fairy story, golden and gleaming with damp against dark-green trees.

Honey rejected Mary Jane's offer to come inside with her.

'It might be dangerous.'

Mary Jane looked at her askance. 'Honey, I won't be in any danger. I've been told I'm going to live till I'm one hundred and ten years old.'

Honey was amazed the medical profession would know that.

'Is that what your doctor believes?'

'No. My spirit guide. He said I'd keep on trooping for a long time yet.'

Honey was inclined to believe it was true, but it was hardly the time to discuss it.

The cottage presently occupied by Dominic Christiansen was as pretty as the others, but the fact that he dwelled therein was somewhat unnerving. He just wasn't the cottage type.

She knocked at the door quite vigorously, the sound sending a couple of house martins fluttering from the eaves.

Though she'd given it a good hard bashing, the door wasn't answered.

A second bout of strenuous knocking also failed to elicit a response, yet she was certain somebody was in. No proof, no sign of anyone, just that odd feeling you get: pure instinct.

The ground to either side of the path was covered in soft moss — not the best place to walk wearing heeled boots.

Leaning to one side, she tried peering through a window but saw nothing. She just wasn't close enough. There was nothing for it but to step off the path to look through the window.

The moss squelched beneath her boots.

She saw the alcove to the window side of the fireplace was fitted out floor to ceiling with shelves. A pine-framed mirror above the fireplace reflected the other side of the room, though it was positioned at a difficult angle so she couldn't really work out what she was seeing.

For a brief moment she thought the light inside the room changed slightly, as though somebody were in the hallway and had just crossed the gap that was the open living room door.

She sidestepped further onto the moss-covered path running between the cottage wall and the rampant flowerbeds behind her and smelled the musty wholeness of damp earth.

Gripping the windowsill, she stood on tiptoe and took another look. She wasn't sure whether she yet again detected movement, though Dominic's car was nowhere in sight. A definite asset — if she could gain entry and have a quick snoop around. She wasn't at all sure what she was likely to find, but it did strike her as a good idea.

Clambering back from loamy earth to mossy step, she hammered unrelentingly at the door using both fists as well as the odd bash of the knocker.

The unexpected happened and caused her to wonder why she hadn't tried it before. On turning the handle, the door creaked open.

For a moment she stood eyeing the opening, reassuring herself that it couldn't have been shut properly. Old places were like that. Not everything was a perfect fit. Old places were also prone to ghosts. She'd never encountered a ghost and had no intention of ever doing so. After assuring herself that ghosts were only found in big houses, not homespun cottages, she stepped inside, finding herself in a flagstone-floored hallway with cream-coloured walls. No sign of paranormal activity.

'Mr Christiansen?'

Her customary bravado seemed to have gone walkabout. She didn't like entering his home without permission. Old-fashioned, perhaps, but uninvited guests tended to be given short shrift.

The silence from within was deafening. No footsteps, no heavy breathing, not even the scuttling of a mouse.

She could have turned away and gone back to the house, but it seemed too good an opportunity to miss. Nobody was at home and the door was open. He wouldn't notice a thing, not if she closed the door afterwards.

Once over the threshold there was no turning back. She turned right into the sitting room, smelled as well as saw the sweet peas bursting from the vase in the window, the mirror over the fireplace, the collection of books ranged along the shelves.

His book collection made her smile. *Winnie-the-Pooh*, *Swallows and Amazons* and Longfellow's epic poem, *The Song of Hiawatha*.

OK, it was a rental. The books probably didn't belong to him.

Returning to the hallway, she was immediately reminded of how bright the living room had been. Not that she needed much light to see by. The only other room was the kitchen, which she barely glanced around.

Nothing much so far, but what had she expected to find? Was there anything here that shouldn't be? And then it hit her. There were no personal papers. No letters stuffed behind the mantel clock or in a kitchen cupboard, and none in the small bureau beneath the stairs in the hallway, the latter only holding pens and paper.

She paused to take stock. If she was not going to find any personal items down here, perhaps there were some upstairs. It was a small thing, but vital.

Climbing the stairs, she made herself a promise to avoid his underwear drawer, interesting though it might be.

There was only one bedroom, with a bathroom next to it. In days gone by there would have been two bedrooms, the lavatory facilities in a small wooden structure at the bottom of the garden. The bath would have been made of zinc and hanging from a nail outside the back door. Back then, the cottages were occupied by farm labourers and their families, numerous children packed into one bedroom or sharing with their parents, even sleeping in the living room.

But the cottage had been modernised, and Dominic would not need to shuffle down the garden in the middle of the night.

Tentatively, she opened the glass-fronted bathroom cabinet and found little out of the ordinary except for a bottle of very expensive aftershave. She liked the shape of the bottle and one thing led to another. She unscrewed the top and took a sniff. It was absolutely fabulous, and breathing it in made it almost seem as though he were standing there in front of her. She rolled a drop of it between her fingers. It felt soft and sumptuous, like liquidised silk.

With hindsight she should have looked and not touched. The blasted bottle slipped out of her hand and into the sink.

'Shit!'

The sink was full of glass. And the smell! First and foremost, she had to gather up the pieces, put them in the bin and rinse the bowl. Her brain clicked in. Forget the bin. She would have to take the debris with her, otherwise Dominic would realise that someone had been here.

Panic is a wonderful boost to brainpower. She carefully gathered the shards of glass into some cellophane packaging she found in the bin, wrapped the lot up in toilet paper and headed for the bedroom.

She felt a little flutter of fear. In her encounters with the opposite sex, she had only ever entered a man's bedroom when invited.

Now, here she was, tripping across the brown carpet of the bedroom of a man she barely knew.

A quilted duvet covered the double bed. The walls were white, the curtains brown and white stripes. The rest of the furnishings were pretty ordinary too: a dressing table, a chest of drawers and a wardrobe.

There was underwear in the top drawer of the chest — not entirely unexpected of course, and she had no reason to believe there was anything suspicious about his underwear. Yet despite her promise to herself, she just had to take a look.

White boxer shorts. The smell of laundry liquid wafted up from the drawer. They smelled fresh and were crisply white. Perhaps a little too crisp. Underwear should never be crisp. Too itchy.

She was just about to open the second drawer when she heard the sound of a car approaching from the lane. She hoped it would pass by, but heard it pull up outside.

She thought about running out of the house, claiming to have been waiting for him, but somehow she didn't think it would be well accepted. And what about Mary Jane? Presumably she was still outside, or at least her car was. Hopefully she would manage things so that the game would not be given away. In the meantime, Honey had to deal with things in here.

There was no way she could leave without being seen, though it did occur to her to climb out of the window and down over the wisteria. Problem was that although wisteria appeared to be a vigorous climber, its looks were deceiving. A few feet down it was bound to give way. She could see it now in her mind's eye, the wisteria breaking and her sprawled at the feet of whoever was driving the car, probably Dominic.

The only course of action was to hide. Fast!

The wardrobe offered a minimal possibility, but under the bed was the more expansive option. OK, it was probably the first place he would look — that's if he suspected there was someone in the house. Would he suspect? Quite possibly. She tried to remember if she'd closed the door behind her. She thought she had, but panic set in again.

Under the bed it had to be.

The carpet was soft against her belly as she slid beneath the bed, carefully clutching the pieces of broken bottle. The draped edge of the bedspread touched the floor all around, keeping her hidden. He'd have to bend down and look under the bed to see her, but she convinced herself that he wouldn't do that. Not unless he slid his shoes underneath then couldn't find them.

She lay there, glad that whoever cleaned this cottage regularly vacuumed beneath the bed so she wouldn't break into a sneezing fit.

He came up the stairs. From the sound of his footsteps, it was easy to imagine the springiness of his ascent. Dominic Christiansen was a fit man. He moved positively and fast, as though he could get things done and quickly, without fuss, without anyone objecting. One look at him and nobody was likely to object to anything he did.

She prayed he would go into the bathroom, perhaps lock the door. If he did she might be in with a chance of sneaking out.

He didn't do that. The bedroom floorboards vibrated with the fall of his footsteps. She cursed him for entering his bedroom, although the man had every right to do so. After all, it was his bedroom and she was here uninvited.

Although he couldn't see her, she curled herself up into a tight ball. She even closed her eyes, as though if she couldn't see him then he couldn't see her.

The bedsprings made a squeaky noise as he sat on the bed. One spring wasn't that far from her ear and a strand of hair got tangled up in it. No chance of a quick exit now! The bedspring was pulling on her hair and hurting. She bit her lip to stop from crying out and wished he would get up and lock himself in the bathroom. At least it would give her a chance of escape.

Thud. One shoe came off. Thud. The second shoe.

The shoes! The dreaded shoes! He was standing in his socks!

Through the crack where the bedcover didn't quite reach the carpet, she saw his socks come off. Then his trousers landing in a heap on his shoes! Then a tie. Then a shirt. Then . . .

There was no getting away from the fact that she was now lying beneath the bed of a naked man. Oh lord! Now what?

Her caught hair pulled at her scalp as he got up from the bed. She heard his feet padding across the floor.

If she was going to escape, it had to be now. Carefully, very carefully, she attempted to untangle her hair. Perhaps it was nerves, but no matter how hard she tried, her fingers behaved like toes. What her hair was up to was open to conjecture — it felt as though she'd turned into Medusa and one of the snakes that made up her hair was making love to a bedspring.

She didn't know how long she was there fighting with the combined forces of curled metal and hair, but she heard his footsteps returning. Worse still, she saw the tips of his toes peeping through the thick pile of the carpet. He was still naked.

She heard him heave a sigh — a very big sigh. Suddenly the cover was lifted and there was his face.

'Are you coming out from under my bed or do I have to come in and get you?'

'Um. I was just passing and needed to use the lavatory.'

'Sure,' he said, lying full stretch on the floor, gazing in at her, his hand supporting his jaw. 'That's fine by me, but the bathroom is along the landing, not under my bed.'

Excuses came fast. 'The door was open. I thought you were here. And then I thought I heard you but it couldn't have been you, so it must have been somebody else. Because here you are.'

It sounded like nonsense.

'You thought someone was here? You saw someone?'

'Not exactly. A shadow. Somebody keeping out of sight. And then I got my hair tangled in one of your bedsprings.'

Bearing the discarded pile of clothes in mind, she dared to look at the rest of him. He wasn't naked. He was wearing a towelling robe. It was white and she glimpsed a monogram on the breast pocket. He stayed very still. She was glad about that, seeing as all he had on was that robe. But it didn't last.

'Right,' he said. 'Your hair still trapped?'

'I'm afraid it is.'

He began to manoeuvre himself beneath the bed, his body eventually ending up lying full length beside her. She was inclined to warn him about carpet burn, but kept her mouth shut. She wasn't ready to answer questions relating to her experience on the subject.

'Get your head as low as possible and keep still,' he said.

She did as ordered. His fingers worked in her tangled mane strand by strand. He had to lie pretty close to do this. She tried not to notice the warmth of his body through the towelling robe. The robe smelled good. His body smelled better. The close proximity of a man in bed is always arousing. Under the bed seemed doubly so. On reflection, she supposed it was something to do with the fact that beneath the bed is a far more confined space than actually being in it.

However, this was no time for acting on what her hormones were up to. At last she was free and there was work to be done.

'I've got something to show you,' she said as she wriggled forward.

'So there was a reason for your madness.'

'I'm not mad. I'm perfectly sane. I heard you'd moved in here, presumably to keep an eye out for this Tarot Man. I appreciate you looking out for me.'

'OK. No problem, but just run this shadow past me again. Are you sure somebody was in the house and that my front door was unlocked?'

'That's what I said.' She was suddenly in a hurry to get out of there, especially from beneath the bed.

'What's that smell?' he said, once they were standing upright.

'Aftershave,' she answered without really thinking, then suddenly remembered the broken bottle she'd left beneath the bed. She wasn't ready to own up. 'You probably used too much.'

Hopefully he would accept the excuse. After all, they had recently spent time together in a confined space with only a bathrobe between them.

What could have happened next didn't happen. The gap between them widened in response to somebody hammering on the front door.

'Hey, Honey. Are you OK?'

Dominic looked disappointed. 'Your friend with the pink car?'

Honey nodded. 'Yes. She's been driving me around. Have to go now. Sorry to have disturbed you.'

He grinned. 'You'll be disturbing me all night.'

Honey blushed. There was no denying that Dominic Christiansen had a certain charm, the sort that spelled danger.

'And you've got enough danger in your life,' she muttered to herself as she headed back down the stairs.

CHAPTER TWENTY-SIX

The remains of Keith McCall were removed in broad daylight by a team of men with a tractor, a trailer and a load of turnips. One of them was chewing on a straw, his flat cap worn low over his eyes. Another was smoking, the third whistling.

To all intents and purposes they were farm labourers taking a load of root vegetables from field to barn, though they were far from being that. On closer scrutiny it could be seen that their hands were soft and white, their complexions unblemished by outdoor living.

Once the work was complete, every vestige of the decomposed corpse removed, the convoy headed towards the road that led to the sausage factory, where they disappeared from view.

Special Branch was informed that their search for Keith McCall was at an end. The search for Peter Orlov, son of Ivan, alias the Tarot Man, was still on.

* * *

'You look peaky. Let me buy you a coffee.'

Honey allowed Mary Jane to lead her by the arm. She couldn't have protested if she'd tried.

They entered the Foxcub Café, which was housed in what had been the estate dairy. Mary Jane sat Honey down in a chair while she collected two cappuccinos and two slices of carrot cake.

'OK. Talk,' said Mary Jane, pushing the coffee and cake in front of her face.

'Somebody's trying to kill me.'

'Hah! I told you so. Didn't I tell you so?'

'You told me so.'

Honey's voice wavered as she fought to hold back her emotion. She'd hardly slept a wink all night thinking it through.

'He wouldn't even tell me the reason why. Just that I was to be careful. I mean, how can I be careful if I don't know who wants to kill me? A description would have been useful.'

Mary Jane popped a few stray crumbs of cake from her lips into her mouth.

'Your father did warn you.'

'My father's dead.'

'It doesn't matter. He still warned you.'

Honey sighed and covered her face with her hands.

'What am I going to do? Hire a bodyguard?'

'Does Doherty know?'

'I've tried phoning him. He's still not answering. Bugger him and that bloody course. Why are men, especially policemen, so set on this team-building malarkey? What does it actually do for them?'

Mary Jane rolled her blue eyes heavenwards as she sought a solution to the question.

'Men are men and are not our immediate problem.'

'Except for the one who wants to kill me.'

'You need something to take your mind off things. How about we take a walk around the animal compounds. Animals have a calming presence.'

'I think that applies to cats and dogs, not carnivores that are inclined to eat you!'

Despite Honey's negative attitude, Mary Jane was already on her feet. Having no alternative suggestion, Honey followed.

They left the café and entered a gate marked, *Private*, which led to the back of the house, the so-called tradesmen's entrance.

The pot rooms, laundry rooms, silver rooms and crockery stores were ranged on the lower level immediately beneath the rooms they were programmed to serve. The servants' hall was beyond this and next to the scullery where huge sinks ran along one wall equipped with equally large scrubbing brushes. In the distant past, this room had been the domain of hordes of scullery maids, their hands red raw from scrubbing huge roasting pans and piles of plates. A brand-new commercial dishwasher had dispensed with all that.

The side door was a heavy wooden affair with clear glass panels at the top, not that they let much light in.

The big bins were to their left. To their right was the climbing wisteria. Ahead was the parkland, acres of grass rolling beneath oak, elm and ash trees, some of which had been growing there for five hundred years. Most of it was enclosed now, keeping the animals one side, humans the other.

The stone steps led down onto the gravel drive that served the rear of the house. The smell of animal droppings was strong here.

The path took them into another courtyard surrounded by what had been stables for the hunters, the carriage horses and the children's ponies. One of the buildings had also housed the coachman and his family on the upper floor. They were now turned over mostly to storage areas.

The muted roar of a lion sounded ahead of them. The entrance was at the back of the building. There was a large caged exercise area at the front.

Mary Jane led the way, marching purposefully through a gate to the rear of the stable yard.

'Giraffe house first.'

The giraffe house smelled of giraffes, or any other ruminating animal, come to that. Heaped straw rustled around the great creature's legs as it positioned them to form a four-pronged protection around its baby. The baby's big brown eyes considered them from beneath its mother's belly.

Normally Honey wouldn't have given it a second glance, but those eyelashes!

'Look at those eyelashes. They're enormous and so, so beautiful.'

The baby was trying to suckle. The mother was knocking it away with her head. The thwacking sounded painful.

Honey wagged her finger at the mother giraffe. 'Poor baby. Mummy, that is so unfair.'

Honey looked the creature in the eyes and she stared back, unblinking.

Honey raised her voice. 'Let your baby suckle, for the love of God!'

The giraffe was so surprised at Honey's loud voice that she hardly seemed to notice the baby had succeeded in suckling on her teat.

'There. It worked,' said Honey, sounding slightly surprised.

'You hypnotised her,' Mary Jane remarked.

'I think it was my loud voice. I've been told it's resonant when roused.'

A door swung open to her left. Honey turned immediately, expecting to see Adrian Sayle, the burly man in safari outfit, calves straining against knee-length socks. Instead she saw a woman in a white coat with horn-rimmed glasses. Her smile was wide, though not wide enough to expose all her teeth. There were just too many. She was wearing white wellington boots, similar to those worn in laboratories.

'I wanted to speak to Adrian. Is he still here?' Honey asked. It was a useful excuse. She didn't really want to speak to him, except perhaps to ask him about his relationship to Dominic Christiansen.

'No, my dear,' the woman said, shaking her head and smiling at Honey as though she were a silly child who'd just asked for a Wall's ice cream in Harrods. 'Adrian was called away. His father's been taken ill. Apparently he's not expected to last, the poor man,' she said, her bottom lip turning down as though she were about to blubber.

'Do you have a phone number for his father?'

'No. I don't think his father has a telephone. It's way out on the veldt, you know.'

'The veldt. You mean Africa?'

She nodded. 'The Transvaal. He runs a mission there. His father was a minister of religion, you see. Now. What do you want in here?'

A likely story, Honey decided. Another of these damned spooks?

'I was just showing her the animals,' said Mary Jane. 'She's had a shock and you know how calming animals can be.'

The woman in the white lab coat and wellington boots looked surprised. The name tag on her breast said Maureen Cline.

'That mostly applies to dogs and cats.'

'Just as I thought,' muttered Honey.

'Do you mind if we take a look in the lion house?'

Maureen looked a little cagey at first.

'We just want to look at them. I promise we're not going to steal them,' said Honey.

Mary Jane backed her up. 'We couldn't. There's not enough room in the car.'

The woman held her head to one side as she made up her mind. Her smile was hesitant, but when it came it was as before, a whole mountain range of white teeth interspersed with a flash of gold Honey hadn't noticed until now.

'Very well.'

The smell of the lion house was exactly as Honey had expected it to be: very urinary, similar to the smell of a leaky domestic cat but on a bigger scale. The lion house itself, however, was modern, big and bright.

'It's empty.' Honey was disappointed. All that smell for nothing.

'They only come in during the winter or when they are ill. The rest of the time they run wild and free out in the park.'

‘Within the fenced-in enclosure?’ Honey asked somewhat tenuously.

‘Of course. We wouldn’t want them to eat the visitors, would we?’

‘Have they ever eaten anyone?’

‘No. Not humans anyway.’

‘Did you know Keith McCall?’

‘Yes.’

‘Did you get on well with him?’

‘Reasonably enough. He was a work colleague. We worked together. That was it. He didn’t intrude into my private life and I didn’t intrude into his.’

There were four cages in total. The middle one was larger than the others. Honey looked through the heavy mesh of the fencing and gate. Unlike the other cages it had three solid walls, the iron bars running only along the front. Straw was heaped up in one corner. A channel ran along the front next to the mesh caging and into a drain. The cover was half solid, half grating. It was built that way so effluent could drain away more freely. Or blood.

‘Well,’ said Honey, turning on her heel. ‘No lions today.’

Mary Jane shared her disappointment.

They made their way back into the house, past the kitchens, up the stairs and along to the office where Miss Vincent worked. She had, of course, already gone home to the little cottage down in the village that she shared with her mother.

Over coffee in the café Miss Vincent had told Mary Jane that her mother was an invalid who watched by the window until she was safely home.

If anyone knew the secrets of who worked here and when, it was Miss Vincent.

‘I need to check something,’ said Honey.

The office was unlit, but enough light filtered through from outside to see one’s way clearly enough. The computer was covered up, the accounts files locked safely away and the post tray empty. Miss Vincent was a tidy soul with tidy ways.

‘She’s very neat,’ Mary Jane remarked.

'Yep! Everything is properly filed in the right place so I should have no trouble finding what we're looking for — whatever it is.'

'You don't know what we're looking for?'

'I'll know it when I see it. I am nothing if not methodical in my approach to a given situation. My mind poses a question and has a small box at the end into which I enter a mental tick when an answer is acquired. Quite simple really.'

It sounded very believable and Mary Jane appeared to accept it.

'Do you want me to keep a lookout?'

Honey was already delving into the staff files. She shook her head. 'Remember, Miss Vincent likes to be home on time. Her mother waits up for her.'

'I thought you already had a list?'

'I do, but it wouldn't hurt to check again. There's something I'm missing . . .'

'Do you think the name of the person who wants to kill you is on that list?'

'Possibly. The same person who killed his lordship.'

'I wonder where he really is? I mean, if the remains were scooped up so nobody could recheck the DNA, then he wasn't cremated, and if that's the case then where is he?'

Honey grunted. Mary Jane had a point, but Honey did not have an answer for that, just as she didn't have an answer for anything else in this case. It was weird, it was huge and it was convoluted. The fact that a government intelligence agency was involved made her nervous. She was out of her league, but hell, she wasn't going to give in that easily.

'This is the oddest case I've worked on. It's also the only one in which my own life has been at stake. I *have* to solve it.'

Mary Jane peered over the reading glasses that she'd had the presence of mind to bring with her.

'You can count on me, Honey. I'm no private dick but I'm going to help you all I can.'

Mary Jane's enthusiasm was comforting. Honey was well aware that her friend from California was as nutty as a fruitcake, but that her heart was in the right place. What did it matter if half the time she lived in another world?

Forcing herself to concentrate and forget she could be a murder victim, she went through the staff files. That was when she finally spotted something.

'Hello! This is interesting.'

Mary Jane peered over her spectacles. 'Found something?'

'I'm damn certain that Keith McCall's name was not on the other list — not as a *current* employee anyway. But it appears here. Hang on while I double-check.'

Details of each employee were kept in a loose-leaf folder. She was one hundred per cent certain that there had not — most definitely NOT — been a current employment sheet for Keith McCall. Miss Vincent had been adamant that he'd left a whole month before Adrian Sayle was appointed. Yet here he was!

She checked again before voicing her finding out loud. She'd understood he was employed as chief ranger, but according to the employee records he was head of security. There was something else that caught her attention. Unlike most of the employees who were paid a monthly wage, McCall didn't seem to have been paid anything at all.

'Another spook,' she said out loud.

'You mean a Fed?'

'No. More like CIA, or MI5 as it is here. But why would an MI5 agent be employed here on a permanent basis?'

'Shady characters.'

Honey thought of Dominic Christiansen. 'You can say that again.'

A thought suddenly came to her. 'He was here on *protection* duties. All that time, Orlov was on the scene too, watching and waiting until the field was wide open. He could choose his time and take his it.'

The nagging question was, why hadn't she seen this sheet before? Also, if the man was self-employed and had presented invoices, why were his details stored with the employees? Surely he should be in suppliers' invoices? But there were no invoices. There was nothing to say he'd ever received a penny. He had to be an MI5 agent.

'I think I need to check Miss Vincent's reasons for this. It's her system after all.'

She was slow putting the record sheet back into the file and springing the clip. Something struck her as not being quite right — quite rum in fact. The sheet of paper seemed brilliantly crisp and white compared to the other record sheets.

* * *

After clearing away the dishes, Miss Vincent sat herself tiredly in front of the television set and turned it on.

Normally she would sip her tea and enjoy putting her feet up and having some time to herself. Tonight she wasn't really following the plot on the TV. She was thinking of Lord Tarquin Torrington.

She'd been nineteen when they'd met, and for a few years she'd enjoyed true passion. Her father had been manager of one of the mines in which Tarquin's family had owned shares. She'd fallen for Tarquin at first sight and for a while everything had been good, though she'd been warned that it wouldn't last. On the plus side he was always generous with his money, even when their more physical relationship was over. She'd refused to believe it would happen, but happen it did, and although he'd taken her into his confidence over many things, and had even given her a very well-paid job, she still hankered for the way things used to be. Eventually she had come to the conclusion that she was just one of many. All she could do was take his generosity for the benefit of both herself and her mother, and like everyone else, be loyal to him and to everything he stood for.

And now he was gone. A tear rolled down her cheek. Gone but not forgotten, and even though she did believe herself to currently be in love with someone else, a very recent acquaintance, she really would always remember.

When the phone rang, she knew who it was and felt that breathless excitement again, just as she had when she was young.

'You're late phoning. I expected you earlier.'

She fidgeted with her dress collar as she spoke, regretting that she may have sounded annoyed that he hadn't rung earlier. She had no wish to upset him.

'I went for a walk in the woods,' he said.

'Oh. How very bracing.'

'I was birdwatching,' he said, 'but somebody came along and disturbed them. I was very annoyed.'

'Oh dear.'

'Are you ready for me?'

Miss Vincent felt a frisson of excitement run through her. She'd never contemplated doing such things as she did with this man, but she couldn't help herself.

'Yes,' she said, her voice timid as she sank into the submissive persona he wished her to be.

'You'd better not be lying. I will smack you very hard if you're lying. Are you lying, Rosemary?'

'No. I mean, yes, but I will be ready by the time you call again. I promise.'

Her mother had died many years ago, but in order to maintain her privacy, she let everyone believe otherwise. Harbouring the tastes she had, it seemed like a good idea, though there had been a desert of a time without a man — the right kind of man — in her life. And now he was here, though she kept his identity top secret. And so did he.

She heard his strong, nasal breath roar down the phone and shivered.

'One lie already, Rosemary. Now take off your clothes and get yourself ready.'

CHAPTER TWENTY-SEVEN

Miss Vincent arrived at the office on the dot of eight thirty, looking as prim and proper as ever: not a hair out of place, her suit sharp and the collar of her white blouse crisp around her crinkly neck. Nobody seeing her would guess what had taken place the night before, a regular occurrence with a man who understood her needs. She'd been a very different creature last night than the one she was this morning.

She had been looking forward to half an hour shared with a cup of coffee and thoughts of the night before. Instead she found that bloody woman from Bath standing there.

She was quick to collect herself. 'Good morning, Mrs Driver. All alone this morning?'

'Yes. My friend Mary Jane is still eating breakfast. She's American but it's amazing how quickly she's adapted to enjoying a full English breakfast each morning.'

'You weren't tempted yourself?'

'No.' Honey had settled for black coffee and a bowl of cornflakes.

Miss Vincent gave a curt nod of her pointed chin.

'How is your mother? Keeping well, is she?' asked Honey.

Miss Vincent's plain features came instantly alive. 'Oh, yes. Yes. Well, what I mean is, as well as can be expected considering her age and her various illnesses. I'm slightly later than usual, but she was a little obstinate with her porridge this morning.'

She glanced nervously at her watch as she gingerly lowered herself into her chair, wincing when she finally got there.

'You're not late, Miss Vincent. It's only just gone eight thirty.' Honey's smile was wide and generous.

'Oh. Yes. It's just that I try to be here by eight fifteen. His lordship always expected me just after he'd had his breakfast.'

'I see. Miss Vincent, I wanted to ask you about his lordship's funeral and the terms of his will.'

She didn't bat an eyelid. 'Well, I'll help if I can, though I wasn't really privy to the details.'

'Ah. I hadn't realised that, seeing as you were so close to him.'

This time Miss Vincent's papery complexion flushed pink. The flattery was a bit thick, but in Honey's opinion, this was a woman who wanted to feel she was that bit closer to Tarquin than any of his other women.

'I thought it odd,' Miss Vincent said. 'Though of course I didn't know his wishes. After all I was not a member of the family.'

Miss Vincent was right. Only family members and their legal advisors were likely to know his lordship's wishes. If that was so, then Caspar may have known more than he'd been letting on — unless the work was purely for the benefit of the government agency. In which case, why go to all that trouble?

Unusually, Caspar was unavailable when she phoned him. Then she wondered about her car, whether it was back where it should be and unclamped. With that in mind she phoned her mother, who answered almost immediately.

'Mother?'

'Who is this?'

'Hannah.'

'Who?'

'Hannah. Your daughter.'

'Oh, yes. Of course. How are you, dear?'

The fact that she hadn't been too sure of her own daughter's identity was a trifle off-putting, but her mother had a busy social life.

'I'm fine. Is my car back?'

'Your car?'

Honey sighed. Her mother often answered a question with another question.

'Have you heard anything from Uncle Percy?'

Honey had tried phoning him but there was no response. It was a long shot but her mother might have heard from him.

'Should I have?'

'No. I just wondered.'

The conversation was short-lived and went nowhere. Once she'd listened to her mother going on about her social engagements, she tried Caspar again. This time he was available.

'I was having a spring clean.'

Honey didn't believe him. She just couldn't imagine Caspar actually having a hands-on spring clean. He had people to dirty their hands for him.

'Caspar, I've no wish to upset you, but did you have prior knowledge of Tarquin's funeral arrangements?'

There was a pause before he answered.

'Tarquin was a little eccentric.'

'Did you know he worked for MI5?'

She'd expected some kind of surprised reaction, but not the sudden explosion of laughter.

'Tarquin? Did you ever see that James Bond film, *From Russia with Love*? He couldn't keep his cock in his trousers! One glimpse of a pretty spy and Tarquin would have changed sides.'

'You still haven't answered the question. Did you know?'

A pause again, then a sigh.

'Yes. He wanted to make his death as dramatic as his life. He did mention going out to the strains of the *1812 Overture* just before . . .'

He stopped. Honey was instantly suspicious.

'Just before he was killed? Were you in touch with him quite recently then?'

She could imagine Caspar's face. He'd been cornered, which meant he wasn't in charge of this conversation. Caspar didn't like not being in charge.

'We had dinner together. He talked a lot about dying. I wasn't sure why — not at the time. But now of course . . . I felt that I was being drawn into something.'

'Had you had much contact with him before then?'

'No.'

Caspar's response was brusque, as though he really didn't care. Yet Honey knew he did care. Tarquin was his half-brother and the legal heir to a stately home. Caspar had been born illegitimate to the Torrington Towers housekeeper.

The family's wealth had been accumulated over generations by shrewd marriage as much as investments. Never mind Tarquin's womanising. The wealth was still there, the glue that held everything together. Honey instinctively knew that it was the lack of status that gnawed at her old friend Caspar, but now he had it he realised he didn't want it.

CHAPTER TWENTY-EIGHT

The business of the bones and the funeral and Tarquin's death in general were the basis of her investigation. If the family and close acquaintances knew little of Tarquin's final wishes, then the path to enlightenment had to be with the professionals. The lawyers.

The offices of Jerwood, Kent and Donaldson, solicitors to Lord Torrington and the St John Gervais family, were in an imposing building of mock-gothic style with lead-paned windows that glittered in the sun and a frieze of shields running along the front above a Norman-style arch.

The double doors with their brass handles opened to the smell of polished mahogany and old papers. The firm specialised in handling the estates of titled families with old money, though no doubt they weren't averse to taking on the newer money of industrial magnates and media barons.

Honey marched in wearing her business suit, the one she usually wore when she went to see her bank manager and wanted to give an efficient and professional impression before asking for a larger overdraft facility.

'I want to see Harald Jerwood,' she said.

The receptionist looked taken aback. 'I'm sorry but he's no longer with us. Will anyone else do?'

Honey was adamant. She'd spotted the name on one of the letters on Miss Vincent's desk and understood he was the senior partner. Nobody else would do.

'No. It has to be Mr Jerwood. There are a few things I wish to clarify with regards to the will. I'm acting for Mr Caspar St John Gervais. Do you know how I might get in touch with Mr Jerwood?'

'I'm sorry,' the woman said again, her expression taut and unsmiling, 'but I'm afraid Mr Jerwood passed away.'

Now this was a blow. 'I didn't know he was ill.'

'He wasn't,' she said, her voice dropping to a whisper as voices do when bad news mingles with past respect. 'He was quite old. But healthy,' she added brightly. 'All the same, we weren't expecting it.'

'Oh dear. How sad.' In a way, Honey didn't find it that sad. Not if he was old. In fact it was quite refreshing to hear of somebody who'd died from natural causes.

'He'll be greatly missed,' the receptionist nodded.

'Perhaps you could tell me the date of the funeral,' said Honey, while rummaging for her pocket diary. There was always the chance that somebody at the funeral would have something to say about his demise.

'I'm afraid that's already happened. It was three days ago.'

Honey stopped mid-rummage. 'How shocking.'

Suddenly, a door to her left opened wide.

'Ah, Vivian. I'm looking for the Harding file . . . Oh. Sorry. I didn't know you had someone with you.'

The woman who had come from the door marked, *Private* was tall, imposing and thin as a reed. Her hair was pulled back into a ponytail at the nape of her neck, which had the effect of accentuating her cheekbones.

'Sorry to interrupt.' Her smile was somewhat superior, though her tone seemed friendly enough.

'That's OK.' Honey offered her hand. 'My name's Hannah Driver. I'm acting on behalf of Caspar St John Gervais in the matter of his brother, Lord Torrington — Tarquin St John Gervais.'

'Alice Belvedere,' she said, looking a tad surprised.

'I'm sorry to hear about Mr Jerwood.'

'Ah, yes,' she said on the back of a sigh. 'Such a tragedy.' She didn't sound that upset. 'I have written to your client informing him of Mr Jerwood's demise and that I shall be taking over his files.'

Her voice was crisp. Honey guessed that the letter she'd sent would also be crisply worded on crisp, stiff paper with an embossed heading.

Now was not the time to wonder why Caspar had not informed her of this — unless the letter had not arrived yet. After all, it was only three days since the solicitor's funeral.

'As I've already explained to your receptionist, I'm acting on Mr Caspar St John Gervais's behalf. I do have a letter confirming this.'

She handed over the letter Caspar had written giving her more or less carte blanche over his affairs, which was swiftly perused before being returned to her.

'I need a few things clarified,' said Honey. 'Perhaps you could do that?'

'Of course. Please come this way.' She held the door open, at the same time instructing her receptionist to arrange coffee.

Honey matched her footsteps with Miss Belvedere's as they made their way to her office. Honey's head was spinning. She felt as though she were drowning in, if not lies, then terrible mistakes. People were either disappearing or dying at an alarming rate — alarming by normal standards anyway. Up until now she had led a charmed — in fact, charming — life. Death and disappearance hadn't figured that largely at all.

The most notable aspect of Miss Belvedere's office was the potted plants ranged along the window ledge. Mostly spider plants, tiny replicas of the main plant hanging green and spidery at the end of pale, lengthy fronds. Her furniture was heavy and well polished. The plants were the only truly feminine touch, with the possible exception of a painting by Utrillo of Montmartre. Honey presumed it was a print, although not necessarily so — the fees of Jerwood, Kent and Donaldson were likely big enough to pay off the national debt.

They sat either side of her desk. Miss Belvedere smiled and explained that she'd known Tarquin for years so was the ideal person to deal with matters.

'So you knew Tarquin well?'

'Yes. Yes, I did,' she replied, her smile businesslike, though the look in her eyes spoke volumes about the memories she entertained in her mind.

'Intimately, I suppose . . .'

'Well, I couldn't really—'

Honey put a stop to her protest before she had chance to lie.

'Look, Miss Belvedere. I am under no illusion about his lordship and his affairs. I get the impression that his main ambition in life was to scatter his seed more widely than a ploughman in springtime. Did you know Caspar St John Gervais as well as you did his brother?'

Her expression turned sour. 'Half-brother.'

Miss Belvedere's direct gaze had transferred from Honey to the files on her desk.

Although detecting hostility, Honey pressed on.

'I can tell from the look on your face that your relationship with his lordship was not purely professional. If you took down a few more things than simply instructions regarding his will, please don't worry about it. My client does not begrudge either of you anything. One way or another, you obviously gave him very good service.'

'How dare you!'

'Right,' said Honey, pleased with herself for catching Miss Belvedere off balance. 'Can I see the will?'

Her crispness even more brittle than it had been before, she began shuffling papers at the same time as stating that a copy had been sent to her client and that Honey should really refer to that.

'I don't remember reading about the funeral details,' said Honey.

'They didn't appear in the original will, only in a later codicil.'

'Really? And when was that added?'

'Well, I'd have to check the file,' she said, shuffling the same papers in the folder in front of her. 'I'm sure we can sort this out. Do excuse me while I check with my secretary. She must have a spare copy.'

'That would be good.'

Miss Belvedere paused by the door. 'Your client may not have liked what happened, but everything was carried out as Lord Torrington wanted it.'

'My client was aware and harboured no objection. But the police have. They've told him an offence has been committed for which he could be imprisoned. What I want to know is, is there an official permission in among that paperwork?'

The moment she was out of the door Honey was across the desk and perusing the file.

It turned out to be less than interesting. In the main it related to Torrington Towers and the land surrounding it. A number of maps were attached with a paper clip to listed rights of the landowner. The land itself was outlined in blue. Honey recognised the rank of tied holiday-let cottages and also those occupied by estate workers such as Adrian Sayle.

She also noted the overgrown field in which sat the blockhouse and the boiler room next to the gate — except that the blockhouse wasn't shown, only a building described as a sausage factory.

The accuracy of the map as applied to the present day would depend on its date. Honey checked it. October 1954. The blockhouse wasn't at all new. It certainly looked as though it should have appeared. But still, lawyers make mistakes, as does the Land Registry, the government department at the heart of property conveyancing and ownership matters.

Honey cast her gaze over the list stapled to the map and immediately deduced it related to various rights of grazing, minerals and such like, which appeared to belong to the estate up until 1984.

Honey was not a lawyer, but intelligent enough to know that something had changed in the year 1984. According to the notes, ownership of mineral rights beneath the land had been forfeited for a period of twenty-five years and then been renewed again.

In a few years' time those rights reverted back to the family. Honey frowned, not able to fathom what that was all about. The rights appeared to relate to land underneath the sausage factory, which was also owned by the estate.

The door opened, heralding Miss Belvedere's return. She looked startled to see the file open.

Honey made comment before she did. 'Is the deal with the mineral rights likely to make the heir to the estate very rich?'

'Ah,' she said, as though everything were plain — which it probably was, to her. 'The leasing of mineral rights is for a twenty-five-year period. After that the rights revert back to the estate, though the lessee has an unobstructed option to continue for as many years as they please. It only attracts a peppercorn rent.'

'That sounds draconian. Does my client have the right not to renew?'

'No. The contract is quite precise.'

'Who is the contract with?'

Seemingly alarmed by the question, Miss Belvedere almost cuddled the file to her breast. For a moment Honey didn't think she was going to answer.

'The government, and in return there are tax concessions.'

Honey narrowed her eyes. 'It's something of a coincidence, Miss Belvedere, that the transfer is for twenty-five years, and the will ties my client to Torrington Towers for the next five of those twenty-five years, the other twenty or so now being behind us.'

'It was a very good deal. It enabled your client's grandfather, and thereafter his father, to recoup inheritance tax and death duties without dipping into capital. It also assisted in the improvement of the estate as a business venture, principally with regard to the safari park.'

'Very handsome, I'm sure. And very unusual?'

'I have to say this firm has never come across anything like it before, but wheels within wheels. This is a copy of the codicil,' she said, sliding a manila envelope across the desk. 'It explains everything.'

Honey glanced briefly at the envelope before slipping it into her shoulder bag. The importance of knowing for sure that his mode of cremation had really been his lordship's last wish no longer seemed to matter quite so much.

'Are you heading back tonight?' Miss Belvedere asked.

Honey told her that she was travelling back on the train and would get a taxi home at the other end.

'Have a pleasant journey.'

* * *

The rail carriage was full of commuters and shoppers going home, away from the city to a place where time, although it had not exactly stood still, still seemed far slower than in London.

Honey alighted at Bath Spa, jostled on all sides by a human tide pushing towards the steps that would take them off the platform, over the bridge and down the steps to the exit on the other side.

Just as she reached the bottom, she saw him. Doherty was waiting for her.

'You're here! What a lovely surprise!'

She wasn't usually that demonstrative in public, but on this occasion she couldn't help flinging her arms around him and burying her face against his shoulder.

Doherty wrapped his arms around her and for a moment they clung there, both acting outside their normal character. She sensed his tension and assumed she was going to get another warning not to interfere with Lord Torrington's death.

‘OK,’ he said softly. ‘We need to talk.’

His car was parked at the front of the taxi rank, a police on-call sign stuck in the windscreen making it look as though he’d only just arrived when in fact he’d left the car there all day. He could have taken a taxi, but he wasn’t thinking straight.

Honey almost fell into the front passenger seat. ‘I’m whacked. How very clever of you to guess which train I was on.’

‘Very,’ he said. ‘But I’m pretty good at guessing.’

She eyed his profile as the car nudged its way out into the early-evening traffic.

‘You didn’t guess. You knew.’

‘I made enquiries.’

Honey sighed and closed her eyes. ‘Are we being followed?’

Doherty was silent.

Honey opened her eyes. ‘Shouldn’t you still be on the course? I thought you had a little more time left.’

‘I left early.’ His grim voice matched the look on his face. ‘I told you not to get involved,’ he added. He sounded angry.

‘And I did not do as I was ordered. Well, naughty me!’

There was a veiled sarcasm in Honey’s response.

‘You’ve left yourself wide open to danger.’

‘I take it you know I haven’t been in Bath.’

‘I know where you’ve been.’

‘And you’re angry with me.’

‘Of course I’m bloody angry with you! I told you to stay away from this. Things are always more complicated and downright bloody dangerous when spooks are involved! This isn’t a straightforward crime. It’s complicated and full of history.’

Honey spun her head to face him. ‘You mean it goes back to my father. How did you find out?’

Doherty had a firm jaw. Today it was set like iron.

‘Something bugging you?’ Honey asked.

He took a deep breath and swung the car into a left-hand turning.

'You're out of your depth.'

'That isn't what's really bugging you.'

Honey studied his face, the set of his jaw, the way he was gazing firmly at the road ahead.

'You've got involved too,' she said. 'I can see it from your face. If you clench your jaw much harder you'll grind your teeth to dust. You know about my father betraying an old friend, so you also know that old friend — or somebody close to him — is out for revenge.'

The car braked as a gaggle of Japanese schoolchildren sauntered across a zebra crossing, chatting nineteen to the dozen and seemingly oblivious to the cars waiting for them to get out of the way.

Doherty slid the car into gear.

'Caspar's half-brother was putting his life in order. He wanted to make amends for some of the things he'd done. One of them concerned his part in the betraying of Ivan Orlov. He took a trip to Russia, went looking for old contacts from Soviet days and raked up stuff he should have left dead and buried.'

'Doherty, you're still in danger of grinding your teeth to dust. You've been got at. You've been told all this by somebody we've both met, although you only know him slightly in passing. Me . . .' She paused. Should she mention going out to dinner with Dominic? 'Can I guess the identity of the person who cut short your little team-building exercise?'

The city was full of tourists, big groups of them decamping from coaches or trailing along behind a tour guide's green umbrella. It was only common sense that he should keep his eyes peeled, watching the ebb and flow of people enjoying themselves and unaware of the traffic.

Honey was pretty good at reading Doherty's mind, even when it wasn't the simple stuff, like sex, beer, eating late and sleeping in.

'You know I'm being stalked?'

'It could have been avoided.'

'I don't think it could.'

Doherty sighed as though he could do nothing but give in. 'We'll get dinner and you can tell me all you've found out.'

Ristorante Martini was on George Street, a Sicilian restaurant run by Sicilians. Not all the staff were of Italian extraction, though — some were Polish and one was French.

The service was excellent, the food good, and there was a comfortable ambience about the place. No table was too close to the next so you didn't feel you were sitting on somebody's lap.

Two courses were ordered plus a bottle of Prosecco. The latter was served at the right temperature and tasted good.

Once the waiter was out of earshot, Honey outlined what she'd found out, including Mary Jane's observation on the residue left by the cremation and the fact that the rooms were bugged.

'There's nothing we can do about Tarquin. Leave it to his colleagues in MI5. It's you we need to worry about.'

Honey met the look in his eyes. 'So where have you been between leaving the course and getting here?'

'Doing what I do best. Investigating with a view to solving a murder.'

'Tarquin was definitely murdered?'

'Somebody was.'

He sounded too casual to be absolutely sincere. Doherty was always dead serious when it came to crime.

'Somebody?'

'The DNA has been tested and identified as being that of Caspar's brother. But . . .'

'You don't trust the people giving you this information.'

He shook his head, his eyes downcast. What he'd told her tied in with Mary Jane's observations.

'And the man responsible?'

'He's getting close.'

'And I'm the next victim.'

His eyes clouded with concern and he held her look as though loath to let it go, as though if he dared blink she wouldn't be there when he looked again.

Honey frowned, thoughts weighing in her mind. 'And it's all to do with my father and the other men in the photograph Mary Jane and I found?'

'Apparently so.'

'Any description? It would be useful if I had an idea of what he looked like.'

Doherty looked down at the empty wine glass in front of him and shook his head.

One of the waiters chose that moment to drop a tray full of glasses. They both looked in that direction before looking at each other.

'I'm frightened,' Honey said.

'I'll be there for you.'

'Mary Jane did warn me.'

'She did?' He looked surprised that Mary Jane knew anything about it all. 'I didn't think you'd confided in anyone?'

'I didn't. My father told her I was in danger.'

His sober expression vanished, replaced by one of disbelief.

'Correct me if I'm wrong. Your father's dead.'

'Correct.'

He shook his head before slapping a hand to his forehead.

'Via the sixth-sense landline, I take it.' There was some humour in his voice, but not very much.

Honey shrugged. She'd always been a little sceptical of Mary Jane's paranormal experiences, Doherty even more so. On this occasion she had every reason to believe what she was being told.

Honey covered her eyes with one hand. Her hand felt cool. Her forehead was warm as toast. Suddenly she felt very tired and very scared.

'I suppose I should be getting on back. Lindsey is a gem, but the hotel is my responsibility. I can't neglect it just because somebody wants to kill me.'

Doherty pulled a so-so face. 'It's up there in the top ten of acceptable excuses.'

The bill settled, Doherty prepared to leave. 'Come on, I'll take you home.'

* * *

After he'd dropped her off, Doherty went home, feeling guilty because he had not told her the whole truth. He would have liked to have her here with him, but this woman was stubborn at the best of times. Yes, they adored each other, but the hotel still ranked high on her list of priorities. He had considered hanging about to keep an eye on her, but he was tired and, anyway, Dominic Christiansen had arranged for somebody to cover him. He hoped it wouldn't be Dominic. The man unnerved him. Not because of his profession but because he was the sort of man women easily fell for. But it wasn't jealousy. At least, that was what he told himself.

Before taking off his jacket, he fished in the pocket for the stub of the return train ticket to London. Absorbed in other things, Honey hadn't noticed him getting on the next carriage down, nor following her in a taxi, nor doing the same in reverse for the return journey. The hardest part had been alighting from the train at Bath Spa and pretending to have been waiting for her. But it had worked. She was home safe and sound — this time.

CHAPTER TWENTY-NINE

Once she'd passed through the double doors of the Green River Hotel, Honey's slant on the world altered appreciably. This was a safe place, a world away from spies, murder and mayhem — or it was until she recalled the goddess card that had arrived. The thought that her stalker knew where she lived made her blood run cold. Suddenly the Green River Hotel — home — did not feel as safe as it should.

'Mary Jane is home,' Lindsey reliably informed her.

Honey pushed the concern away, thinking how attractive her daughter looked, how confident she was. Without a care in the world. She had not informed Lindsey that she was being stalked. She could hardly believe it herself.

'How did she seem?' she asked lightly.

'A bit tired. She drove up from Torrington Towers yesterday and immediately took to her room. She said something about getting in touch with Granddad, though didn't let on why she would want to do that. I've known our American friend long enough to know she's talking séance or one-to-one meditation. Apparently it's the latest thing.'

Honey didn't doubt it but was grateful that Mary Jane had seemingly not mentioned the intrigue surrounding her father, Edmund Driver.

‘I expect she’s taking forty winks,’ Honey commented, though it couldn’t possibly be the truth. Mary Jane was getting on in years and, although the drive up from Torrington Towers must have been tiring, she wasn’t the sort to give in easily. ‘In the meantime I need to get up to speed. Fill me in on what needs doing.’

Lindsey moved around from one end of the reception desk to the other, pieces of paper and electronic gadgets dealt with at a phenomenal rate.

Her statement confirmed what Honey had expected.

‘Not very much. I’ve taken care of the bulk of it and what’s left is trivial. Clint rang to ask if you had any slots for him this week. He’s in need of money urgently.’

‘He’s in trouble.’

It was a statement not a question. He was their casual washer-up who sported a shaved head covered in a spider tattoo.

‘He needs to get away. It’s something to do with getting involved in a fight at a pop concert he was at with a few friends.’

Clint was the sort of person who sold bits and pieces at gigs and nightclubs. Honey had always been careful not to ask what those ‘bits and pieces’ constituted.

‘Tell him we can accommodate him whenever he’s available. Did he say where this “pop concert” — which I presume was a rave — happened to be?’

‘A farm near some old factory. And it wasn’t exactly legal from what I can gather.’

Honey didn’t pry into the details. ‘And your grandmother?’

Honey had heard nothing from her mother. On reflection, perhaps she was recovering from the realisation that her ex-husband, Honey’s father, had not been the bowler-hatted civil servant she’d thought him to be. Ditto Uncle Percy.

Unaware of what had been going on, Lindsey assumed there to be a different and rather mundane reason.

‘I’ve seen little of Grandma since she took delivery of her cat. It’s a sweet little thing, but I’m not sure it’s quite right for her.’

'Is that so?'

What price a cat's happiness compared to a threat on her life?

She felt Lindsey's eyes studying her.

'You look pale. Is this thing about Caspar's brother too much for you?'

'Of course not!' She forced herself to sound full of confidence, not a care in the world. After that she pretended to be besotted with the day's post. The cat was not at the top of her agenda.

Lindsey continued to study her. 'You are looking pale.'

'Your grandmother left me holding the baby, so to speak. I could have done with some extra help, but you know her, there's always something more important to deal with. Something that concerns her and her alone,' she remarked acidly.

Lindsey's gaze remained, just a little hurt at her mother's brusqueness. Honey could feel it in the look that was landing on her and felt guilty.

'I'm sorry for snapping. I'm just tired. Tell me about the cat.'

Some of the stiffness left Lindsey's shoulders. She was coming round, but only just.

'She hasn't got it anymore. The window cleaner left the window open and Samson jumped out in hot pursuit of a pigeon. He hasn't been seen since. Grandma's been out looking for him and so has Stewart. He's not happy about it. He paid over three hundred pounds for that cat.'

Honey shook her head. Her mother's new husband had more money than sense.

Lindsey eyed her anew, although in all honestly the searching look had not really diminished. Just wishful thinking on Honey's part.

'You look like the traveller in *The Ancient Mariner*.'

Honey was jerked from deep and disturbing thoughts.

'Who?'

'You know. The poem by Coleridge . . .' Lindsey looked skywards as she searched for the words of a poem learned in school. 'Da de da de das . . . the traveller walked onwards and turned no more his head, because he feared a demon did close behind him tread . . . Is there a demon treading behind you?'

Too close, thought Honey, and laughed. 'Of course not. I'm off to check the kitchen. Give me a shout if you need me.'

Lindsey was not and never had been a fool. Even as a child she'd been insightful beyond her years.

Honey felt her daughter's eyes searing into her back. Should she tell her the truth and have her worrying, or keep mum until everything was done and dusted — even if it meant she was the one done and dusted and gone for ever.

* * *

The coach house she shared with her daughter was cool and had a safe atmosphere. The stray cat was sitting in a basket by the fireplace. So was a note. On opening it she found it was from Smudger, her head chef.

> *Hope you don't mind, Mrs Driver, but Albert is homeless. My landlady said pets weren't allowed, though she hasn't noticed him up till now. So I brought him in with me. Trouble is he shot into your place and refuses to come out again. Hope you don't mind too much. Will discuss further when you have a moment.*

The cat opened one eye to scrutinise her before jumping onto the sofa and curling up beside her. For some reason she couldn't possibly explain, its contented purring further added to the overall feeling of security. Anyway, she hadn't the heart to throw it out. She put in a quick phone call to Smudger.

'It can stay here. OK?'

He was speechless.

She presumed Lindsey had provided the basket and no doubt she'd also been feeding it. Cats weren't really Honey's thing, but its presence made her feel quite relaxed. The cat's purring intensified when she rubbed at its ears and throat, a pair of big yellow eyes fixing her with a hypnotic stare.

Whether it was down to its stare that her thoughts returned to the subject of mineral rights, she couldn't be sure. It was like somebody had grabbed hold of her collar and jerked her backwards.

Basically, someone had been making free with the family's mineral rights. If that was so, surely there should be signs of mining such as winding wheels, propped entrances and piles of discarded aggregate in the form of huge slag heaps? Perhaps not. Things had moved on a bit from the days when Wales was the coal-producing capital of the world. And this wasn't Wales. Neither was it the nineteenth or even the twentieth century. But whatever was being mined, surely there should be some sign?

It could have been her imagination, but she was sure she saw the cat's eyes glowing.

'You're right,' she said, as she continued to stroke its ears, which sent it purring like a freight train. 'Local knowledge is everything. Perhaps I'm missing something. In which case I know the person to ask.'

The cat snuggled down beside her hip as she spoke into her mobile phone.

'Caspar. Are you aware of any disturbances around your ancestral home — as in mining disturbances? Piles of earth, obnoxious ironwork?'

She heard him suck in his teeth. He would have loved living in a stately home if it was not also a safari park, but it would have to be his own choice. Caspar was not the kind of man one told what to do. He pleased himself.

'No. And that is emphatic, my dear Honey. There are no mines on the Torrington estate.'

She needed to call on local knowledge. Local gossip meant the village pub, which meant driving all the way back to Wyvern Wendell. She considered inviting Doherty along but there was no response from his mobile so she left a message. It struck her as odd that he wasn't answering, but guessed he had important reasons.

'I'll be in plenty of company. The village pub is well patronised so I shouldn't be in any danger.'

That was what she hoped. She told Lindsey she wouldn't be long. Mary Jane overheard and asked if she'd like company. Honey declined. She quite fancied a drive in her own car at her own pace and without the horn blowing and rude gestures that Mary Jane's driving attracted.

Streetlamps lit her way as she drove along the narrow road that wound downhill into the village between boxy hedges ripe with berries.

Wyvern Wendell was hardly the liveliest of places to live, but it was pretty and had a shop that doubled as a post office. Rows of lopsided gravestones surrounded the church, its square tower dominating the village skyline. She passed the garage with the old-fashioned petrol pumps out front and an ancient enamel sign advertising Castrol oil. The pub was at the heart of the village, the eaves of the roof frowning over square windows, the lead panes sparkling like diamonds.

She glanced in her mirror, and although she did glimpse the odd set of car headlights, nobody appeared to be following her. Reassured that she was safe, she headed for the pub.

Everyone knows that the pub is the centre of village gossip. If you can't gather local knowledge there, you can't get it anywhere.

The village was quite large and rapidly being eaten up by a suburb of the nearby market town. The pub was a welcome remainder of what the village had once been like. The walls were far from plumb, the windows small and the roof thickly thatched.

The woman behind the bar had dark hair and brassy earrings big enough to hold a pair of velvet curtains.

Honey ordered a white wine spritzer. She could have murdered a vodka and tonic, but wine diluted with soda water was best, considering she was driving. The woman added two chunky slices of lemon from a plastic container.

Honey grimaced but made no comment. She liked lemon but that container looked old, the lemon not often used.

She asked a few customers about mining thereabouts. Thoughtful frowns were followed by a shaking of heads.

'Not round 'ere.'

Honey asked the woman behind the bar the same question.

Bright-red lips were pursed in concentration.

'No. No,' she said, repeating the word with a brisk shaking of her head.

Honey sighed.

'Perhaps they haven't got round to it yet,' the woman suggested.

Honey had to concede she had a point.

The landlady was curious. 'Are you working for the new bloke up at Torrington Towers?'

Honey conceded that she was.

'Fancy that. I wouldn't want to step into the shoes of a bloke who was murdered, even if he was family. The place is cursed. Stands to reason, don't it,' she suggested while tugging at one pendulous earring.

The landlord barrelled forward, nudging the landlady to one side in the process.

'Don't listen to 'er. We'll welcome the new bloke whenever he gets here.'

'You will?'

'You bet we will. We want the safari park and the house to stay open. Have you any idea how much business it brings to the village?'

'I can only guess.'

'A bloody good living, that's what. There was sod all in this village before the old lord set it up. It was a pound to a penny that all the small businesses 'ere — including this pub — would have gone bust by now without it.'

Two old men were bent over a table in front of the window playing draughts. Two others were flinging darts into the dartboard. There was something about their flickering eyes that told Honey neither was concentrating on the game.

Both darts players were heavyset with hard faces. Neither looked the sort you'd want to bump into on a dark night.

Another man was hunched in a chair pulled close to the fire where a single log glowed in a bed of embers and smoke, his gaze fixed. A Jack Russell cowered beneath his chair. When Honey returned its stare, the dog curled back its lips showing a formidable set of teeth, number eight on a scale of nought to ten.

'Don't touch the dog,' hissed the woman behind the bar when she noticed Honey eyeing it.

'I wasn't going to.'

'It has a bit of a bite.'

'So does this lemon.'

Her tongue prickled. Her lips tingled. The lemon had been incarcerated in that plastic tub a long time, floating in a bath of citrus extract.

The fact that the men at the dartboard and those at the table were all listening and watching made her want to throw something into the midst of them, something to make them move. Resisting that urge, she concentrated on what she was there for.

'So you're certain there are no mines around here.'

The landlord shifted slightly. The landlady picked up a cloth and began polishing the brass beer pumps.

'Might have been. Years ago.' He had the voice of a heavy smoker.

'How long ago?'

He shrugged. One of his rolled-up shirt sleeves rolled up further. Honey spotted a tattoo of a naked lady and the name Rita. The nude bore little resemblance to the blousy bird behind the bar.

He pursed his lips and shrugged again. 'Maybe fifty. Maybe a hundred years ago.'

The answer didn't make sense. The rights were leased only twenty years ago and there was only five years to go, longer if the government had their way.

'What did they mine?' Honey asked.

'Stone. Bath stone. They used it to build the posh houses. The Georgian crescents and all that. Other cities too. Even London.'

Even London. He said that as though Honey should be awestruck by the fact.

'Interesting.' Actually it wasn't really that riveting, except that Honey couldn't understand why anyone would lease such an underground facility, especially the government. Perhaps they were using the stone to repair the buildings in Whitehall? That didn't seem likely. So what would they want with it if it wasn't the stone? There would be nothing left. Just caves, great big open caverns . . .

'Miles of them tunnels, there are. Some says that in ancient times people lived down there — in the caves and all that. And some even says there are drawings round there.'

'Was that what Professor Collins was investigating?'

He looked at her blankly. At the same time she got the impression that her question had put off the aim of the men throwing darts. They stood stone like, still listening.

'He was a funny bloke. Used to eat his supper here most nights. I didn't like him much,' said the woman, who Honey was now certain was the landlady, Rita. She was shaking her head as though she were being offered something deeply distasteful on a plate. A Michelin-star meal when she was strictly a fish-and-chips or Cornish-pasty type.

'Any particular reason?'

'His eyes were too close together. And he used to get drunk.'

'Well, this is a pub.'

'And lewd,' said the landlady, lowering her voice to such an extent that Honey wondered whether he'd had a naughty grope of 'Rita' as she was bending down changing a beer barrel. Her next comment scuppered that particular image.

'He liked the company of men, if you get my drift. Definitely a left 'ooker.'

Honey hadn't been expecting this. It seemed odd, given his behaviour when she'd dined with him. Sexual chemistry could be unpredictable, for sure . . . But, to Honey's ears, it didn't seem like the same man. The landlady had to be mistaken. The man she'd dined with had to have been bi, if not straight.

'Do you buy your sausages locally?'

Honey had no particular reason for asking the question. Just something dumb to round things off.

'No. Nobody makes pork pies locally.'

The response struck her as odd seeing as there was a pork pie and sausage factory nearby. Should she mention it? She decided not. Pies and sausages were not a priority issue.

* * *

Lindsey had not taken the university route when she'd left school. Her busy mind was not made for channelling into any one subject or a syllabus as tight as a whalebone corset. Her mind was free, her friends were varied and she loved running her mother's hotel. Honey Driver would never admit that her daughter was a better manager than she was, but Lindsey knew, and that was all that mattered. Meeting people from all over the world fed her mind as much if not more so than any textbook. Dozens of tourists came tripping into reception, characters of every persuasion. She'd studied them all. Some were easily read, the majority quite charming, but there were always exceptions. Getting to know them and read them took her a little bit longer, but doing so had made her quite instinctive about their guests' characters.

To this end she had also become very good at reading her mother's mind. She knew when she was happy and when she was frightened. And at present her mother was frightened. She was so jumpy, and although Lindsey had thought about mentioning it, she knew it would be denied.

Her first instinct had been to ask her outright what was going on. Her second was to sit back and wait to be told.

Her mother had worried about other crime cases she'd worked on, but this time Lindsey sensed something different and far more serious was going on. She'd never shown such anxiety before, and she wasn't forthcoming with the detail. To Lindsey's mind she should be, seeing as it involved Caspar St John Gervais, and when she'd spotted her mother's notes left casually on her desk, she could see there was a circle around the name Professor Lionel Collins. The name had rung a bell and by the end of the day she had made the connection.

Her grandmother also seemed to be keeping things close to her chest. She'd even forgotten to rebuke Lindsey when she'd inadvertently called her Grandmother instead of the customary Gloria. She'd told her granddaughter long ago that to be called Grandmother, Gran or even Nan made her feel very old.

She'll never be any different, Lindsey thought to herself, even when she is ninety.

There was nothing for it but to work things out for herself, and to her mind it all began and ended with Caspar St John Gervais.

Lindsey took it into her head to pop around to La Reine Rouge and speak to Caspar, but first she had a lunch date.

The name Professor Lionel Collins had finally risen to the surface. Daphne, one of her old school friends, had a degree in geology and archaeology, and had studied under the professor. On the pretext of catching up on old times, Lindsey invited her out for lunch.

The Boathouse pub nestled on a riverside curve just off the main A4. The car park was large, and although it wasn't quite midday, it was half full.

Lindsey parked her bicycle against a post beneath a tree.

Daphne gave her a little wave from a table as far from the bar as it was possible to be.

At least it'll be quiet, she thought to herself. The bar had the atmosphere of a mother's meeting. There were a number of 'yummy mummies' indulging in an early lunch along with their pre-school offspring.

They greeted each other with air kisses and brief catch-ups before ordering a light lunch and mineral water.

It did not escape Lindsey's notice that Daphne's gaze frequently strayed to the mother and toddler groups.

'Am I reading your broody gazes right?'

Daphne blushed at being discovered.

'I'm about three months. You didn't notice?'

'Not your bump,' Lindsey admitted. 'Just the look on your face. There was a time when your gaze only strayed to shoe shops or rugby players with tight butts and firm thighs. Now it's straying to the under-fours.'

Daphne shrugged. 'I decided it was time to settle down. Is there anyone special in your life?'

Lindsey was forthright. 'Yes. There is. He's asked me to go travelling the Andes with him. In fact the idea is to replicate a trip done years ago by an explorer and two horses. He's got it in his head to travel the whole range of mountains from the far north of the North American continent to the far south.'

Daphne's eyes opened wide.

'Are you going to do it?'

Lindsey thought of her mother, the hotel and the familiar surroundings of the city of Bath. She also thought about Sean. He wore glasses, a dreamy look and mismatched clothes, underneath which was pure masculinity.

'I'm tempted. Very tempted.' She thought again about her mother, the fear she was presently wearing in her eyes and not admitting to. 'But I have a few things to deal with before I commit.'

Daphne shook her head. 'You always were more responsible than the rest of us.'

Lindsey didn't deny it. Anyway, she wasn't here to talk about the way they used to be. There were more pressing matters.

'You once mentioned a Professor Lionel Collins you used to study under. I can't tell you why I want to know, but I wonder if you can tell me anything about him.'

A small frown appeared between Daphne's finely plucked eyebrows, accompanied by a barely discernible shrug.

'He was a dish, but he wasn't interested in women. Can you give me a hint as to what this is about?'

Lindsey shook her head. 'Not really. It was just that his name came up.'

'In connection with . . . ?'

Lindsey chewed it over. There seemed no harm in hinting. 'The death of a friend's brother. His name was linked.'

Daphne grinned. 'Was your friend's brother very good-looking?'

This question coupled with Daphne's earlier comment about the professor not being interested in women brought instant enlightenment.

'He was gay?'

'Absolutely.'

Lindsey took a moment to let this new information sink in. Yet her grandmother had dropped enough hints about the professor's designs on her mother, taking her out to wine and dine her, for it to be confusing.

'Are you sure?'

'Absolutely. One hundred per cent. And it was a crying shame for the female population. Here—' she swiped at her mobile and held it up for Lindsey to see — 'they've not gotten around to taking his picture down from the faculty pages just yet. He's the hottest thing since Indiana Jones. Am I right?'

* * *

Cycling from the Boathouse to La Reine Rouge, Lindsey considered her friend Daphne. She was reaching forward into a new life. OK, having a baby didn't float Lindsey's boat, but it made her think. She was no longer a child and her mother was perfectly capable of looking after herself.

It hadn't always been that way. She'd been like a twirling top after Lindsey's father had died, not sure of where her life was going. The only thing she had been sure of was making a decent living in order to bring up her child.

Lindsey knew how much her mother had put into the hotel, even though it wasn't a career she'd willingly gone into. She'd done it for her daughter. Gratefulness flooded over her as never before. Should she take up Sean's offer or continue to be a dominant presence in her mother's life? The jury was out. She'd think about it.

Caspar looked surprised to see her.

'My dear! To what do I owe this rare occurrence?'

As usual he was smartly dressed, not a thing out of place: crisp white shirt, mottled cravat at his throat, blue striped blazer and dark-blue chinos. His dress sense and presentation were directly opposed to her darling Sean's. In a way she found it quite funny and it made her smile. However, she saw dark circles beneath Caspar's eyes that had not been there before.

He indicated she should take a seat in an off-white armchair. It looked early eighteenth century.

Lindsey thanked him. 'I'm concerned about my mother.'

He nodded silently, eyes averted and a tightening around his mouth. She sensed immediately that he knew more than he was letting on.

'I want to know what this is really all about.'

The first flush of guilt was quickly quashed and replaced by a bland and uncompromising stiffening of his jaw. If Caspar hadn't decided on the hospitality business, he could easily have gone on the stage.

'My dear!' He chuckled softly. 'I really don't know—'

'Professor Lionel Collins. Do you know him?'

'Now look here . . .'

'No! You look here. I can't help getting the feeling that my mother's been steamrollered into a situation in which she's out of her depth. I'm concerned for her. I want to know what this is really all about.'

'My dear . . .'

'I'm not your dear, so please don't keep repeating yourself and stop buggering about. My mother went to dinner with a man claiming to be Professor Lionel Collins. She reported to my grandmother that he was all over her like a rash.'

Caspar sat bolt upright. Lindsey guessed he'd always considered her the beating heart of the Green River Hotel. The backroom girl, eyes fixed to a computer screen.

'I really cannot comment on your mother's choice of male companions . . .' He recovered quickly, throwing in the chuckle that smacked of evasion.

Lindsey's stance remained adamant. 'Don't play ignorant. I happen to know something of the professor's history. A good-looking man according to a friend of mine, but not at all responsive to the interest of women on campus. From what I've learned, there is no way he would have made overtures to my mother. So what's the truth? What's going on here?'

Caspar's shoulders slouched. He looked deflated and unsure what to do next.

'Excuse me, I need to make a telephone call.'

He left her alone in the room, sitting stiffly upright in the handsome antique chair. Her face was stony and pale, her jaw painfully clenched. She was afraid for her mother. Very afraid.

Instinct was like a cold frost gradually creeping over her skin. Something bad was about to assault her ears and she found herself wishing that Mary Jane was here to translate what was happening to her. The professor of the paranormal regarded instinct as part of a person's natural make-up before it had taken a backseat to reason.

The sudden chiming of a grandfather clock startled her, but the instinctive fear remained. So did the conviction that Caspar knew a lot more than he was letting on.

Her eyes filled with tears and she couldn't think why. Just tension, said the voice inside her head. You could do with a good cry.

By the time Caspar came back from making his private call, her eyes were moist and a stray tear had trickled down one cheek.

‘My dear, I’m afraid . . .’ Caspar curbed whatever excuse he’d been about to use. Lindsey, Honey’s daughter, was crying and, no matter what he’d been told to say, he swiftly backtracked.

With a flourish, he retrieved a white silk handkerchief from his breast pocket.

‘My dear child. Please. Dry your tears.’

He looked out of the French doors to the beautifully kept courtyard garden, his hands clasped behind his back. The sight of Japanese maple and a host of other plants whose names he did not know helped him make a very serious decision, one that might cost him dearly.

Suddenly he turned round. ‘Damn them all! I don’t care what happens. You deserve to know the truth!’

CHAPTER THIRTY

'Nice day. Nice car.'

Fred Cromer, the garage owner in the village of Wyvern Wendell, was placing the keys to a vintage Ford Capri back on one of a line of brass hooks above his oil-covered workbench.

'Early model,' he said, as his eyes swept over the smooth-looking bloke who had brought in his car to have it checked for an oil leak. It seemed odd that such a handsome car — a BMW at that — would have anything wrong with it. Still, the customer was always right.

Dominic nodded at the Capri. 'Yours?'

Fred Cromer beamed. He was rightly proud of the old car.

'It is. I hire it out. Just in case you're interested.'

'I wouldn't mind having a go.'

Dominic Christiansen ran his hand over the bonnet. With the other hand he paid his bill.

'It's still warm. Has it been hired out today?'

Cromer nodded. 'This morning.'

The government employee, light on his feet, followed Cromer into the dark interior of the ramshackle garage. His own car was shoved forward from a deep pit, the keys in it, ready for a quick getaway.

Somewhere beneath the accumulation of grease and oil was a concrete floor. Car and engine parts sat on wooden benches and shelves fashioned from roughly hewn wood.

'Fancy a cup of tea?'

'No thanks. Have you had the car long?'

'Bought it about three months ago from some young fella who was digging around here. Irish, I think he was. A lot of these hippy types, students for the most part, came here when they were doing a bit of digging around the Torrington estate. Sold me this van too just before he shoved off.' He indicated a Volkswagen camper van. 'Another classic. I do love a classic car. Made to last they were. No bits and bobs of electronic stuff to make it go. Sheer mechanics. Bit over the top though, all these flowers and things. But that's hippies for you.'

Christiansen nodded. 'I suppose it is.'

'I've got 'is log book with 'is name on and everything.'

'Can you describe him?'

Fred Cromer looked at the suave young man with narrowed eyes.

'You a copper?'

'What makes you think that?'

'Well, for a start I can't find anything wrong with your car, and secondly you ask a lot of questions.'

'Ok. I admit it. Now tell me more. Describe him, this Irish man.'

Cromer ran the back of his hand beneath his nostrils and sniffed.

'Had long, light brown hair, a beard, and wore those wire-framed glasses like John Lennon used to,' said Fred, while wiping the excess grease from his hands. 'And a bandana around his head. You know. Usual stuff. Baggy jeans. Sandals. Makes me laugh. There they all are, these hippies, pretending to be different than normal folk, and all ending up looking the same as one another. Silly buggers.'

Christiansen stood with his hands in his pockets, head slightly bowed. He was thinking how much more he knew about the previous owner of the camper van than Fred did.

'What name did he give you?'

The way he'd formulated the question made Fred look up from his hands.

'You sound as though 'e might 'ave 'ad loads of different names.'

'Hippies don't always give the name they were given at birth. Not dramatic enough. I've heard of guys called Soft-Voiced Sid, Radillion Rainbow, all manner of different handles.'

'Ah! I see what you mean. Patrick Casey. Yes,' he said after further thought, 'that was it. Patrick Casey. It'll be on the log book too. And the address.'

Christiansen felt a jolt of hope run through him. He knew that neither the name nor the address were authentic. The Tarot Man was good at covering his tracks — whether in his professional or casual capacity.

Dominic paid the bill and didn't wait for the change. Fred saw only the tail lights of the sleek car fading into the rain.

* * *

On the way back to the cottage that he was living in for the duration of this project, Christiansen stopped off at the telephone box and rang the usual number. A crisp voice answered. He told him what he intended doing.

'You can't tell her any more than you've told her already. We need her to flush him out.'

'Surely it's only fair that she knows what he looks like. She has to know what she's up against.'

CHAPTER THIRTY-ONE

Honey woke up shivering to the sound of the wind howling and the casement window thrashing back and forth. She was still dressed, a fact that somehow surprised her. She remembered going to the pub and asking questions, but surely she'd arranged to go straight home afterwards?

She recalled it being too late, and that she'd ended up begging a room at Torrington Towers. She also vaguely recalled having a bottle of cheap wine.

Her throbbing temples were proof enough that the wine hadn't been very good. She presumed that Miss Vincent or one of the other women had dumped her in here on the bed.

The room was in darkness, but surely it was morning?

Her phone began ringing. She reached out for the table lamp, switched it on and picked up the phone.

'Mother. Are you OK?'

Lindsey sounded agitated. Placing a cool hand on her aching forehead, Honey tried to remember a time when she'd heard her daughter sound so upset.

'Mother. Where are you?'

'At Torrington Towers. You see, I went to the pub last night to ask a few questions, and—'

'Mother. Get out of there. Get back here as fast as you can.'

Honey went to the window and pulled back the curtain. The branches of trees were blowing wildly in the wind and stair rods of rain were coming down sideways.

'Lindsey, I'm not quite finished yet. My, the weather's certainly taken a turn for the worst.'

'Mother, never mind the weather. If you don't get in your car right this minute, I'm coming down to get you. You're out of your depth. Completely out of your depth. You see, Professor Lionel Collins wasn't Collins, and Caspar's brother wasn't who he was either. It's a trap, Mother. A trap to get—'

The line went dead. The flashing green light told Honey the battery had died.

Head spinning, she fell back onto the bed and closed her eyes.

Behind her closed lids she thought about Lindsey's phone call. There had been more than agitation in her daughter's voice. There had been fear.

Honey sat up too swiftly, sending her head swimming.

Swinging her legs over the side of the bed, her feet hit the floor and her head swam. The most positive thing she could think of to do was to take deep breaths, at the same time willing her eyes to settle down and stop acting as though she were swinging on a trapeze. Once they did settle down and she could focus, she spotted a note left on the bedside table. It was from Miss Vincent.

> *The editor of the* Western Daily Press *called. He said you can get him at home this evening. Hereunder is his home number. He says he has some important information for you. Urgent.*

Honey frowned. What information? He'd already apologised to Caspar, so what else did he need to do?

Her mind was like a notebook. She went through the possibilities quickly, simply because there weren't that many. The only possibility was that the editor had discovered the identity of the person who had passed misinformation to the reporter. Someone had given the reporter a lead, but who and why?

Unfortunately her mobile phone was dead so no chance of using that.

Miss Vincent had fought her way to work through the foul weather and informed Honey that the power was down so she couldn't use the cordless phone either.

'Do you have a mobile?' Honey asked.

Miss Vincent looked at her as though she'd suggested something quite lewd might be happening over breakfast.

'And nobody else is in. You could use the payphone in the cafeteria. That might still be working.'

* * *

If it hadn't been so important, and if Miss Vincent hadn't lent her a pair of stout wellington boots and an oversize raincoat, Honey would have stayed put until the storm had blown itself out. Reminding herself that this was England and that the storm could last for days, she decided she had no choice.

Swamped in wet weather gear, she trudged off in boots two sizes too big for her, head bowed against the howling gale and driving rain.

The payphone was not exactly in the cafeteria but adjacent to a stone wall some distance hence and very much outside.

In an effort to hold with tradition, it was one of the old red telephone boxes, a ploy to tempt the visitor away from their mobile phone and enjoy a bit of nostalgia. Honey couldn't see that getting soaked through was much of a nostalgia trip, but hey, what did she know.

Heaving open the door to the telephone box was a two-handed job. It weighed a ton!

Luckily the phone box took credit cards. Nostalgia wasn't everything, and the modern visitor wasn't likely to have enough change.

Honey rang the number and asked for Geoffrey Monmouth, the man who would disclose the source of his story. If she was guessing correctly, the source must have had a reason for imparting the wrong information and only Geoffrey Monmouth knew the person's identity.

Someone answered and told her that Geoffrey was away at present covering a body found in a mudslide somewhere in Shropshire.

A body found in a mudslide . . . The words sent a chill running down her spine. She asked where he was staying and was given the address and telephone number of a pub in Much Wenlock.

'And I'm going to stay there too,' Honey said out loud once the old-fashioned phone was back in its cradle. It did pain her that she didn't have time to phone the Green River, just to check that everything was all right, but she trusted her daughter to take care of things. Her aim was to travel to Shropshire and take a room in the same pub as Geoffrey Monmouth. Face to face he wouldn't have the nerve to lie or fob her off.

CHAPTER THIRTY-TWO

The Tarot Man was already there.

The engine of the old red truck idled as he checked things out. The inn in which the archaeology team had stayed looked the most likely place to start.

If the interior of the Black Dog was any reflection of the exterior, there wasn't much to look forward to. The paint was peeling. The dog on the old wooden sign looked as though it had mange, the paint from one ear hanging like a ribbon covering one jowl. He swung into the parking lot ranged along the front. The white-painted lines delineating the spaces were as decrepit as the inn sign. Two vehicles were parked out front. One of them was a tractor.

It had been a long journey. The ground was firm beneath his feet and it felt good to stretch his long legs, to tense and release the muscles and take a deep breath of evening air.

Behind the roof of the pub the branches of trees made bare by an early north wind spread like black veins against a blushing sky.

Without bothering to lock the truck door behind him — this was a village after all, not a big city where anything with wheels was fair game — he headed for the warmth of the pub.

The door was oak-panelled, grey with age and braced with reinforcements of cast iron.

Heads turned as he and the night invaded the clogging warmth and staleness.

Conversation ceased immediately. He guessed they didn't get many visitors through here. The finding of a murdered girl was probably the most sensational thing that had happened in years.

He bid them good evening. They looked surprised that he was well spoken as they eyed him suspiciously. Not that they went overboard to be friendly, though one or two bobbed their heads. Their mouths remained tightly shut. He didn't let it get to him. He'd been in other out-of-the-way places where everyone knew everyone else and strangers were observed and not accepted until their credentials were known.

Isolation didn't so much breed contempt as insularity, an inbuilt wariness of those not sharing the same history, the same family name, the same sins and introvert thoughts.

Despite television, good transport and the telephone, old habits died hard. Old hostilities towards outsiders stayed pretty much the same.

He could feel it in their eyes as he made for the bar and ordered a beer. They were as wary as the people of the Middle Ages would have been, wondering who he was, what he was doing here, what sort of trouble he would stir up. Would he steal their money, rape their women?

A log fire crackled and spat in a cast-iron dog grate set into an inglenook fireplace. A live dog — a Jack Russell — pricked its ears and met his eyes.

Something unseen and unheard by anyone else passed between them. The dog whined, got up and resettled beneath a fireside stool.

He addressed the woman behind the bar. 'Do you have rooms?'

She had a double chin, greasy with sweat and pink, either from drink or sitting too close to the fire. He favoured the first theory.

Her small blue eyes stayed fixed on him as she nodded. Her lashes were golden blonde, like ripe straw and just as spiky. She looked surprised by his request and uncertain whether she should let him have a room, until he got out his wallet.

'Cash,' she said, her eyes now fixed on the wad of money emerging from the handsome leather case.

Her fat fingers folded over the bills before slipping them into the pink patch between her breasts.

'I'll need a name.'

'Geoffrey Monmouth.'

'First floor, second door on the left,' she said, handing him a key.

He recalled the white-painted sign outside: *Bar Food Available*.

'Are you still serving food?'

'It's a bit late but I can do you a ploughman's.'

'That's fine.'

'Cheese or ham?'

He chose ham. 'And a pint of beer.'

'Do you want it in your room?'

'No. Here.'

After sliding over some more money, he took his beer and made for an unoccupied table.

The table was round and small — possibly the smallest in the bar — and he had trouble tucking his legs beneath it.

A slight murmur of conversation resumed, though it was still subdued. To his ears it sounded like the humming of a piece of machinery or an old-fashioned tape recorder, the sort with big reels that made a hissing sound.

The ploughman's came: crusty bread, yellow butter, thickly sliced ham with just enough fat, a little salad, a lot of pickle, a touch of coleslaw.

The beer was warm and straight from the barrel. It would be the only beer that night. He needed to keep his wits about him. He needed to ask questions, though subtly and without arousing suspicion.

He left the bar, following the sign saying, *Residents Only*.

The bedroom had a floor that creaked with each footstep. A double bed, clean white pillowcases, an old television sitting on a chest of drawers, a wardrobe — possibly Edwardian vintage, definitely pre-First World War — a chair, and a card hanging from the headboard of the bed stating that the bathroom was to the left along the landing. No en suite facilities. He hadn't expected anything else.

He lifted the curtain and looked outside, his eyes searching the shadows thrown by trees and thick bushes on the other side of the road. There were few street lights. The denser part of the darkness formed frames around squares of light falling from cottage windows. Twilight was turning into night.

The village was quiet out of respect for the murdered girl. It was Halloween, yet no kids were out trick or treating. Down in the bar he'd seen a black-and-white notice on the wall advertising a Halloween party, yet no one was dressed in costume and he'd detected less than a party spirit.

The silence was suddenly disturbed by the sound of a car. The Tarot Man looked in the direction it was coming from. A pair of small headlights popped like surprised eyes through the darkness. A yellow Citroen slid to a halt beside the old red truck. Honey Driver had arrived. She'd got the message. Things were about to get interesting.

CHAPTER THIRTY-THREE

'Hi,' said Honey, bouncing into the bar as though she were a regular. 'I phoned you about a room. You have kept it for me, haven't you?'

The woman behind the bar exchanged looks with all the other heads that had turned to give Honey the once-over.

Honey noticed the cessation of conversation. 'Is something wrong?' she asked.

The woman behind the bar looked away from the curiosity of her customers and back to Honey.

'It's just that we don't get many people asking for rooms at this time of year. Do you want food as well?'

'If it's available.'

'I can do a ploughman's.'

'That'll do nicely. I don't suppose you sell wine by the glass,' she said as she handed over the money.

'The Black Dog don't even do wine by the bottle,' somebody said.

There were chuckles and grins.

'The room's at the back,' said the woman. 'It's not as big as the one at the front, but I've already let that. Would you like your ploughman's by the fire?'

It seemed a good idea. No wine, so Honey settled for a port and lemon.

'On holiday?' the landlady asked her, suspicion written all over her face.

'Business,' Honey said. 'I'm a tax inspector.'

Heads turned at her pronouncement. One or two downed their drinks and left. Honey smiled to herself, confident she wouldn't attract any further questions. She was left with time to think.

'You said you've already let the other room. Was it to a man named Geoffrey Monmouth?'

The landlady eyed her suspiciously. Being in the hospitality trade herself, Honey could read her thoughts. She thought this was an assignation — two separate rooms booked but only one bed likely to be slept in. Two married people were the norm, though not married to each other.

Honey decided to enlighten her. 'He's a journalist.'

The landlady almost looked disappointed. 'Oh. I suppose he's up here about that poor girl they found.'

'Girl?' Honey frowned.

'The girl they found buried in a mudslide. They've not named her yet, of course. I expect he's up here about that.'

* * *

It was nearing nine thirty and she was tired when Geoffrey Monmouth entered the bar. She knew it was him purely from the look thrown by the landlady, one that darted to him then back to Honey.

A bush of a beard covered the lower part of his face. A broad-brimmed hat was pulled low over his features.

Shutting the door firmly behind him, he leaned against it, looked at Honey and swiped at his nose.

After ordering himself a soft drink, he came and sat opposite her.

Honey felt the landlady's eyes weighing them up, perhaps salivating that a lovers' tryst might be going on here. Some chance! One glare from Honey and she turned away.

Honey turned back to Geoffrey, cradling her drink tightly, as though warming it through might improve the taste. His eyes, even the shape of his face, seemed oddly familiar and she was instantly on her guard.

'I read the newspaper's apology,' she said to him. 'Caspar was grateful for that, but it still doesn't excuse why you used his name in the first place. You said you had an informant. Can you give me a name?'

She noticed him fiddling with the cuffs of his tweed jacket. At the same time he looked at her, then away again. Probably embarrassment. He didn't look like the sort with something to hide — unless he was a consummate actor.

'I didn't mean any harm. It's just that I had a scoop and thought the details were bona fide. My source assured me they were.'

'But you didn't check.'

He looked down at his hands, stilling his nervous fingers as he did so. 'My source told me he was close to the family, especially to Lord Torrington. And I was . . . well . . . to put it mildly, in need of funds fast. I'd been gambling and drinking and got involved with this woman . . .'

Suddenly Honey realised what he was getting at.

'Am I getting this right? You usually pay for information, but on this occasion you were paid to print what you were told?'

'I'm sorry.'

'Who was it? Give me a name?'

She couldn't help eyeing this man with the utmost disdain.

'Christiansen. Dominic Christiansen.'

Suddenly he seemed to look past her, his jaw tensing as he did so.

Honey glanced in the same direction. She saw nobody, only the stairs leading up to the first-floor rooms.

'Excuse me,' he said.

She presumed he was heading for the men's lavatory. Ten minutes went by. He didn't come back and she thought she heard his old truck start up and drive off.

Oh well, she thought to herself. It's not the first time I've been stood up.

The landlady asked her what time she'd like breakfast in the morning.

Honey asked if nine thirty would be all right.

'Ooow, no. Sorry, love. It 'as to be before nine. I'm off up to where they discovered that girl, see 'ow they're getting on. It's better than telly.'

* * *

'Shit.' He cursed under his breath, as the engine of his truck stuttered into life.

Everything had been going his way just then at the bar. He'd felt closer to Honey than ever. Then, he had recognised the boyfriend from the time he'd watched them both on their weekend away at the cottage. He'd faded into the shadows back then, knowing the security services would be close by.

He would do the same now.

CHAPTER THIRTY-FOUR

Her meeting with Geoffrey Monmouth had both upset and angered her. She badly wanted to phone Dominic Christiansen and have it out with him, but she'd omitted to add his number to her phone and she'd left his card back at the Green River Hotel. Besides, her phone's battery was dead.

She found the door to her room and inserted the key, only to find it was unlocked. That in itself was no big deal in an off-road inn where visitors and predators were thin on the ground.

Naturally, because it overlooked the fields at the rear of the inn, the room was in darkness. But there was more to it than that. She knew someone was in the room.

Heart beating wildly, she stood with her back to the door, listening for the sound of breathing. Female instinct is a funny thing, and not in the least bit magical. Honey's belief was that the female subconscious picks up on certain things even before the more physical senses kick in. Sight, taste, touch, sound and smell. It was the last one she was picking up on — a smell she'd come across before.

Her heart was motoring and her legs had turned to jelly. The only weapon she had to hand was her overnight bag. Was the weight of her make-up bag likely to knock an assailant aside? Quite possibly. So did she go on or back off?

Her hand tightened on the sturdy handles of her bag. The decision was made.

On!

She fingered the wall for a light switch, found one and switched it on.

'What the hell do you think you are doing here, lady? I told you to back off. What is it about that statement that you don't understand?'

Doherty was sitting in the only chair in the room, elbows resting on knees, thunderous expression turned squarely on her. It was like being faced with a loaded shotgun — she was in his sights and about to get blasted.

In three swift strides he was towering over her. His expression was angry. 'Get a good hold on your bag, get back down the stairs, into your car and get out of here.'

'Steve, I am not a child!'

'I want you out of here.'

His attitude made her see red. 'You have no right to order me out of here! I will not go!'

'Now just you listen to me,' he growled. 'There are things happening here that you know nothing of.'

'You are so right!' she shouted. 'And that's why I'm here. To find out what the devil's been going on. And before you tell me yet again that I'm out of my depth and it's none of my business, things have moved on a bit since Caspar drew me in to this. It's about me, Steve. It's also about my father and a lethal legacy. Somebody is out to kill me and I want to know who it is.'

Now she'd gotten started, the accusations were flying thick and fast, each accompanied by her finger stabbing at his chest. Who cared if her next-door neighbour heard their raised voices? The tension she had been under finally boiled over. Tears streamed down her face.

On swiping her hand across her eyes, smearing her make-up in the process, she saw that the anger had gone from his face. He was looking at her thoughtfully. She was instantly taken back to when they had first met. He'd looked at her like that back then too.

'I didn't think you cared,' he said softly.

'About my father? Of course I care. Just because I don't remember much about him . . . This whole thing has got to me. I want to know what he really did — something bad obviously, that somebody would want to kill me for. I mean, what's it got to do with me? I barely knew my father and I certainly didn't know much about his job, and neither did my mother for that matter.'

He sat down again in the chair, hands clasped in front of him.

She shook her head. 'I find it so hard to believe.'

His eyes locked with hers. Honey sensed again that feeling of being weighed up, and wondered exactly how much Doherty had known about all this. She had to ask him.

'I get the feeling I was set up from the start. Is that what you think?'

He trailed a thumb across his chin as he thought it over before coming to a decision.

'I think Geoffrey Monmouth was used as a filter for a government agency, though probably didn't know it. Sometimes they'd feed him outright lies, but most of the time he was fed small things that might trigger other things. It's amazing what you read in the papers.'

For a moment his face creased into a smile. His complexion looked grey and there were lines beneath his eyes. We're all tired on this case, she thought to herself.

'So Caspar was set up?'

He nodded. 'Partly.'

Honey frowned. 'Partly? What does that mean?'

He shook his head. A faint smile played around lips that a romantic novel would describe as sensual. A respectable girl would have been told that such lips were best avoided. Was she a respectable girl? Not where Doherty was concerned.

This was no time for salacious musings. She wanted answers and had the impression that Doherty knew more than he was letting on.

'OK, so they used Geoffrey for their own purposes.'

'Define "they",' she said, her tears gone and her resolve toughened.

'MI5. MI6. Either of them. The people your father worked for.

'Just one thing I have to point out,' he said. 'I spoke to Geoffrey Monmouth down the road at Holmleigh Guest House. He was very apologetic and said he'd published the information in good faith. He went round to apologise to Caspar. Did you know that?'

Honey was stunned. She shook her head dumbly.

'He didn't mention it.' She frowned. 'You just said that you met Geoffrey staying at a guest house?' She shook her head again. 'That can't be right. Geoffrey Monmouth is here. He's staying in the other letting room. I met him earlier . . .'

'How did you contact him?'

'There was a message waiting at Torrington Towers. My battery was down and the power was disrupted by the storm. I went to the phone box to contact him but somebody told me he wasn't there and gave me the number of where he was staying. Here,' she said, jerking her chin.

Doherty sprang to his feet. She saw his hand pass swiftly to a lump beneath his jacket. Her heart almost stopped beating. Since when had he carried a gun? Policemen didn't carry guns, not unless they were in a special unit or had been given special dispensation.

'Which way?' he asked, his hand already on the door handle.

'To the front,' Honey said softly, waving her index finger weakly towards the front of the building.

After warning her to stay put, Doherty vanished through the door, though not before ordering her to lock it behind him.

He wasn't gone long. When he came back he confirmed that the man calling himself Geoffrey Monmouth was gone, along with the red truck. They both knew now that the man Honey had been talking to was not Geoffrey Monmouth.

Honey took a deep breath, scared at how close she'd been to the Tarot Man. 'I would still like it confirmed,' she said falteringly. 'Just so I can sleep tonight.'

'Have you still got that message?'

She nodded.

'Phone him.'

'My battery's flat. Remember?'

He shook his head. 'I would prefer you didn't use mine. There's no knowing what electronic devices our false Monmouth might have.'

'There's a payphone outside.'

'Goodness. Two in one day!'

Honey took the card from the pocket of her jacket.

Doherty had got up from the chair and positioned himself between Honey and the door. Now he moved aside.

'Right,' she said, all strident confidence and grim determination. 'You're coming with me. I've no wish to wander outside by myself.'

On the way out, they passed through the bar where the landlady was wiping down the tables. She looked up when she heard them, surprise registering when she saw Honey was with another man.

'Well I never!' Her expression said it all. Honey was a hussy — worse still perhaps.

'I'm just going outside to use the phone,' Honey said to her.

It was possible that she might offer use of the bar's phone, but neither Honey nor Doherty wanted that. A phone box was more impersonal and not so traceable.

'We don't 'ave one,' remarked the landlady in a throaty voice that betrayed her cigarette habit. 'No point paying for one when there's a phone box outside, only across the yard in fact.'

She purposely addressed Doherty, as though informing him that Honey could find it all by herself without undue supervision.

Catching on to that fact, he said, 'I'm her bodyguard. No knowing what dangers lurk outside village pubs at night.'

What he said seemed to strike a chord with her.

'We won't be long,' Doherty told her.

'Right. But if you're not back in ten minutes I'm calling the police.'

'I am the police.'

Unlike the red telephone boxes that used to be found on the corner of every city street, this one was in tip-top condition and smelled of polish and disinfectant. Honey guessed that somebody in the village made it their personal job to take care of it. Perhaps it was the pub landlady, though she wasn't too sure about that.

The landlady at the guest house didn't sound too happy about getting Geoffrey Monmouth to the phone.

'I'm a woman alone. I don't hold with knocking on my male guests' bedrooms at this late an hour.'

'It's terribly urgent,' said Honey. 'A matter of life and death in fact.'

Her response that she would do as asked was begrudging. Honey heard her slippers scuffing away from the phone. It seemed she was gone an age. At last a groggy-sounding Geoffrey Monmouth was on the phone. Honey duly asked him for a description of the man who had passed him the information regarding Caspar's brother.

'Smartly dressed bloke,' he said. 'Upper-crust type, but foreign — kind of. Spoke well though.'

'How tall?'

'I don't know for sure. I'd guess about five feet eleven. Perhaps six feet.'

'What about his hair? What about his eyes?'

'Very fair hair, blue eyes, about thirty-eight years old and athletic, gangly but strong; looked as though he could run a marathon without a sweat.'

Honey was immediately uneasy. He was describing Dominic Christiansen.

'Mr Monmouth. Do you know a middle-aged man, portly, of average build, who wears tweed jackets and has a nervous habit of intertwining his fingers?'

Judging by the silence the real Mr Geoffrey Monmouth was totally confused.

'I'm not sure. I'd have to think about it.'

'Do you look like that, Mr Monmouth?'

It was a silly question and earned her a reprimanding look from Doherty. They'd both made up their minds that the gentleman who'd fled the front letting room at the Black Dog was not Geoffrey Monmouth.

'No. I'm not middle-aged and I'm not portly.' He sounded quite affronted.

Honey thanked him and put down the phone.

Doherty was eyeing her expectantly. 'Well?'

'He doesn't know anyone who looks like the man I met here.'

Doherty looked thoughtfully over his shoulder. 'I already know that.'

'How did you find out about Geoffrey Monmouth?'

'Government departments are notorious for not speaking to each other. That fact also applies to their computer systems. The key is to grab some amateur hacker who knows how to get them to talk.'

'And you know somebody who can do that?'

Doherty grinned. 'Yeah. Your daughter.'

The trill of his phone pierced the air only seconds after he'd said it.

'Your daughter,' he said to Honey. 'She wants to talk to you. And after that she wants to talk to me.'

Recalling their earlier truncated conversation, Honey grabbed the phone.

'Mother! Are you OK?' Lindsey sounded frantic.

'Of course I am. I have my own bodyguard to look out for me.'

'He needs to.' Lindsey's voice was tight with fear. 'You may want to sit down when I tell you this. Better still, put it on loudspeaker and Steve can catch you when you faint. And Mother, do remember to recharge your phone regularly and not wait for it to run out.'

'What is it?'

'You're going to be shocked.'

'Get on with it.'

'It's powerful stuff.'

Honey and Doherty's heads touched as they both attempted to listen to what Lindsey had to say.

'It's Caspar. Caspar is at the bottom of this.'

The rest of what she said made Honey's blood run cold.

The moment the conversation was over, Doherty was shepherding her towards the door.

'I think I might kill Caspar when I get hold of him,' he muttered through clenched teeth.

'I'm quite capable of doing that myself,' muttered Honey, her blood like ice in her veins.

CHAPTER THIRTY-FIVE

It was easy to hide in London. There were so many people, so many places in which to get lost.

The man who had posed as a middle-aged journalist was annoyed he'd had to run. He was sure he could have persuaded Honey Driver to come with him if her policeman boyfriend hadn't shown up. He'd seen him on that first occasion when they'd stayed at the cottage. He had hoped to get closer then, but the fact the boyfriend was there, plus Christiansen loitering close by, meant it would have been foolhardy.

The woman had even made the mistake of climbing into his car, en route to her date with the buffoonish professor — no matter that he was a virtual stranger . . . He could've killed her a hundred times over. But with Christiansen's eyes on her, she was untouchable.

He was in no doubt that his appearance and whereabouts would be instantly passed on to MI5 by those two. Not that his appearance would stay the same. Altering one's look was vital if one wanted to keep a step ahead of one's pursuers. And, God knew, it was second nature to him by now. Geoffrey Monmouth, Adrian Sayle, Patrick Casey . . . the lies came to him as easy as breathing.

He chose a hotel in Paddington where he could stay for one night's rest without attracting undue attention. Paddington was a place people passed through on the way to somewhere else. Just like him.

After purchasing a newspaper from a shop close by, he settled in, opened the paper and read about what he had done. The *Daily Express* carried the headline in thick black type. He didn't bother with all the details. He already knew them. The Tarot Man always kills when the weather is bad — pouring down, just like it was now.

What they had failed to grasp was that there were two aspects to his killing habit. On the one hand he was intent on pursuing those with a hand in the killing of his father. On the other, he liked killing young women. He'd originally only left cards with those he regarded as responsible for killing his father. But as time passed, he began leaving them with the dead girls too, though only ever the goddess.

His father had been a double agent, finally settling in the Soviet Union where he'd met his mother. It was his father's old friends from university, agents for MI5, who had plotted and succeeded in killing him. He blamed them and would always blame them, and once he'd found out, he'd wanted his revenge. If the men who had killed his father were dead, then he killed their immediate next of kin. Blood for blood, so a child, brother or sister of that person, though not a wife. Wives were not of the same blood.

The girls he murdered were a different matter. Killing them wasn't about vengeance. He liked doing it. As far as he was concerned, killing was better than sex.

He stretched himself in the chair, thoughts of how the last girl had died giving him greater satisfaction than any orgasm ever could. But it wasn't just the killing, it was the prospect of being caught. As if the day job, working for what was no longer the Soviet Union but a corrupt administration, wasn't enough, he thought to himself. Moscow knew of his hobby, but although they had admonished him, they had never forbidden it. Neither had they ceased to use him in covert operations against the West. He was good at his day job and they needed him.

He sighed and stretched, casually considering that it was merely the death of yet one more high-class whore and that soon there would be another, but this one, this one, was the greatest prize of all. A little older than his other victims, she was the daughter of the man responsible for his father's death. Honey Driver.

He'd watched her for a while, noting her habits, her contacts, both relatives and friends. Unfortunate about the policeman, but hopefully he wasn't that good at his job.

'We will see,' he muttered as he raised a tumbler of whisky in front of his face.

After downing his drink he gazed out of the hotel window, sweeping over the traffic to the buildings on the far side of the carriageway. He looked down to the kerbside below where taxis deposited guests in front of the hotel entrance then drove away, their wheels disturbing the surface water and sending it washing into the gutter. A taxi rank took up the rest of the kerbside parking, taxis coming, going, disgorging passengers and picking up new ones.

One car that was neither a limousine nor a taxi was parked at the kerb. It wasn't flash. It wasn't lit. It was ordinary.

He tensed.

He moved away from the window, turned off the light and lay on the bed, hands folded behind his head. Closing his eyes, he slept, timing himself to wake up when he needed to. He'd always had this skill: switch on, switch off at will. The gulag had influenced his behaviour when he was young. Before his death his father had been political commissar to a load of ingrates, subversives and murderers. Like them he'd felt exiled to somewhere he had no wish to be, trapped and unable to escape. He'd felt he deserved better and had taken his frustration out on the inmates, and sometimes on his son, but not as he grew older. As time went on he encouraged his son to participate in torturing those who kept him there, blaming the Western democracies for every crime committed.

'They have had so much for so very long, whereas we have so little. So hate them. Despise them. Kill them.'

His mother had been unknown to him, though his father had hinted that she was still alive but had fled to the West. The original high-class whore.

What he'd meant was that she'd been titled, from good family, and had only married him to save herself. Once the opportunity had arisen, she'd escaped to the West, leaving husband and son behind. Neither of them had forgiven her, himself less so than his father.

Exactly four hours later, his eyes blinked open. Without turning on the light, he went to the window. The car was still there. The driver's side door opened. He saw a figure get out, stretch and enter the broad entrance where the light from reception fell onto the pavement. Another man got out from the passenger side and followed. Both had the broad shoulders and confident demeanour of purposeful men.

He held still and counted. Twenty minutes later the first figure came back out and got into the car. Then the other man.

Neither one looked up. There would be no point. They — whoever 'they' were — knew where he was. They probably knew more about him than he did himself, he thought, then smiled. Well, not quite everything.

Filled with a mix of elation and anticipation, he packed his bag, dragged on his clothes and headed for the stairs. Not the lift. The stairs.

He kept going until he came to a set of doors and a sign marked, *Private. Staff only*. He went on through, past the kitchens, now in darkness. Past the night porter's lodge, the man snoring in front of a black-and-white movie on a portable television.

It was two in the morning and the rain was still falling. Whoever was sitting out front in the car wouldn't bother themselves to do a walk round, foolishly believing that their quarry would be reluctant to slip away in the rain. A bad mistake on their part. His judgement, however, had been good.

Ripping the red beard from his face, he let it fly off into the wind and rain, over a hedge. From there, it tumbled across a field and into a ditch.

The stormy weather was blowing in from the west and he would be travelling to meet it. Swiping his hand across his nose, he set off, jubilant that everything he wanted to achieve was finally within his grasp.

CHAPTER THIRTY-SIX

Doherty had found out all he could about the case Monmouth was reporting on.

'A young girl buried in mud with a rope around her neck. Buried alive, according to the pathologist. I asked if the perp left a tarot card on the victim. The answer was yes. A blue one.'

Doherty was given further information that brought a dead, disbelieving look to his eyes.

They drove away from the Black Dog, each engrossed in their own thoughts, staring ahead through their own individual car windscreens.

There were similarities between the deaths. The first victim was found at the side of the railway line buried in mud with marks of a rope around his neck. Yet it seemed amazing that the same person who'd killed a young girl was also the one responsible for the original killing.

They stopped at a pub, parking the MR2 and the bright-yellow Citroen side by side outside.

As usual in this isolated part of the world, heads turned when they entered — strangers were a rare sight.

They took two drinks and sandwiches to a corner table out of the earshot of the few other people in the bar.

Honey apologised for being ready to swing at him with her handbag. 'I really appreciate you turning up.'

He reached out and stroked her face. 'I'm glad I did. Our man in the tweed suit checked out too quickly not to arouse suspicion.'

Honey shivered. 'You don't need to tell me that. I've already guessed he was after me. I just don't understand his reasons.'

'I'm going to tell you a story,' he said.

'About this Tarot Man?'

Honey sensed his reluctance to continue but also his steely determination that he had to go ahead.

There was great power in the look that held her gaze, as though he knew damned well that she was going to take all this as total bullshit.

'The Tarot Man is the son of one of the old-time Soviet spies. Peter Orlov. Son of Ivan. You've seen the photograph.'

'Have I?' She frowned and was about to say that she'd never seen a picture of Peter Orlov when the penny dropped. They were speaking of the father, not the son.

'His father was a double agent,' Doherty told her.

'How did you find that out?'

Doherty tapped the side of his nose. 'I have my sources . . . And besides, the spooks aren't the only ones who take sneak peeks into secret files.'

'What secret files?'

He grinned. 'Caspar. His brother left them with him for safekeeping. They should have been destroyed but never were.'

Honey was almost afraid of the determined look in his eyes, but also peeved. He'd played things close to his chest, but there was more to it than that.

'So, Caspar finally came clean. But, besides that — and getting my daughter involved on the technical side — did you break into a government department? I take it they still have filing cabinets?'

'I do have a few favours to call in, and the Shropshire police were pretty forthcoming. As for Lindsey, she's just looking out for her mother.'

He looked away. She was sure she saw his shoulders heave. It could have been a shrug. It could have been a sigh. She wasn't sure.

'So what do we do next?'

'You do exactly as we say.'

Neither of them had seen Dominic Christiansen and two other well-dressed men enter the pub. All of them looked resolute, Dominic more than any of them.

'I'm going back to Bath,' said Honey. She got up so swiftly, the chair toppled slightly. Dominic caught it before it hit the floor. 'I have a hotel to run.'

Dominic pressed her shoulder hard so she couldn't help but sink back into her chair. Doherty knew better than to attempt anything. He just shook his head disconsolately and muttered a few choice words under his breath.

Dominic's voice was resolute. 'Perhaps I didn't make myself plain enough. You're coming with us. You have a job to do.' His pronouncement was directed at Honey.

She cocked her head defiantly. 'I don't work for you.'

'You do now.'

Doherty was told to stay put. One of the agents was to remain with him.

Honey was manhandled outside and shoved into the back seat of the shiny black BMW next to the other agent. Dominic sat in the front next to the driver.

'Almost an army to collect me. I must be important,' she declared loftily, though inside she quivered like reeds in the wind.

'You are.'

Never had two words of confirmation been so chillingly given and also received. Her mind was clear. All the bits and pieces had clanged into place. MI5 wanted to apprehend the man they called the Tarot Man. She could understand that.

The man was a killer. Unfortunately, he'd taken it into his head to kill her — a fact she was far from happy about.

'So I'm the Judas goat. Am I right?'

Christiansen hesitated before answering.

'We didn't want to get you involved, but he is not an easy man to flush out. His prime target was Lord Torrington.'

Honey gazed out of the car windows without really seeing anything. Everything was a blur, with the exception of the intention of this man and the plan that had been concocted to flush out the killer.

'Professor Collins wasn't killed at his house, was he? That scenario was for my benefit. The professor was Tarquin's cousin.'

'Whatever makes you say that?'

Honey glared at him. 'There's no point denying it. I've heard the whole story from my daughter. And even before that, I knew I smelled a rat. The real professor was gay, but the man who took me out to dinner was most definitely not. Unless he was one hell of an actor . . . Then, when I saw the professor's headshot online, it finally made sense. Tarquin is still alive. Am I right?'

His silence said it all. She was correct, but Tarquin was an important man in their operation, more useful alive than dead. The Tarot Man had to be stopped, but without arousing suspicion. She knew beyond doubt that their quarry would not live long enough to stand trial. They would put him down just as they might a mad dog. In the meantime, she was the bait to lure him, the daughter of the man who had played a part in his father's death.

An hour and a half later the castellated battlements of Torrington Towers loomed before them.

'How will you lay the trap?' she asked, sounding a lot braver than she actually felt.

'You'll be staying in one of the cottages on the estate.'

She quickly guessed it would be one of those close to where Adrian Sayle lived. It was funny but she hadn't seen him for a while. The last time he'd been in the company of

Miss Vincent, the latter gazing up into his face like a loyal cocker spaniel.

'So I just have to sit there until he comes calling.'

'Something like that. Don't worry. We'll be close by.'

'What if I don't want to do this? There are such things as civil liberties, aren't there?'

Dominic Christiansen looked at her as though she were naive to the point of stupidity.

'There are special dispensations,' he said grimly.

* * *

Doherty sat passively in the back of the car as they hurtled towards Bath.

He knew there was no point doing anything else. The door locks would be automatic. The man left to guard him was sitting in the passenger seat next to the driver. If there had been only one man he might have chanced an attack. As it was there were two of them, and he had no doubt they both carried guns. His own had been taken off him.

In police training he'd been taught to gain the trust of terrorists and kidnappers by talking. Let them think you're totally calm and that they are in control. Eventually they might regard you as a friend.

That was what he did now.

'So. Any chance I might have your names? Just in case anything goes wrong and I have to make out a full police report.'

Their jaws remained clamped shut, their eyes staring at the road ahead.

'So you're definitely not Flying Squad. By now I'd know your names and what time you left the pub last night. Or your old woman's bed. Or your girlfriend's.'

Still no response, which brought him to the conclusion that their training in this situation had been at variance with his own. They'd been told to keep their mouths shut.

'Oh well. Might as well catch up on the kip.'

Folding his arms, he stretched out his legs, settled himself comfortably in the seat and closed his eyes. Ten minutes later he began to snore, though only lightly. He'd had a hard time away in the Brecon Beacons and he was due a rest. His eyes were tired. So was his body. But his ears remained sharply tuned to whatever the two men up front might be saying to each other, and also to the speed and sound of the car.

The journey was along winding roads before joining the motorway. They pulled in at a service station. One by one each went to relieve themselves, though they insisted one of them accompany Doherty.

On their way into the concourse, they were faced with a horde of football fanatics. In the normal course of things Doherty would have skirted them, partly because it was quicker, and partly because barging through would cause trouble.

On this occasion he barged through, breaking into a sprint halfway.

'He's a pig and he's trying to arrest me,' he shouted, waving his hand in the general direction of the agent and using the well-known colloquial term.

The gaggle of football fans were not fond of the police force.

Shouting obscenities for past grievances that may or may not have occurred, the agent was overcome. Doherty charged onwards, finally gaining a lift with a Polish lorry driver, who gratefully accepted the fifty pounds he offered.

CHAPTER THIRTY-SEVEN

There was food in the cottage, the heating had been turned on and her car had been parked outside, driven there by one of the spook brigade. All in all, it was very cosy. These guys had thought of everything. Her car was here so she was here. The Tarot Man would know that.

Christiansen stood in the middle of the living room. His presence made it look crowded, albeit a tad upmarket.

He was wearing a crisp white shirt, a knitted silk tie loosely knotted. His jacket was of dark burgundy, his slacks navy blue. The whole outfit was complemented by dark-blue loafers and his silky, slick hair. She still thought he looked like a medieval knight, even though she was no longer attracted to him as much as she had been.

She made herself comfortable in a chintz-covered arm-chair, carefully adopting an optimistic air. Nobody was going to bump her off without a fight.

'So. Where will you be?'

A suspiciously wishful look came to his very blue eyes.

'Close by.'

'And what do I do?'

'Just act natural.'

'Can I have a gun?'

'What?' He looked as though he were about to burst into laughter.

'To protect myself.'

Smiling, he shook his head. 'No. There's no need. We're fully armed and here to protect you.'

'No, Mr Christiansen. You're not here to protect me.'

'Whatever makes you say that? We're here to apprehend a murderer.'

She shook her head. 'No, you're not. You're here to kill him.'

The smile diminished, though his confidence remained, worn like armour against the slings and arrows of anything Honey or anyone else could throw at him. He had the confidence of a man who knew he played an important role in this world. He'd probably had that air of self-importance from a very early age. Perhaps, like Tarquin, he too was titled.

He left quietly, leaving her sitting in the chair. All pretence of being unruffled vanished with him. She stiffened at the thought of what she was here for. She'd been told to be compliant, but she'd never been submissive in her life. Never done as she was told but rather what she wanted to do, and right now she had no intention of being the bait in the trap. The question was, could she escape this predicament without these professional protectors of the realm noticing?

It had been impossible to escape their presence in the car, but she'd weighed things up on the way down once she knew she was to be installed in the cottage to await her fate.

The thing that had most surprised her was that she was to be left here alone. She had expected someone to supply the muscle, not just to protect her but to prevent her from escaping.

Her conclusion was that whatever was guarding her was electronic. There had to be a camera somewhere, some kind of surveillance that would flash like a Christmas tree if she so much as moved.

Flicking from one TV channel to another gave her something to occupy her right hand more so than her brain.

She certainly wasn't ready to go to bed. Her mind was in a state of planning. She had to have some kind of weapon. Perhaps not a gun. A kitchen knife would do.

A rummage through the kitchen drawers produced a carving knife, the modern sort that looked as though it were made of plastic rather than steel. It was in a shade of bright pink, not quite the colour one associated with an offensive weapon, but lethal all the same. It just might hold him off should the cavalry not arrive in time.

She settled on the late-night news channel, which led on an item about the girl found dead in Shropshire and the suspicion that she'd been buried alive. Her blood ran cold.

Other items of news followed, including the lowdown on the worsening weather situation. Storms and gales of gigantic proportion were set to batter the West Country and two months' rainfall was expected to fall in one day. Not good, as it had already been raining on and off for a few days now.

A sudden flash of lightning was closely followed by thunder.

Honey looked out of the window. Low-lying cloud rolled over the trees that formed a barrier between the cottages and the single-track country road, obliterating the moon. Forked lightning speared the sky. Thunder rolled and the whole world seemed to throb with electricity.

The rain came down in bucketloads, followed by more lightning, more thunder.

The TV went dead. The lights went out.

Honey moved quickly. She could be wrong, but whatever electronic gadgets surrounded her relied on mains electricity. Even batteries could be put out of action by a thunderstorm.

Should she or shouldn't she? Was she safer here or out there on her own?

She decided on the latter. Being the cheese in the mouse trap didn't suit her at all. She'd take the chance that she was right and the surveillance was out of action.

Slipping her feet into her shoes, she swooped on her car keys conveniently left on the coffee table and headed for her car.

Outside a maelstrom raged, whipping her hair around her face, stinging her eyes and sending twigs, leaves and even branches tumbling around in a dervish dance. A bin from the end cottage hurtled past, its rubbish festooned like a treasure trail through the dying foliage. Further away on the far side of the lane beyond the garden, leaves fell in torrents of red, brown and orange before scuttling off like frightened mice along the tarmac lane.

'Where to?' she asked herself as she turned the ignition key.

Home. She was going home! Hopefully Doherty would have made his escape and already be there.

The car bumped along the track, the branches of trees waving and creaking along the route. She glanced in her rear-view mirror but could see no sign of pursuit.

When the lightning flashed she could see the smoke from the sausage factory twisting as the wind wound it upwards.

Then it came to her that it couldn't be the factory — it was too far. The smoke, steam or whatever was coming out of something else, and the only source had to be one of the vents above long-dead ancestors' private access to the railway station. The chimneys were no more than six feet high. Most were covered in ivy or hidden behind suitably decorative landscaping, the lords of the manor not wishing the brick-built constructions to spoil their views. But why would there be smoke? It was just a disused railway tunnel.

Her mind went back to when she'd seen Dominic outside. He'd given no excuse for being there but had looked decidedly pensive.

Tunnels, sausage factories with few employees and a forest of weeds and brambles around it, land leased by the government and spooks of one kind or another all over the place.

Some kind of secret installation? Back in the Cold War they were everywhere, hidden beneath the most inconspicuous buildings.

The urge to run for home was very strong, but her curiosity would not be ignored, though fear of what was stalking her wouldn't go away.

* * *

Thanks to the Polish lorry driver, Doherty had got back to Bath well ahead of his guardians, picked up his car and headed for Torrington Towers. Everything seemed to centre around that place and he thought he knew why. The Tarot Man had been there in disguise but in plain sight for a very long time, and what with Miss Vincent's list of employees and what they were paid, plus smaller things like broad-brimmed hats and a tell-tale runny nose, he thought he knew who it was.

The nighttime roads were plagued by roadworks and speed restrictions. He'd taken the step of phoning the local police responsible for the village of Wyvern Wendell but was told they were rather busy.

'A lot of trees have come down in the storm and there's flooding in places. Can you tell me what it's about?'

'I think somebody is going to be murdered. I'll need backup.'

'Just one moment, please.'

He was passed to a senior officer, the sort who wears a uniform and carries a baton but totally lacks street cred.

The fact that Torrington Towers and the village of Wyvern Wendell was in Somerset should have clinched the request. It didn't.

'Look, Doherty, I cannot send men to you purely on a hunch — which I presume this is . . .'

'No. It is not. It's got a lot to do with MI5. You can check with them if you like.'

'Now it sounds as though we're heading into the realms of fiction,' the senior man said sardonically.

Doherty swore as he slammed down the phone. It was all down to him and him alone. Uttering a couple of other well-known swear words, he slammed his foot on the throttle and hurtled south.

Security at Torrington Towers refused him entry.

'We have a dangerous incident on our hands,' the man at the gate gabbled, his eyes glowing with a mix of excitement and fear.

Doherty had seen this kind of look before. The security job had veered from routine to something unusual.

'I'm a police officer,' he said. 'Can I help?'

'Not unless you're used to dealing with lions,' said the man. 'The electricity failed. We've had more than six trees fall onto the electrified fence. It's dangerous to be out tonight, officer, but if you want to help, get yourself a gun and head for the old railway tunnel. There's game down there, small creatures they can hunt and eat.'

Doherty didn't have a gun but that was not going to stop him.

'I'll see what I can do,' he said, and roared off in the general direction pointed out to him.

CHAPTER THIRTY-EIGHT

Honey finally reached the entrance to the tunnel. Steam and smoke were rising from one of the chimneys. The rain was coming down in torrents. A single light on a long iron arm hanging at the side of the arched entrance helped her find her way.

Luckily she had a hooded coat with her, which she struggled into while still behind the wheel. Better than getting wet too early, she decided.

The coat was heavily padded and the hood was large. She pulled it over her head as she got out of the car, slamming the door behind her.

The light hanging on a curved iron bracket adorned with entwined leaves threw a watery light before the tunnel entrance. Beyond the pool of light there was only blackness — a solid blackness, no movement. Nothing except night.

Where there were no puddles, the ground was slippery underfoot and the smell of burning was quite strong.

She hesitated to go further. Someone was burning rubbish in the tunnel. That's all it was. Just rubbish. In this downpour it made sense to do so. Oh well. She might as well have a quick look while she was here, though for that she would need a torch.

Feeling in her pocket she found a Maglite, a tiny thing armed with a series of LED light bulbs, far brighter than an ordinary bulb.

The wind howled around her as she flashed the beam over the tunnel entrance, then around at the bushes and trees, their branches waving like frenzied arms.

In the midst of all that movement she picked out something that did not move: a solid black shape — no — not black. Dark green. The dark green of one of the estate's Land Rovers, the sort the rangers used to drive around the safari park.

And then she saw him.

Adrian Sayle stepped swiftly between her and the Land Rover. She knew for sure now who this really was. Peter Orlov. Getting the job of ranger meant he'd been able to discover the whereabouts of the men or descendants of the men who'd killed his father. His disguises had been excellent. The broad-brimmed hats, the bushy red beard, one man with a stoop, another with perfect posture. The only thing Orlov hadn't been able to disguise was his rather vile habit of wiping his nose on the back of his hand, one he hadn't been able to control.

She spun round, her feet sliding through the slop of mud as she headed for her car. She should have gone home. Curiosity killed the cat, and it might well kill her if she didn't get out of there.

It was so sudden, she thought she was mistaken. Adrian Sayle, Peter Orlov, the Tarot Man moved before she had chance to open the car door. He grabbed her shoulder fiercely and she yelled with pain. With the sharp light of her Maglite, she saw the steely glint of a needle, then felt its tip nick her arm. Her feet slid from under her.

'What are you doing?'

'I'm going to kill you.'

'Why?' she asked as her legs buckled under her.

There was no gloating laughter. No cackle of glee, just an ice-cold voice speaking in an ice-cold tone.

'I think you already know the answer to that. You're your father's daughter and that's enough for me.'

His eyes glittered with excitement at the panic he saw in hers.

She felt her arm growing numb where the needle had gone in. She tried to raise her other arm and rub at it but found she couldn't.

All her limbs were going numb. She tried to shake his hands away from her hair, but whatever drug he'd injected was taking swift effect.

Next, the roughness of a hemp rope tightened around her neck.

'You paid Geoffrey Monmouth to report Caspar's death.'

By virtue of the numbing effect of the drug, her words were mumbled but he heard her.

'I never give notice, but your case was special. A little rash of me perhaps, but your father's reaction was even rasher when he found out what my father was doing. He was directly responsible for his death.'

She wanted to shout for help, but her tongue lay like a pork sausage in her mouth, and her lips felt as though they were smeared with starch. Her words came out slurred and unrecognisable.

The world whirled around her as she was lifted off the ground, her arms flapping helplessly downwards as though her bones had melted away, her legs like two sodden bags of mud.

The wind whipped her hair across her eyes but she could still see where she was destined to end up. The yawning mouth of a pit was directly beneath her, dug close to the wall of the tunnel.

Even her scream of pain as she landed at the bottom of the pit was subdued to a squeal — like a rat caught in a trap, or smaller, a mouse possessing too small a voice to be heard.

Clods of clay landed on top of her. She heard a grating sound followed by gushing water.

At a guess he'd pulled a drainpipe away from the tunnel wall, directing the unrelenting flow into the pit. The clay would hold the water and also mix with it into an orange sludge.

Honey knew she would drown here. The back of her head was already submerged. Her face would be covered first unless she could raise her head and keep her nose above water.

Suddenly somebody else spoke. 'Peter! I've got the map.'

It was a woman's voice, one Honey recognised. Miss Vincent. She immediately recalled the puppy-dog expression on Miss Vincent's face whenever Adrian Sayle had appeared.

Then the man's voice. 'Give!'

Miss Vincent's pale face appeared and Honey saw her look of horror.

'You can't do this!'

Honey heard the clang of a spade against bone. Miss Vincent had received her response from Peter Orlov and groaned as she fell with a splash into the mud, just outside the circle of light.

In this, his moment of sweet revenge on the one hand, and feeding his own perverted taste for killing on the other, he had no more time for the woman who had helped him achieve his aims. With manic intent he continued to shovel mud into the pit, his arms working with frenzied excitement, so frenzied, so obsessive, that he was no longer aware of what was happening around him.

Thin and of late middle age she might be, but Miss Vincent had been fiery in her day and some of that fire still burned deep inside. She began to crawl.

Using her fingers like claws, she moved on her belly further away from the circle of light. Thorns from brambles tore at her hands and her fingernails began breaking under the strain. Still she crawled on, until one set of fingers landed on something that was not mud. The toe of a shoe. Someone else was here. Her face a mess of blood and bone, she pointed before falling face forward into the mud.

Steve Doherty stepped over her, his eyes narrowed against the darkness and the rain.

The light hanging from the bracket at the side of the tunnel bravely fought the night and the weather. He could see all he needed to see. He knew all he needed to know.

A lone figure was bent over, shovelling sopping mud into the pit at the side of the tunnel entrance with alarming efficiency.

He guessed the pit always filled with water when it rained. In time, the foundations on that side of the tunnel would subside.

It was then he saw something else moving in the darkness, something heavy and moving on all fours. He heard the low rumble of a growl deep in the lion's throat. He saw the figure with the spade start and half turn, the shovel braced like a shield before him.

The sudden crack of a pistol shot split the darkness. The bullet went haywire as the man slipped in the mud, the lion taking full advantage of the situation, standing four-square and threatening.

The shooter was the man who had called himself Adrian Sayle, real name Peter Orlov. And his bullet went arcing over the head of the snarling beast, missing its target by a mile.

Much as Doherty didn't care whether Orlov, the Tarot Man, got mauled or not, water was pouring into the pit where mud had already been thrown. It was only a matter of minutes before yet another young woman was plastered in clay.

Orlov turned, crouching over a job unfinished, his gun pointing not at Doherty but down at the woman, Mrs Honey Driver.

Just as he was taking aim to make the killer shot, a pair of spiderlike hands wrapped around his ankles and threw him off balance. Miss Vincent!

He lashed out in a backward kick, his heel slamming hard against her face. She gave one last groan and collapsed into the mud.

When Doherty turned back towards the tunnel, both the man and the lion were gone. He hoped the lion was in command of the game and that Orlov was dead meat.

* * *

Never, ever had Honey been so glad to see Doherty's face. She managed a mumbled response. Luckily she had been wearing a pretty thick jacket with puffy sleeves and the needle had only nicked her.

'He's gone,' Doherty said, as though reading her mind. 'And so's the lion. I think it ate him.'

* * *

The first thing she did after having a bath back in the coach house at the Green River Hotel was to sit with Doherty in the kitchen while he tossed a dozen or so crevettes in a mixture of garlic and butter. The salad was good too, and so was the bottle he fetched from the hotel cellar.

They went through all that had happened.

It had all started with the report of Caspar's death, a lie woven as part of an intricate plan to capture an elusive bogeyman whose family history was caught up with Honey's own family.

'My biggest surprise is that Caspar was in on the plan. I don't think I can ever forgive him for keeping me in the dark. Using me in fact.'

'The same applies to Christiansen and his bosses.'

'That's different. Caspar was a friend.'

Doherty arched an eyebrow. 'You said the most telling word — "was". That's past tense. I take it you don't think him such a good friend now.'

'You bet I don't,' she said, almost choking on a mouthful of wine.

Doherty set the plates on the table. 'You said he did try to explain things to you.'

Honey shook her head. 'OK, he explained to me that he'd long suspected his half-brother's involvement in international espionage and, despite his success in the hospitality industry, had always felt inferior to the legitimate heir to the family title.'

They both agreed that the reporting of his death had been a trifle melodramatic. But the headline in the local paper had drawn Honey's attention, and she in turn had told Caspar, who in turn had been persuaded to do as the spooks wanted. Everyone had to be convinced that it really was Caspar's brother who'd been found dead at Bradford on Avon. Caspar didn't relish the prospect of deceiving his dear friend. But if that was what it took to save his brother . . .

Doherty went on, 'The Tarot Man chose the wrong man to kill. Nobody quite seems to know how that happened, but they think Miss Vincent might have had a hand in it. Peter Orlov was good at befriending women who were past their prime. Miss Vincent was totally loyal to his lordship, but considered herself in love with Orlov.'

Honey interrupted. 'I get it. Collins was the body cremated once Caspar had followed instructions and identified him as his brother. And the ashes had to be disposed of. Mary Jane was right about that, though she wasn't right about there not being a body. There was, but not the one it was supposed to be. If they'd been tested there was a chance the ashes would have shown a different DNA.'

'Correct.'

'And he never was found dead at his home in Dunster. That particular charade was put on for my benefit.'

Doherty shook his head. 'Dominic Christiansen is not to be trusted. Not like me.'

Honey slapped his wrist.

'Stop looking so smug. And the map?'

'There's a mass of underground store rooms, passages and top-secret items beneath the estate of vital importance to the Western world, or at least it used to be in the days of the Cold War. I don't know the exact details, the underground facility is still kept under wraps. Just in case. Peter's father was sent to infiltrate and map it all. Present-day Russia is merely a different name for the Soviet Union. It still prods and pokes, hoping to find things out.'

Honey eyed him over the top of her glass. 'There's something you're not telling me.'

Doherty held up his hands in surrender. 'I've been offered a transfer to Christiansen's department.'

'And?'

'I turned it down. I mean, do I look like James Bond?'

Honey smiled. 'You do to me.'

'Nobody needs to fly off to foreign parts anymore. The baddies are here, babe, and yours truly can be a British secret weapon guarding the home front. Although there is another option I've been considering . . .'

Honey was only half listening. She had picked up the phone and punched in Caspar's number.

'Ah, Honey. I'm so glad you didn't come to any harm . . .'

She didn't give him chance to continue but turned the phone onto loudspeaker so that Doherty could hear too.

'I'm resigning,' Honey stated in a no-nonsense voice. 'I've had enough of crime. You'll have to find somebody else to do it.'

'Oh! I really didn't think you would take that attitude.' He sounded quite affronted. Not that Honey cared. Being affronted beat being killed any day of the week.

'Well I am!'

She had never raised her voice to Caspar in the past, but she did now. No matter what he offered her, she would stand firm.

'Well I do hope that our new Crime Liaison Officer will get on with Inspector Doherty as well as you do.'

Doherty grabbed the phone from her. 'The prospect won't arise. I'm taking early retirement.'

Honey's jaw dropped. Doherty had hinted a few times about making changes in his life, but up until now they'd mainly centred on them getting married. The idea was there but she wasn't sure about the will on both their parts.

'Oh.' Caspar sounded quite peeved, but still attempted to bring Honey round. 'My brother sends his regards. If you ever want a day out he'd be pleased to show you around. I think he'd also like to take you to dinner again. To make up for things, if you know what I mean.'

Honey turned her back on him. 'Tarquin St John Gervais can go to bloody hell!'

* * *

SIX MONTHS LATER

'Are you cold?'

'No. Quite warm in fact.'

Honey rolled onto her back, arms behind her head, staring at the deep-blue sky. The aquamarine sea kept up a gentle slapping against the hull of the yacht they'd bought between them.

Every day she woke up and thought herself extremely lucky. That last case could have been her swansong.

Wearing a pair of threadbare shorts, Doherty was sitting at the stern of the boat trying a spot of fishing. He wasn't terribly good at it but both he and Honey took the view that practice makes perfect. Nothing could compare with this.

Bath was over a thousand miles away and nobody back there was enough of a draw to make them return.

Her mother was happy with her new husband who indulged her something rotten. Her daughter was trekking around the world and on the last occasion she'd been in contact suggested she might be pregnant. To Honey's surprise both she and Sean were quite ecstatic about it, but wouldn't be cutting short their journey.

'This kid will have an alternative lifestyle,' Lindsey had told her.

She envisioned Lindsey carrying a backpack, a pair of tiny hands waving from the opening.

As for everyone else . . . her mind went back to that moment under the bed in the cottage. It made her smile. Where was Dominic Christiansen now, she wondered, and was just about to voice her thoughts but thought better of it. He was out of her life and it was best it stayed that way. Doherty was well and truly in it. The world was their oyster.

THE END

THE JOFFE BOOKS STORY

We began in 2014 when Jasper agreed to publish his mum's much-rejected romance novel and it became a bestseller.

Since then we've grown into the largest independent publisher in the UK. We're extremely proud to publish some of the very best writers in the world, including Joy Ellis, Faith Martin, Caro Ramsay, Helen Forrester, Simon Brett and Robert Goddard. Everyone at Joffe Books loves reading and we never forget that it all begins with the magic of an author telling a story.

We are proud to publish talented first-time authors, as well as established writers whose books we love introducing to a new generation of readers.

We have been shortlisted for Independent Publisher of the Year at the British Book Awards three times, in 2020, 2021 and 2022, and for the Diversity and Inclusivity Award at the Independent Publishing Awards in 2022.

We built this company with your help, and we love to hear from you, so please email us about absolutely anything bookish at feedback@joffebooks.com

If you want to receive free books every Friday and hear about all our new releases, join our mailing list: www.joffebooks.com/contact

And when you tell your friends about us, just remember: it's pronounced Joffe as in coffee or toffee!

ALSO BY JEAN G. GOODHIND

HONEY DRIVER MYSTERY SERIES

Book 1: MURDER, BED & BREAKFAST
Book 2: MENU FOR MURDER
Book 3: WALKING WITH MURDER
Book 4: THE JANE AUSTEN MURDERS
Book 5: MURDER BY LAMPSHADE
Book 6: MURDER BY MUDPACK
Book 7: MURDER AT THE ROMAN BATHS
Book 8: MURDER FOR CHRISTMAS
Book 9: MURDER AT THE MANOR HOUSE
Book 10: A CROOKED MURDER
Book 11: MARRIAGE IS MURDER
Book 12: A BESPOKE MURDER
Book 13: MURDER RUNS IN THE FAMILY

Printed in Great Britain
by Amazon

50997392R00155